Nicole Richie is a bestselling author, philanthropist, designer, actress, mother, and the daughter of music legend Lionel Richie. In addition to writing hot, contemporary novels, she has launched a signature jewellery and accessories line, House of Harlow 1960, and is designing her new fashion line, Winter Kate.

Watch an exclusive video from Nicole on *Priceless*, and find lots more information at nicolerichie.celebuzz.com

ALSO BY NICOLE RICHIE

The Truth About Diamonds

Priceless

NICOLE RICHIE

HarperCollins*Publishers*
harpercollins.com.au

HarperCollins*Publishers*

First published in the USA in 2010
by Atria Books, a Division of Simon & Schuster, Inc.
First published in Australia in 2010
by HarperCollins*Publishers* Australia Pty Limited
ABN 36 009 913 517
www.harpercollins.com.au

HarperCollins*Publishers*
25 Ryde Road, Pymble, Sydney, NSW 2073, Australia
31 View Road, Glenfield, Auckland 0627, New Zealand
A 53, Sector 57, Noida, UP, India
77–85 Fulham Palace Road, London, W6 8JB, United Kingdom
2 Bloor Street East, 20th floor, Toronto, Ontario M4W 1A8, Canada
10 East 53rd Street, New York NY 10022, USA

ISBN 978 0 7322 9235 5

Cover design by John Vairo Jre. adapted by Pricilla Nielsen
Cover and author photographs by Randee St. Nicholas
Printed and bound in Australia by Griffin Press.
60gsm Hi Bulk Book Cream used by HarperCollins*Publishers* is a natural, recyclable product
made from wood grown in sustainable plantation forests. The manufacturing processes conform
to the environmental regulations in the country of origin, Finland.

5 4 3 2 1   10 11 12 13

To the priceless moments in your life

Priceless

Chapter ONE

As the beautiful young woman
strode through the international arrivals terminal at JFK, several
people turned to look. A flight attendant noticed the way she carried herself, the clothes she wore, her shoes, and guessed she'd
just walked out of first class. She was right. A young man pulling espresso paused, distracted by the girl's obvious sexuality and
lovely figure. She felt his gaze and turned slightly, favoring him
with a brief smile that made his hand jump, causing him to scald
himself. A man in a Savile Row suit lowered his *Wall Street Journal*
and raised his eyebrows. Hmm. Charlotte Williams was back. Her
father would be happy. The market would go up. He folded his
paper and called his broker.

Charlotte descended the escalator, scanning the crowd waiting
for arrivals. She smiled; there was Davis. He caught her eye and
smiled back. He already had her bags.

"Hello, Davis, how nice to see a familiar face so soon." She
shook his hand.

"Miss Charlotte, it's a pleasure to have you back in New York.
The city has been very quiet without you."

She laughed. "I doubt that, Davis, but thanks. Is the car very far? My shoes are killing me." She'd worn sweats for the flight, but just before they began their descent, she'd changed into her city clothes. Louboutins, which were pinching her feet after only a hundred yards, a Marc Jacobs dress from spring '09, with a wide wrapped belt, a cashmere sweater coat. Still comfortable and easy to wear but appropriate for public viewing.

He shook his head. "Just outside, Miss."

Indeed, the long, low Mercedes was parked right in front, in a red zone, a cop very slowly writing a ticket for it. He saw them coming and looked around, making sure no one saw Davis slipping him a folded bill. Charlotte kicked off her shoes and relaxed as Davis expertly navigated the traffic back into town.

It was very good to be home.

HOWEVER, NO ONE except the staff was home to welcome her. The housekeeper was the same, but a young man she hadn't seen before was working on the plants. She looked him over and decided to save him for later. Sitting on her bed, she surveyed her room.

"Your father had it repainted for you." The housekeeper was unpacking her things, silently evaluating and appreciating the silken underwear, the fine labels: La Perla, Aubade, Eres.

"How did he manage to do that and yet have it look exactly the same?" Every doll, every picture, every photo was precisely where she had left it the year before.

Greta shrugged. "He spent a lot of time in here while you were away." She looked around. "And he paid a designer to draw a map of where everything was." She smiled at the memory. "It was quite a task."

Charlotte frowned, tucking her long blond hair behind her ears. "Why was he in here so much?" She pulled her feet up onto her bed, pausing at a glance from Greta, removing her shoes.

Greta smoothed her gray uniform over her hips, before heading out the door. "He misses your mother, and he missed you. He's going to be very glad to see you tonight."

"Do you expect him for dinner?"

"No. I think later than that."

Charlotte nodded. It was rare that her father was home before ten; it had always been that way. She'd eaten dinner alone every night, once she no longer had a nanny. She would curl up in his study, after her homework was done, and fall asleep waiting for him. If she closed her eyes, she could still remember the feeling of being lifted from the chair, the smell of whiskey and cigars, the roughness of his stubble as he kissed her, the smooth wool of his suit jacket. They would sit by the fire while he told her about his day, spinning fairy tales about the world of money and the knights and dragons that lived there. He was wonderful, when he was with her, and Charlotte loved him deeply. He just wasn't there very much.

But while his work had kept them apart, it had also paid for this triplex on the park, a pony stabled at 89th Street (until the stable closed), a new Jaguar for her eighteenth birthday, an apartment in Le Marais for her year in Paris, and all the clothes and jewelry she could ever want. She had a lot to be grateful for. If she felt she'd missed out on a lot, too, she never said so.

———————

CHARLOTTE CALLED SOME friends and set up an impromptu welcome-home dinner for herself. Then she threw open her closet doors and walked in, stepping between the racks, flipping hangers. The closet was nearly twenty feet long and curated like a gallery. On one side were pants, suits, jackets. The other held dresses, skirts, shirts. Everything from Abercrombie to Alaïa. Floor-to-ceiling shelves held four dozen pairs of shoes, each in a clear plastic box. Sometimes, when she'd been a bored teen, she would rearrange her closet by designer. Or decade. Or color. She'd been bored a lot.

Her favorite section held her mother's clothes, those her father had kept. Her mother had died in a car accident when Charlotte was seven. On her way back from a party, for once without her husband, stone-cold sober and apparently driving below the speed limit. Another driver, drunk, high, traveling at nearly eighty on a cross street, had run the light at Fifth and rammed her car from the side, killing her instantly. He, of course, had gotten out of his car and walked away. Charlotte barely remembered her, though the house was filled with photographs. Jackie Williams had been a great model, internationally known and instantly recognized, and Charlotte had inherited her slanted green eyes and wide mouth. Her death had rocked the fashion world, and Charlotte's main memory of that time was that the phone never stopped ringing. Her father had come home from the funeral and pulled it out of the wall, locking himself in his study, drinking and sobbing incon- solably. When he'd come out and found Jackie's assistants packing up her clothes, he'd flown into a terrible rage, firing them on the spot and carefully smoothing each garment, delicately replacing them on their padded hangers, closing the closet door quietly.

Now Charlotte had a world-class collection of semi-vintage couture, and she knew the details and history of each piece. Many of them were one-offs, worn in runway shows and tailored for her mother. Jackie had been taller and thinner than Charlotte, who had a little more curve to her figure, and many of the pieces simply wouldn't fit. But many did, and she loved pulling something unique from the collection.

Tonight she picked a simple slip dress by Galliano, one of his less flamboyant pieces, and looked at herself critically in the mirror.

She knew she was beautiful, and she knew she was attractive to men, but she couldn't help comparing herself with her mother. Or, rather, with the images of her mother, because she'd never really known her mom. The public Jackie had been aloof and elegant, famous for her platinum hair and regal bearing. Charlotte was sexier, warmer. Her hair had honeyed streaks mixed with the pale cream, some of them almost dark. Her mother's hair had been board-straight, but hers was tousled and curled and hard to control. She was feeling a little nervous, strangely, going out for the first time, and reached for her war paint, leaving her hair loose and wild. Her skin needed no foundation, but she dusted it with shimmery blush to bring out her cheekbones. In Paris, the women had worn minimal eye makeup, and she followed their lead, simply shadowing her lids with a pale aqua that brought out the subtle turquoise in her eyes and finishing with a razor-thin line of liquid eyeliner. Several coats of mascara and matte red lipstick later, she was ready.

Jewelry. She'd nearly forgotten. In the center of her closet was a Chinese chest, priceless in itself, its many lacquered drawers holding a small fortune in jewels and precious metals. Her father loved to buy jewelry and was something of a snob about it. His wife's collection had included dozens of antiques alongside important contemporary pieces. Charlotte opened drawer after drawer, looking for the perfect thing. A single cabochon emerald on a long golden chain hung between her breasts and added green to her eyes. Time for battle.

Chapter TWO

When Charlotte had left for Paris the year before, Le Petit Champignon was relatively new, perching precariously on Jane Street. She'd adopted it, loving its richly delicious vegetarian cuisine. The chef was famous for saying, "Just because it's vegetarian doesn't mean it has to be good for you," and the rich sauces and abundant butter showed he was as good as his word. Apparently, the news had gotten out, for when Davis dropped her in front, there was a line.

"Will you call, Miss?"

She nodded. The one time she'd ridden the subway home, her father had taken her aside.

"Charlotte, the world is full of interesting people. However, it isn't necessary to become intimately acquainted with a hundred of them in the unventilated confines of a subway car. Please call Davis when you need to go anywhere. That's what he's for."

Jean-Claude, the maitre d', recognized her as soon as she walked in.

"Miss Williams! Paris's loss is our gain. I saw your name on the list and hoped it was you. I have your favorite table ready."

Two people were already there, James and Zeb. High school friends. They stood to embrace her.

"You're even skinnier than when you left, you bitch. How is that possible?" Zeb was gay and not all that subtle. "Don't the French eat nothing but lard and cheese?"

James shushed him. "Keep your voice down, Zeb. We're not at the club yet. Maybe she took up smoking; it keeps you thin."

Charlotte wrinkled her nose. "Thin and stinky. Not likely. I think Zeb's memory has just been affected by all those club drugs and pretty boys he likes to inhale."

"I don't inhale the boys."

"Just swallow?"

Zeb giggled.

James poured Charlotte a glass of 2007 Malbec and raised his own.

"To the lovely Charlotte. Welcome home, my sweet." She and James had briefly been friends with benefits, and when he smiled his pussycat smile at her, she remembered his . . . gifts. She wondered idly if she should rekindle the relationship. There was nothing else on the horizon.

The door was flung open, and Clara, Jane, and Emily burst in. The three weird sisters. Only Jane and Emily were actually sisters, a twist of fertility making them eleven months apart in age but in the same school year. Alternately sworn enemies and best friends, they were a force of nature. Clara was the peacemaker, a cousin of some sort. There are a lot of relationships among the super rich of Manhattan: cousins, second cousins, related by marriage, related in secret. There aren't that many people living in 10021, and when you don't need to work, there's a lot of time to fill.

"Charlotte!" There was squealing. And hugging. And cheek kissing.

Eventually, they settled down to the serious business of catching up.

Over appetizers, the sisters brought her up to date on all the gossip in their small circle.

Emily was appalled. "And did you know that Bebe was secretly sleeping with her boyfriend's sister? I mean, come on, this isn't reality TV." The candlelight flickered on her dark, wavy hair, her perfect nose the product of superior plastic surgery.

Charlotte was amused. "Younger or older sister?"

"Older. She was away at Vassar when Bebe started dating Tim, and she came back for spring break and apparently thought little Timmy should share his good fortune." She sighed. "It all got very East Village, apparently." She cut into her spring roll thoughtfully.

James grinned. "Whatever that means." He refilled their glasses. Charlotte could tell she was getting a little drunk, because he was starting to look better and better.

Clara had news, too. "Do you remember Jemima Rhodes?" They all did. "Her mother lost her job when Bear Stearns collapsed, and they had to sell the beach cottage. We were all gutted." (The beach cottage was a sixteen-bedroom mansion overlooking the ocean in East Hampton.) "I mean, where are we going for Fourth of July this summer?" She dropped her voice. "I heard they were going to *rent* someplace." A pause. "On the *North Fork*." The three women shuddered, delighted.

Charlotte picked at her salad, enjoying the familiar sound of pointless gossip. You could always rely on these three to know everything that was going on. Emily and Jane were the middle daughters of a large family who'd owned most of the Upper West Side since the 1920s. The UWS connection made them the token "artistic ones" at their ultraconservative Upper East Side school, and they were allowed a little leeway in terms of behavior. Clara was a slightly inbred blue blood whose family had come over on the *Mayflower* and made their fortune shortly thereafter. Charlotte wasn't quite sure how they'd made the money. Button hooks? Buggy whips? Something archaic. No one in Clara's family had worked for generations, but they did a lot of Good Works and Sat on Boards. Clara had been very successful at school and at one point rashly expressed a desire to go to MIT. No one of her class ever tried that hard, she was informed, and she dropped it. Stiff upper lip, maybe, but backbone? Not so much.

James got up to go to the bathroom and met Charlotte's eye meaningfully. She sighed. Why not? She waited a moment, then followed him. She knocked softly on the bathroom door, and he pulled her in.

"Charlotte Williams, of all people, fancy meeting you here." James was nuzzling at her neck, his hands reaching around behind her, starting to pull up her slip dress.

She grabbed his wrists firmly. "James."

"Hmm, you want to play a little? I can do that." He flipped his hands around, grabbing hers and pinning them above her head. His head dipped, aiming for her breast.

"James, no." Her tone was clear, and he paused.

"What's up, dearest? Don't you want to make up for the past year? We can fuck once before the main course and again before dessert. It'll be just like old times."

"And that," Charlotte said firmly, pushing him away, "is the problem." She sighed. "You're a sweet boy, but I'm just not feeling it. Do you know what I mean? After all, a year of French men kind of elevates your standards."

He pouted. James was extremely good-looking and couldn't keep track of all his women. Charlotte pushing him off wasn't going to dent his ego for more than a second.

"So why did you follow me?"

Charlotte shrugged. "I'd finished my appetizer and had time to kill."

James straightened his pants and washed his hands. "You're a bit of a bitch, Charlie, my sweet."

Charlotte nodded. "You're not the first to say so, love."

And with that, she walked out, leaving the door open.

Chapter THREE

It was incredibly loud and hot in the club. The pulsing bass lines could be physically felt in every pair of panties in the place, which might explain the glassy expressions and elevated heart rates. Drugs, of course, may have had something to do with it. Not that there were drugs there. That would be illegal.

If you'd walked down this particular side street in Alphabet City, you'd have thought someone was having a party. No lines. No signs. No ropes. Just the distant sound of very loud music. You had to call ahead to get into this club, and if they bothered to answer the phone, you'd get an arrival time, and that was it. Your driver pulled up, the door opened, and you were let in. Charlotte simply texted the club owner. Regular cell-phone calls were for regular people.

He was waiting for her with a hug at the top of the stairs, and he embraced the other girls, too.

"Charlie, it's been an age. I think I was on the West Side Highway when you left." He laughed. "That was two spaces ago!"

Charlotte smiled at him. Only a handful of people got to call her Charlie, and Nick was one of them. He'd been at school with her, and she'd helped him get his first club off the ground. Clubs like

Nick's tended to move: it's not the space, it's the mix. You had to stay one step ahead of the police, two steps ahead of the East Village hipsters, and three steps ahead of the bridge-and-tunnel crowd. Nick was a master. As soon as he found one location, he started looking for the next. A warehouse in DUMBO. An abandoned department store above Harlem. A townhouse being gutted in the West Village. His clientele were the young, the rich, and the bored. They came to him to be entertained, to see their friends, to watch the show.

"Who's here?" Charlotte leaned closer to hear his answer.

He took her hand and pulled her to one side. "Actually, lovely, Taylor is here. I nearly told you not to come, but then I thought enough water might have flowed under the bridge by now."

Charlotte felt herself get colder, despite the sweaty heat of the club. "Oh."

Nick pulled back and looked at her. "Ah, I see I was wrong."

"Is she with him?"

"Are you crazy? No, love, she's long gone. He's with Stacy Star tonight. And her girlfriend. And her girlfriend's girlfriend." He coughed. "Celebrities, what can I say?" Charlotte raised her eyebrows, but Nick just shook his head. "Ignore him, sweetheart. You were always too good for him, anyway."

Charlotte sighed. During her first year at Yale, she'd fallen deeply in love with Taylor Augustine. He was a couple of years ahead of her, studying European literature, and was totally gorgeous. He considered himself a beat poet for the twenty-first century, and he mumbled a lot. He and Charlotte hung out in bed most of the time, reading poetry and smoking weed. Then, suddenly, he decided that was too bourgeois and dumped her for a fiery political science major who thought shaving her underarms was bowing to the Man.

Charlotte had been devastated. It was literally the first time she couldn't have something she wanted, and she hadn't handled it very well. Not well at all. Drunk and furious, she'd torched the political science building.

Luckily, her father was able to step in and offer to rebuild those parts of the building that hadn't burned to the ground, and he and the Yale board had agreed that Charlotte should spend her sophomore year elsewhere. Europe might be far enough, they thought, and the Sorbonne acquired a new student and an updated computer system.

And now here she was, back less than a day, and already she'd run into him. Sometimes life was just a bitch.

AS SHE WALKED into the main part of the club, she saw that things hadn't changed much while she'd been away. Anyone who was young, gorgeous, rich, or horny was there, and most of Nick's guests were all four. Beautiful girls and boys danced essentially naked on podiums all around the club, and everyone pretended not to look at them while at the same time hoping they were being looked at themselves. Same same. She turned to Nick, who was following her in, presumably to make sure she didn't set fire to his club.

"I see you're still working the ugly beat."

He shrugged. "What can I do? The beautiful are drawn to me—why else would you be here?" He looked around, his experienced eyes seeing everything, despite the candlelight and heavy smoke. "There. He's in that corner."

Charlotte took a moment to make him out, but then her heart stopped. Taylor. Still gorgeous, although now he seemed to be working a gangsta look, which is hard when you're from Connecticut and your father is the president of a major bank. The closest he ever got to the threat of violence was hiding from the townies in New Haven. Loose pants, slumped posture, lots of bling, and three girls dressed as sluts from the future on either side. Bottle of Courvoisier on the table. Bottle of Cristal, presumably for the sluts.

Nick squeezed her arm. "Are you going to cause trouble, or are you cool?"

"I'm cool."

"Don't light any fires, promise?"

"That was more than a year ago."

"Do you even have matches?"

"No, you idiot. Besides, look around. The place is full of candles and drunks. About six hundred people are in danger of burning the place down. If the fire marshal comes in . . . "

He quickly put his hand over her mouth. "Don't ever, ever say those two words in my presence again." He raised his finger. "I mean it, it's bad luck. Don't make me block your number."

She laughed and watched him melt into the crowd. In the far corner, as far from Taylor as possible, her dinner posse had set up camp, and James was apparently trying to persuade two pole dancers to let him join them onstage. They really weren't interested, but they were drunk enough to let him try.

Emily and Jane waved her over. She sighed inwardly and headed in their direction. In many ways, these clubs were where she lived or, at least, where the public face of Charlotte Williams lived. Before she'd discovered her inner bitch and realized that people found her entertaining when she was naughty, she'd found clubs scary. And they still made her feel anxious inside, but she guessed everyone felt that way when the world was looking at them. Not that any of her crowd would ever admit it.

"Did you see Taylor?" Jane looked worried.

Charlotte nodded. "It's OK. It's been a long time."

"Did you see who he's with?" Emily looked excited.

Charlotte nodded again. "Stacy Star."

Zeb was beside himself. "I have all her albums. She's outrageous. She worked the runway for Gaultier, and it was beyond fabulous. She's awesome."

Charlotte looked at him. "You're babbling, Zeb. Calm down."

He was quivering like a greyhound. "I can't. She's awesome. I love her."

Charlotte frowned, indicating to a passing waitress that she needed service. The waitress ignored her. "Zeb, I went to preschool with her. Her real name is Stacy Fishbein."

Zeb refused to be put off. "Well, good for her that she changed it, then. I'd change mine if I could."

"What's stopping you?"

"My parents. They think Zebediah is a cool name for a faggot. Fucking hippies. They're so accepting, it's really annoying."

The waitress came over, finally. Charlotte smiled up at her.

"Did Nick make you wear that, or are those your own clothes?"

The waitress was wearing a peekaboo bra, with glitter on her nipples and short-shorts. She narrowed her eyes. "You're a friend of Nick's?"

"I'm a very good friend of Nick's. You must be new, or you'd know me by sight and would already have brought me a Grey Goose and grapefruit, which is what I always have. I never pay, and neither does anyone with me."

The waitress started to laugh. "You're joking, right?"

The rest of the table went quiet. The waitress looked nervous. She looked over at Nick, who was watching her. He raised his eyebrows and made a gesture with his hand that made it clear she was to give Charlotte anything she wanted.

"Uh, I'll get you your drink right away. Sorry." She turned to go.

"Show me your tits." James was being insolent, but Charlotte let it go. New staff need to be taught a lesson sometimes.

The waitress turned back. She was actually very pretty. "No. Fuck off."

Pretty and feisty. That was hot, and James became more interested.

"No, really, take off your bra, and let me touch your tits. In fact, if you know what's good for you, you'll let me see it all. Otherwise, Charlotte will tell Nick you're out of here."

Charlotte sighed. This was too much. "No, I won't, James. Get a grip. Go get us our drinks, OK?" The waitress hurried away.

James was annoyed. "I want the waitress, Charlotte."

Charlotte shrugged. "Well, why not go about it the usual way, James? Talk to her for ten minutes, and tell her she's pretty. It usually works for you, right? Of course, now you've got your asshole behavior to overcome, so it might take you half an hour."

She was watching Taylor. He hadn't seen her yet. Time to make a move.

She stood up, tousling her hair and smoothing her dress. "Come on, James, come dance with me." She felt hollow inside, but she couldn't let anyone see it.

James was sulking. He shook his head.

Charlotte smiled at him. "Come on. We'll make it so hot the waitress won't be able to help herself, and she'll go down on you on the dance floor."

James smiled. He really was a very simple creature. He stood up, elegant and tall, and took her hand.

The dance floor had been full not a moment before, but somehow it had had one of those sudden shifts, where half the people wander off for a drink. Everyone could see Charlotte and James as they walked on, and since most of the club knew who they were, there was lots of whispering.

Charlotte began to dance sinuously. She knew she looked good, and dancing always turned her on. She and James had actually done this many times before; it was how they'd hooked up. There was something about their chemistry that turned dancing into foreplay. She could feel Taylor watching her now and touched herself, shimmying the silk of her dress over her body until her nipples became hard, clearly visible through the thin fabric. James was moving very close to her, their hips pressed against each other, swinging and moving in time. James took her long hair in one hand and wound it around his wrist, pulling her head back so he could start licking her neck. His other hand curved around her breast, squeezing it and pulling on the already hard nipple until she felt herself growing aroused. The dance floor was clear now, and even the pole dancers were watching. Charlotte suddenly twisted away from James and turned her back on him, making him grab her hips and pull her against him, closing his eyes. Charlotte saw the waitress watching and beckoned her over.

"He's all yours, love. Enjoy." She kissed the girl on the mouth, just for fun, and wandered over to Taylor's table.

Taylor watched her approach, his face hard to read. Stacy Star was an easier book.

"Charlotte Williams, the last time I saw you, you were playing with Legos. You grew up so nicely! My girlfriend wants to eat you all up, don't you, honey?"

Honey nodded, sucking her finger. "You're pretty."

Charlotte smiled at her kindly. "You're a moron. You should all go away now. I want to talk to Taylor. Go lick each other in the bathroom."

Stacy started to get pissed off but then shrugged. "Why not? Come on, ladies, I need a touch-up, if you know what I mean." She giggled, then quickly bent over and snorted two lines of coke that had been hidden behind her drink. Rubbing some on her gums, she stood and swayed a little, pulling the other girls with her.

Charlotte sat down, sweeping the rest of the coke onto the floor with the back of her hand. Taylor started to protest but didn't bother. Coke was cheap.

"What's up, Charlotte? Long time no see, baby."

"It's only been a year, Taylor. What happened to Phillipa?"

He shrugged. "She started dating a commodities trader with a house in the Bahamas."

"So now you're seeing Stacy Fishbein?"

"She doesn't use that name anymore. I want to work in the music business, you know. She knows people. She's a hot commodity right now, and she likes me. Why not?" Charlotte said nothing. Taylor lit a cigarette, another new habit. "I graduated, sweetness, and not all of us have Daddy to buy us out of trouble. I have to work, have to get a career going."

"Really? I would have thought that was optional."

He shook his head. "No, I want to work."

She was surprised. He really didn't need to. His family was almost as wealthy as hers. She looked at him again. Blond hair to his shoulders, stubble, a face like a model, he still made her ache inside.

And yet. It passed. She felt the attraction suddenly ebbing and thanked whatever higher power had decided to set her free.

As if he could read her mind, Taylor spoke again. "You still make me hot, Charlotte. Come home with us. Stacy throws a mean party, if you know what I mean. I know you like it. We used to ball all night, remember?"

"I remember. But no thanks, Taylor. It's not worth re-lighting that fire, if you'll pardon the phrase."

His smile faded as she walked away. But hers just grew bigger and bigger.

Chapter
FOUR

Her father had waited up for her, of course. She dropped her house keys on the hall table and paused, listening.

"The lovely girl, the lovely day . . . "

She smiled. Her father had a great voice, a secret she kept for him, and singing together was one of their private pleasures. This was a song he'd made up for her as a little girl.

"A perfect time to run and play . . . "

Charlotte's voice was not a secret. Singing "Happy Birthday" at the age of five, she had silenced a room. People really listened when she sang, and at first it made her shy and frightened. But when Millie, her beloved nanny, had told her father she really had talent, her father had encouraged her, sent her to the best teachers, and, most of all, loved to listen to her. Her voice was deep, smooth, with the barest hint of a rasp.

"Daddy's here, won't go away . . . "

Charlotte followed the sound of his voice, finding him, as expected, standing by the fire in his study.

"And in his arms you'll always stay."

They finished the line together, laughing, and Jacob Williams held out his arms. She stepped into his embrace, resting her head on his shoulder, the cashmere of his jacket feeling just as wonderful as it always did. No cigar smoke anymore—she'd made him quit.

He kissed the top of her smooth head and stepped to the sideboard. "Drink?" He topped up his scotch glass, the ice cubes tumbling together.

Charlotte nodded. "A little."

"Scotch?"

"Brandy."

He nodded, reaching for the bottle.

She curled up on the sofa, the glass warming in her hands, and smiled broadly at him. At home, she could just be herself.

"So, Daddy, what's new on the Street?"

He laughed. "Like you have any interest at all."

She pretended to be offended, kicking her shoes off onto the floor. "Of course I'm interested. Just because I don't understand it doesn't mean it's not interesting. I don't really get Greek philosophy, but I like to listen to people talk about it."

"You do?" His look was quizzical. "Bullshit."

She laughed.

"But since you asked, there was a nice pop in the market today, and quite a few people got very rich."

"What made that happen?"

He looked into his glass. "I was in a good mood, I sold, I bought, and lo and behold, the market rose."

"Goodness, what power you wield. Can you do something about world peace? Or, better still, the price of couture?"

He shook his head. "Those things are beyond me. But you don't need to worry about the price of couture. You got wealthier today by about three million dollars."

Charlotte paused, about to sip her brandy. "Really? I didn't even feel as if I was working."

"You weren't. I didn't even have anything to do with it. Your mother set up a fund for you before she died that I can't even touch. But today it did well, all on its ownsome."

"Huh, who knew?"

"Colloquialisms, Charlotte? I didn't send you to Paris to forget to speak English. I sent you there to learn French."

She ignored him. "What else? Are you seeing anyone?"

He frowned, hard and quick. "No, of course not."

She frowned back at him, mockingly. "Why not? You're not too old."

"I should damn well think not."

"And you're still very good-looking."

"You're biased."

"Maybe." But it was true. Jacob was still handsome. Tall, healthy and fit, superbly dressed, and one of the most powerful men on Wall Street. He'd been featured on the covers of *Time* and *BusinessWeek* and in the party pages of *Vanity Fair*. He attended functions with a variety of actresses and models, some as young as his daughter, but that wasn't what Charlotte meant. He knew what she meant.

Sighing, he looked her in the eye. "Charlotte, when you are older, you will understand. I believe there are only one or two people in the world with whom one can have a true connection. When you've been fortunate enough to find and marry one of those people, you are reluctant to settle for less. One can have lovers, those are easily found, but true love rarely strikes twice."

Charlotte snorted. "God, Dad, you sound like a Hallmark ad. Why don't you try going out with women who are closer in age to you than they are to me? Someone you'll have stuff in common with?"

Jacob stood. "Lord, child, you used 'stuff' in a sentence and then ended it with a preposition. I can't continue this conversation." But he was smiling.

Charlotte put down her glass and reached for his hand. Jacob pulled her up, held her in the curve of his arm, and started to dance.

She grinned up at him as they moved slowly into the hall, dancing gravely.

"The lovely girl . . . the lovely day . . . "

They stopped at the bottom of the stairs, Jacob dipping Charlotte low as they finished the song together. Then he pushed her toward the stairs.

"Go to bed, little one. Get your beauty sleep, not that you need to be any prettier, Lord knows."

He watched until she was out of sight, then closed his eyes, trying to hold the image. Decisively, he turned and headed back to the study. It was morning in Tokyo, and there really is no rest for the wicked.

Chapter FIVE

Jacob was long gone when Charlotte came down to breakfast the next day. Sipping her latte, she wandered around the apartment.

"Looking for me, Charlotte?" Greta surprised her. She'd caught Charlotte watching the young man she'd seen the day before, who was deliciously bent over, repairing something in the kitchen. "Admiring my new appliances?"

"Is that what you call him?" Charlotte kept her voice low, but Greta raised hers.

"Watch out, Andy, the mistress of the house is after you."

He straightened, turning around to regard his audience. Broad grin. White teeth. Dark skin.

"You know my heart belongs to you, Greta."

"I know, but she's new in town."

Charlotte protested. "I'm not really new, I'm just back again."

He shrugged. "Maybe you missed the memo. Young and pretty is out, older and wiser is in." He grinned at Greta and turned back to work.

Greta walked out, crooking her finger at Charlotte as she did so.

They went into the conservatory, with its curving glass walls overlooking Central Park. It was winter still, and the warmth of the room
and the tangle of exotic plants felt surreal against the background of
ashen trees below.

"Now, listen here, Charlotte." Greta had been with the
Williams family since before Charlotte was born, and she had
become another mother to Charlotte after her own had died.
"You keep your hands off Andy. He's a man, like any other, and
likely to get his head turned by you, but he's happily married,
with two small children, and you have no interest in any of that.
Leave him alone."

Charlotte narrowed her eyes. "I have no idea what you mean,
Greta."

The older woman snorted. "Please. I've seen the kind of trouble you can cause. Burning down a building was comparatively
civilized for you."

Charlotte was offended. "Greta, you're exaggerating."

"I am not. We went through three pool boys at the summer
house one year. And you were only seventeen, so Lord alone knows
what you could do now that you have more experience."

Charlotte giggled. "Yes, that was a great summer."

Greta looked firm. "For you, it was fun; for them, it was a
disaster. Some people need to work, you know."

Charlotte was unbowed. "Look, Greta, I didn't make them do
anything they didn't want to do. They weren't much older than I
was. We were just having fun."

"Hmm. Well, my point is that you're not seventeen anymore,
and people like Andy have responsibilities beyond protecting rich
young women from sunburn and over-chlorinated swimming
pools."

Charlotte put up her hand. "OK, Greta, I get it. I hear you. No messing with Andy. You have my word."

"That and a MetroCard will get me anywhere. Promise?"

"I promise."

Greta looked at her for a moment. "Are you looking forward to going back to Yale in the fall?"

Charlotte thought about it. "No, not really."

"Why not?"

"Because I don't find the studies very interesting, and because people are going to remember the whole stupid building thing. I wish I'd gone to Juilliard instead."

"To study singing?"

The younger woman nodded. "I don't think I would make the same decision now."

Several years earlier, at the ludicrously expensive private school Charlotte had attended, the college counselors had been discouraging about Charlotte's chances of a musical career. "The kids who go to Juilliard are going to be professional musicians," they'd said. "You don't have a classically trained voice. You've been gaining a traditional education. If you wanted to be a musician, you should have gone to a music school. No, Miss Williams, you should consider your voice a wonderful gift from God, something lovely to share with your future husband and children. Have you considered medicine? Or the law? A law degree could offer you freedom to follow multiple careers. Yale is an excellent school. Think about Yale."

Embarrassed, Charlotte had shut down, taken the information about Yale, filled out the paperwork, and let the school handle the whole thing. Unsurprisingly, Yale had accepted her sight unseen, the historical relationship between the two schools as strong and preferential as ever.

"Have you been to see Janet yet?"

Charlotte smiled. "I'm going later this morning. We're going to do a lesson and then have lunch."

Janet was Charlotte's voice coach and one of the limited number of people Charlotte felt truly comfortable with. You wouldn't think to look at Janet, in her Stevie Nicks handkerchief hemlines and general love of the witchy look, her long gray hair defiantly undyed and untamed, that she was one of the leading music teachers on the East Coast, but she was. She guided many members of the Philharmonic, frequently held master classes for members of the Metropolitan, and taught the talented children of the wealthy. Charlotte loved her.

"In fact, I'd better go get dressed right now." She turned back at the door. "I think there's a leak in my shower. Do you think Andy could come and take a look?"

Greta opened her mouth to chastise her but then realized she was teasing. Charlotte headed upstairs, still giggling.

Greta sat for a while, thinking. She wasn't sure what was going to become of Charlotte, to be honest. She had so much—looks, money, opportunity. But to Greta, Charlotte would always be the sobbing seven-year-old, calling for Mommy in the night, her father too anguished to hear. A few weeks after Jackie had been killed, a nanny had arrived, found by Greta, and Miss Millie and Greta had raised the girl between them. Jacob was a doting father, but he spent all his time at work. And something had changed in him when Jackie had died. Greta saw it; so did Davis. Miss Millie had been a wonderful nanny, though, very loving and firm, and Charlotte had recovered and eventually started to flourish. Seven years of relative peace had passed, but then one of Millie's own children had needed her back in Louisiana, and she'd had to leave. Charlotte hadn't ever really gotten over the loss, and Greta missed her colleague and friend, too. Early in Charlotte's teen years, things had started to go badly, with boys and God knows what else. It was hardly surprising; there was no one there to set an example, although Greta had done what she could. Now Charlotte was a young woman, and there wasn't much Greta could do to protect her anymore.

In fact, there wasn't anything anyone could do.

Chapter

SIX

Leaving the triplex an hour or so later, Charlotte decided to walk across the park instead of making Davis get out the car.

"Are you sure, Miss?" Davis looked concerned. "The park? Alone?"

"Oh, for goodness sake, Davis. It's Central Park in broad daylight, not Tompkins Square at two A.M. I've been taking care of myself in Paris for the last year. I even took the Metro alone, with only a fresh baguette to protect me."

Davis wasn't known for his lightheartedness. He went pale. "Your father wouldn't like it, Miss. It won't take me a minute to pull the car around."

She shook her head, pressing the elevator button. "No, Davis. I'll call you if I need a ride back from Janet's, OK?" She knew she was making him anxious, but that wasn't really her problem. Her dad could take care of himself, and so could she.

After the warmth of the apartment, the chill of the park was a shock. She greeted the doorman and pulled her Ungaro cashmere coat tightly around her. She'd forgotten how cold the city could

get, especially once you stepped out of the protective canyons of
the avenues. Joggers wearing earmuffs and gloves passed her, their
breath clouding, their eyes focused, the tinny buzz of their iPods
like passing insects. Charlotte had never enjoyed running—she
was more of a yoga and Pilates girl, although mostly, she was a
"naturally skinny and likes a big salad" kind of girl.

She found herself thinking about her mother. She wished she
remembered more, but her memories consisted of brief scenes,
scents, her mother bending down to kiss her good night when she
and her father were going out, the smell of Chanel No. 5 and finely
milled face powder. Clearly, Jackie had loved her, and she'd taken
her everywhere. One of Charlotte's favorite pictures was of herself
as a toddler, backstage at some runway show, covered in makeup
and surrounded by topless models, all of whom were smiling
down at her like soft-hearted, long-lashed giraffes. She was grinning back, toothless and happy, and at the side of the frame sat
Jackie, getting her hair done, her glance proud. In Paris during
the last year, she'd been greeted as a prodigal child, welcomed to
all the fashion houses, embraced and clucked over by designers
whose names were permanently etched on the pages of *Vogue*. Stories of her mother were told with great affection, and photos were
brought out that made Charlotte catch her breath. Many of them
were pictures of her as a baby with Jackie. Some were of Jackie
pregnant, candid shots of her helping other models get ready for
shows she was too spherical to work. And in some, she could see
her father, relaxed, smoking his cigars, watching his beautiful wife
with hot eyes and a warm smile.

More than one designer told Charlotte she should be a model,
but the aging models who'd held her at those long-ago runway
shows shook their heads at the idea. "No," they'd said firmly.
Finish college first. Get an education. Your mother would have

insisted, and she would have been right." One woman, Nadia, who'd parlayed a successful modeling career into an even more successful career as a booker, said she wouldn't even represent her if she asked.

"*Non, non, non.* Your mother was my dear friend, and she would curse me from her grave if I even suggested such a thing. Modeling is a cruel business, *ma chérie,* and she would keep you from it. She had fun, because she loved clothes and designers and other models, but it isn't the way it used to be. It is a big business now, and there is too much money at stake for friendships to be worth very much." She'd made a very French noise of disgust. "And besides, the models these days are all children, girls who didn't even get their periods yet, girls who should be climbing trees and kissing boys and running away." She had turned to look out at Paris and sighed. "If Jackie were here, she would be fat and happy, and you would have a dozen brothers and sisters, *chou chou.*"

Now, walking through the park her mother had also loved, Charlotte thought about this. Her memories of Jackie couldn't be trusted, they were melded with the information she'd gathered from the press, from books, from documentaries. There was one about the fashion of the '80s that had an interview with her mother, and she must have watched it a hundred times. It was long before she was born, and Jackie only talked about one particular designer, but Charlotte could recite every word, anticipate every head movement, every smile.

She kicked along through the leaves on the bridle track, wondering if her mother really would have wanted more children. She'd wished for a sister all her life, and when she was little, she'd hoped her daddy would remarry, maybe even someone who already had children, maybe several children. The big apartment was lonely and too quiet. Once she was older, she had turned her attention to friends from school whose families she could temporarily join. But those families were almost as cold as hers, sometimes worse. Sisters and brothers rarely played together, shuttled from one after-school activity to another by one nanny or another. Parents worked or shopped or spent time with the needy poor or the neurotic rich, and hanging out with the children was something you paid other children's mothers to do. It was no wonder she and her teenage friends were such a tight bunch; they just needed someone to play with.

From thinking of her mother, her mind turned naturally to Miss Millie, who had stepped in shortly after her mother died. Dark-skinned, fine-featured, sharp-tongued, Millie Pearl had been an incredibly important part of Charlotte's life. Whenever she stopped short of doing the truly stupid thing, when she refused that hard drug, when she didn't get into the car full of drunken frat boys—that was Millie's influence. She'd taught the young woman to value what was inside, to think for herself, to judge people by what they did, not what they wore. And she'd loved the girl deeply, hugging her frequently, brushing her long hair every night, and singing to her, making her feel special and safe and surrounded by a warm structure that supported her growth like a trellis in a garden. Charlotte had missed her very much when she left and had been desolate and depressed for several weeks. Then she'd sadly reached the conclusion that people you love were prone to suddenly leaving, and she'd polished herself a hard, shiny shell and kept it on from that time forward.

She was about halfway through the park, past the reservoir, when a young man approached her. He had something in his hand, and she instinctively took a step back in case it was a weapon. It wasn't. It was a pad and pen.

"I'm sorry, aren't you Charlotte Williams?"

She nodded, slowed a little. Maybe she knew him?

"I'm Dan Robinson from the *New York Sentinel*. I was wondering if you had a statement to make?"

She was confused and immediately on her guard. There were a lot of crazy people in the city, and then there were reporters. One had to be careful. Her dad didn't trust the press, and neither did she.

"A statement about what?" She started walking again, quicker this time.

"About your father's arrest." The reporter's eyes were bright, and he could tell he had surprised her. Her step faltered.

"I think you must be confusing me with someone else. My father is at work."

"He was at work. Now he is under arrest for embezzlement."

Charlotte felt and heard her phone ringing in her bag. She pulled it out. It was home. Then another call came in, from Emily. She answered the first one.

Greta's voice sounded shaken. "Charlotte, where are you?"

"I'm on my way to Janet's. Greta, there's a reporter here who says Daddy has been arrested. What's going on?"

"Come home, Charlotte. Or go to Janet's if you're closer. Davis will come and pick you up."

Charlotte looked up at the skyline. She could see the Dakota.

"I'm closer to Janet's. Tell Davis I'll be there in ten minutes. Is it true?"

Greta sounded like she was in tears. "Yes, Charlotte, but we don't know anything yet." There was a pause. "Please hurry, Charlotte."

She hung up. Emily had long ago gone to voice mail, and as she looked, she saw text after text coming in, voice mails piling up, phone calls on top of phone calls. She looked up. The reporter was still there, a tape recorder in his hand now, stretched out to catch her comments, her first thoughts on whatever it was that was happening. She drew a breath.

"Miss Williams? Do you have a comment? Your father is accused of perpetrating a massive fraud, embezzling millions, possibly billions, of dollars. The SEC claims to have been following him for years. What do you have to say?"

Charlotte narrowed her eyes at him and stood tall. "I have absolutely no doubt that my father is completely innocent and that his name will soon be cleared."

"It's your name, too, Charlotte." The reporter was very still, hoping she would say something that would make his editor proud.

But instead, she said something that would have made Miss Millie proud. "A name is just a label, Mr. Robinson. It doesn't tell you anything about someone's character."

And then she turned on her heel and walked away.

Janet opened the door, smiling, her arms open wide. She had her hair piled on top of her head, antique chopsticks holding it up, rhinestone cat-eye spectacles glinting. She really was one of a kind.

"It is so wonderful to see you, Charlotte. Give me a hug, for goodness sake. I want to hear all about Paris." Then the elderly woman paused, looking at her young friend more carefully. "What has happened? Are you all right?"

Charlotte pushed gently past her and went into the kitchen, where she knew there was a TV. "Can I put on the TV, Jan? Something bad has happened to Dad."

Janet gasped and rushed after her, finding the remote underneath a fluffy gray cat and switching on the TV. The cat was annoyed and stalked off, tail twitching.

"Calm down, Brutus, you weren't watching anyway."

Janet McTavish was, as her name suggested, originally from Scotland, but four decades in the United States had softened her accent considerably. She and her favorite pupil stood and waited for CNN to tell them what they needed to know. And then, suddenly, there was a photo of Jacob Williams, and the announcer was talking.

"Today, Wall Street was thrown into disarray when one of its giants, Jacob Williams, was arrested for securities fraud. Spokesmen for the SEC and the FBI issued the following statement."

The video cut to a press conference, where a man who didn't look very threatening was talking about Charlotte's father as if he were a criminal.

"For more than five years, the SEC and the FBI, working together, have been building a case against Mr. Williams, who has held the confidence of some of our country's leaders, many of our major banks, and thousands of individual investors. At times, we didn't think we would ever gather the evidence we needed, so complicated was his web of transactions and funds, but now we are confident that we have a watertight case against him. He is being held without bail in Manhattan, and a preliminary arraignment is scheduled for the morning."

Janet took Charlotte's arm and guided her to a chair, displacing poor Brutus again, who simply left the room in disgust.

"Goodness, child, you're as white as a sheet. Let's get you some whiskey."

Charlotte silently shook her head.

"A cup of tea, then?"

Another shake.

Janet snapped her fingers in Charlotte's face. "Charlotte, wake up." Charlotte jumped. "Your father is innocent, and there has been some mistake. You need to pull yourself together so you can help him."

There was a knock at the door, and suddenly, Davis was there.

"Miss Charlotte? Are you ready to come home?" He coughed, which was about as distressed as Davis ever got. "I'm afraid there are journalists and photographers at the building. We will be unable to avoid them."

Charlotte shook herself. She was young, but she was tough. She turned to Janet. "I will take that whiskey, thanks. Davis?"

"I'm driving, Miss."

"Of course." She thought for a moment. "Did you already contact Mr. Bedford?" Mr. Bedford was her father's lawyer.

"He was the one who alerted us first, Miss. He is with your father downtown."

"What about Marshall?" Michael Marshall was her father's partner. He'd been with Jacob a while, although he played a less public role than her father did.

Davis looked pained. "I haven't been able to reach Mr. Marshall."

"Maybe he's also been arrested?"

Davis shrugged, something she'd never seen him do before. For some reason, that small gesture of hopelessness on his part worried her deeply.

Charlotte looked around Janet's kitchen, cluttered and small yet as beloved to her as the stately kitchen in her own apartment. She'd had many of her happiest times in this place, singing with Janet, learning what her voice could do. She guessed those times were over for a while. If not forever.

"I'm sorry, Janet. I guess I need to go home."

Janet gave her a quick hug. "Oh, for goodness sake, you've nothing to be sorry for. I'm sure it's all an error somewhere or just someone jealous over some money. It usually is. You'll be back to see me next week, I expect, and we shall laugh about it."

Charlotte got up and walked through the living room to reach the door. The faded sofa, the enormous Steinway grand that dominated the room, the rich ruby and blue of the Oriental carpet, all precious sights she'd missed in Paris. She felt as if she were sleep-walking. Brutus regarded her balefully from the top of the piano, but his sister, Cleopatra, purred at Charlotte's feet. She bent to stroke the soft black fur, and it was as if someone else's hand was doing it. Somehow, the gentle purring of the cat reminded her that the world wasn't over; there was just a problem to be dealt with, and it would all be all right. The cat looked up and slowly blinked her big amber eyes affectionately. Charlotte straightened and turned to Davis, feeling the blood returning to her fingers and toes, her mind clearing.

"OK, Davis, let's go face the hordes. The apartment first and then downtown."

Davis smiled briefly, relieved to see that she was taking charge. "Yes, Miss."

But when they got home, they found downtown already waiting for them.

CHARLOTTE STAYED VERY calm as she pushed through the photographers and reporters at her building entrance and paused in the lobby to talk to the building manager. Jacob Williams was not the first resident to provoke media interest, and the manager was sanguine.

"Miss Williams, rest assured that no member of the press will be allowed into the building without your prior permission and that no photographers whatsoever will be given access. You've known Davy and Felipe since you were a child; you know their discretion can be relied upon."

Charlotte did know. The two doormen had seen many a drunken return to the apartment and had never so much as made a peep, not to her and certainly not to her father. Their discretion wasn't because of the Christmas bonuses each resident gave them, either; it was pride and honor. Or it could be a total lack of interest in the goings on of their spoiled tenants, but she preferred to think it was honor.

She smiled at the building manager. "I know, Mr. Rockwell. I am very grateful to all the staff. We will, of course, cover any additional expenses you incur . . . " She let her voice trail off politely, but her message was clear. *Spare no expense. Keep them out.*

Mr. Rockwell nodded. "This is your home, Miss Williams. You will be secure here, and when Mr. Williams returns, we will all be glad to see his reputation restored."

All of this made Charlotte feel much better, at least until the elevator opened onto the triplex foyer and Greta was waiting for her.

"There are gentlemen in the library, Miss. They wanted to enter your father's study, but I locked the door and told them they had to wait for you."

Charlotte took a deep breath and tried to fight down her rising sense of panic. "OK. Please tell them I have returned and will be with them shortly. Have you offered them coffee?"

Greta looked scandalized. "No. They are the police. They think your father is a criminal."

"All the more reason to treat them with civility, don't you think?" Charlotte headed up to her room. "Please serve them coffee." She paused. "On the Sèvres china, please."

Charlotte walked into her room, closing the double doors behind her with a click. Leaning back, she waited until her head cleared. What. The. Fuck. When she'd burned that building down at Yale, her dad had sent a lawyer to meet her at the police station, and he hadn't been far behind himself. Every time she'd gotten into trouble in her teens, Davis had shown up, whisking her away.

She had never, ever had to face anything difficult alone, or at least not for very long. She felt totally lost and terrified, but she knew she had to pull herself together. She looked around her room and realized that everything she needed was right there. "If you walk into a nest of vipers," her father had told her, "walk in looking like a million bucks. It'll confuse the snakes." A Chanel suit seemed like appropriate armor, with gorgeous shoes for a little "fuck you." Full makeup but not slutty. Smooth, tight hair in a diamond clip. Everything very under control. Yes, she was a twenty-two-year-old girl, but she was going to act as if she dealt with the authorities every day of her life. Secretly, she wanted her mommy, but dressing up in Mommy's clothes was the best she could do. It was small comfort, but it was comfort.

As she came down the stairs her knees were trembling, and at one point she stumbled, grabbing the banister for support. She saw Greta waiting below, her face drawn. Charlotte straightened, swallowing her own fear in the hope that she would alleviate Greta's. Like a swan, she told herself. Calm and serene above the water, paddling like mad underneath.

She made it down the rest of the stairs without falling.

WHEN CHARLOTTE ENTERED the library, she looked like the cover of a magazine, and all three men in the room instinctively got to their feet. The dark suit made her hair glow, and her smooth skin and unusual features were stunning.

"Gentlemen." Charlotte extended her hand. "I'm Charlotte Williams. I understand there has been some mistake about my father."

The first man, who was short and somewhat round, introduced himself.

"Miss Williams, I'm Philip Mallory, NYPD. I'm acting as the liaison between the NYPD and the two other agencies involved in the investigation." His tone was bland, calm. He could probably see her hand was shaking, but he just seemed to file that away.

"The SEC and the FBI?" Charlotte was equally cool. "I assume you gentlemen represent one each?" She smiled, getting them to smile back at her, unable to stop themselves. *OK, Charlotte, they're just men,* she told herself, *just men. Men love you.*

"I'm Jim Scarsford from the SEC." Taller than the cop, handsomer, and dressed in what Charlotte immediately saw was an Armani suit. She guessed you had to dress like a banker to catch a banker. She smiled briefly at Scarsford and turned to the last man.

"Sam Dale, FBI." He could have come from anywhere, been anything. Sandy hair, pale eyes, small mouth. His extreme normalness was probably an advantage in his work. Your eye would just slide right over him. His suit was Men's Warehouse, all the way.

"Can any of you gentlemen tell me where my father is?"

Scarsford cleared his throat. It was unfortunate for him, but the SEC agent found Charlotte attractive and appeared to be struggling a bit to remain focused on the fact that she was a subject in an investigation. "Uh, yes, Miss Williams. Your father is being held at an FBI facility downtown. He is safe, of course."

"Of course. Why FBI, may I ask? Is he being charged with a federal offense?" Charlotte was impressed with how calm she sounded. She didn't feel it, but she sounded it. All those deportment lessons finally paying off.

Mr. Dale answered. "Yes, he is. Securities fraud is a crime with far-reaching implications and victims in multiple states. In fact, your father is accused of defrauding investors from more than fourteen different countries."

Charlotte smiled again, although she feared she might throw

up at any minute. "Really? That sounds very energetic of him." She paused, crossing her legs and settling herself more comfortably, the red soles of her shoes seeming to distract them. Jim Scarsford started to go scarlet, the color climbing his neck. "My father's lawyer has been present throughout, I assume?"

The FBI agent nodded. "Yes. Your father hasn't actually answered any questions or spoken to agents from any of the agencies involved yet, although we hope he will. If he wishes to prove his innocence, he's going to need to talk to us."

Charlotte's expression remained calm. "I imagine he'll do whatever he deems most sensible." She stood. "Now, gentlemen, I assume you need something from me, or you wouldn't be here. How can I help you?"

The cop pulled out a piece of paper. "We have a warrant to search your father's study. The warrant allows us to remove his computers, his files, and any other materials we consider pertinent to our investigation."

Charlotte took the piece of paper and folded it without looking. "I'll need to consult with my attorney, of course. Will you gentlemen excuse me while I call him?"

Once outside the door, Charlotte ran for the bathroom and made it just in time. Resting her clammy forehead on the sink, she unfolded the paper and looked at it. It was, as they had said, a search warrant for her dad's study. It was signed by a judge she knew, one who'd eaten in their home several times. *Traitor.* It was probably only a matter of time before they searched the whole place. Her room. Her closet. She retched again and waited there a while until she felt composed.

Wiping her mouth, she looked at herself in the mirror. A little pale. She pinched her cheeks and opened her eyes wide. *Pull your-*

self together, Charlotte. She entered her father's study and called the lawyer.

"Arthur?" The line wasn't very good, and it sounded as if he wasn't alone.

"Charlotte? Are you at the apartment?"

"There are police here, Arthur, with a warrant for Dad's study."

The lawyer sighed. She'd known Arthur Bedford all her life, and she'd never heard him sound stressed before. "Your father has been accused of some very serious crimes, Charlotte, and the FBI and the SEC are totally within their rights to search the apartment."

Charlotte looked out the window. Everyone was carrying on as normal. Tourists were climbing into horse-drawn carriages. Children were playing. Did no one realize the world had ended?

"The warrant only covers the study. I'm in it right now. No smoking guns. No piles of cash."

Arthur had lost his sense of humor. "Don't touch anything, Charlotte. Don't take anything out."

She frowned. "Why would I, Arthur? The sooner they clear this all up, the sooner we can sue them for defamation of character."

Another sigh. This was beginning to make her feel anxious.

"Dad is innocent, right, Arthur?"

"Charlotte, I wish I knew." She heard the sound of louder voices. "Let's talk in an hour or so, OK?"

She stood there a moment, lightly touching the things on her father's desk. His laptop was there. A detachable flash drive. Keys to his files. Nothing was hidden, no secrets there. *Fine. Let them come.*

She collected the key to her father's study from Greta and went back into the library. She decided to address Dale, the FBI agent.

"My lawyer advises me that my father wants to see me. Will that be allowed?"

Surprisingly, Dale turned to Scarsford.

Charlotte raised one eyebrow. "I thought the FBI was holding my father?"

Scarsford looked annoyed at Dale, briefly. "They are, but the SEC began the investigation. I'm the lead investigator."

Charlotte started to feel the tiniest flicker of anger, deep within her fear. "Gentlemen, let me be crystal-clear. You think my father is guilty of something. You think he is a criminal. But I assume your suspicions don't extend to me?"

A short pause, each waiting for the other to catch the ball.

"Or do they?"

The cop caught it. "Not at this time, Miss Williams. The investigation is just beginning."

"I thought your case was watertight? That's what you've told the media. You've hung my father before you've even begun? That's not very sporting of you, is it?"

She walked to the window and looked out for a moment, composing herself and pulling together every ounce of inner strength she possessed. She wanted her father to walk through the door, laughing, telling everyone what a good joke this had been. But when she turned back to the investigators, she looked as if she were serving tea rather than an ultimatum.

"If at any time during this investigation I feel I am not being treated with the utmost respect or that I am being deliberately misled in any way, I will cause problems for each and every one of you that will make you wish you had not been born. My father and my family are connected at the highest levels of government, of society, and internationally. Please remember that you have been welcomed into my home and treated with civility. Do me the courtesy of extending the same civility."

She took a deep breath.

"Now, will whoever's in charge please answer my simple question: May I see my father?"

Scarsford smiled. "Of course, Charlotte."

"Miss Williams."

The smile didn't wobble. "Miss Williams, sorry. Once our people have begun to search your father's study, I will take you to him myself."

"Very well." She extended the key to him. "Here is what you need. Nothing has been disturbed or removed since my father left for work this morning. We have nothing to hide." She looked Scarsford in the eye. "Can you say the same, Mr. Scarsford?"

He flushed.

 EIGHT

It was actually an hour before they could leave the apartment, and during that time, Charlotte was able to talk to Emily on the phone. Emily seemed more amused than anything.

"It's just ridiculous, Charlotte! There are photos of your dad on CNN, for crying out loud. And not very flattering ones, either."

Charlotte made a face. "That's hardly a problem right now, Emily. When this is all cleared up, I'll make sure to update their file photo, OK?"

Emily was unchastened. "Well, he looks heavy, is all I'm saying." She giggled. "Maybe he'll be like Martha Stewart and get in shape in jail."

"Emily." Charlotte's tone was sharp. "Don't even joke about it. It's not funny."

She could hear her friend pouting. "It is a little bit funny, Charlotte. It's silly. Why on earth would your dad steal money when he's so wealthy? The po-po are so stupid."

Charlotte happened to be looking at Detective Mallory as Emily said this, and she thought she'd rarely seen a man who looked less stupid, but there you go.

"Shall I come and visit you?" Emily sounded giddy. "I can wear dark glasses and cover my head with a shawl and creep in."

"Don't you dare, Emily. Stay away so you don't get dragged in the mud, too. Besides, I'm going to see Dad soon, so I won't be here much longer."

"OK, Charlotte. I'll call you later, OK?" Emily hung up, presumably to call all of her other friends and revel in schadenfreude.

Charlotte was getting a pretty good handle on her anger now, and she found herself irritated by her friend's lighthearted response to her crisis. Not once had Emily said she was sympathetic or said that she felt bad that Charlotte was going through this or offered to do anything concretely helpful. Oh well. To be fair, she wasn't sure what she would do if the situation were reversed. She smiled at the thought of Emily's parents getting in trouble. For what? Shoplifting at Zabar's? Buying non-fair-trade coffee?

Jim Scarsford, watching her from across the room, saw a brief smile soften her features for a moment, then fade away. Mallory came over and spoke to him.

"We're good here. You can take her downtown now, if you want. Or keep her waiting some more. It's up to you. Sometimes if they get worked up enough, they make a mistake, you know, blurt something out in frustration that they wouldn't have otherwise."

Scarsford frowned at his NYPD counterpart. "I doubt she knows anything. She's been away in Paris for the last year, and before that, she didn't seem interested in anything but boys and clothes. I doubt Charlotte Williams is a criminal mastermind."

Mallory looked less sure. "She would have been arrested for arson if she'd been anyone else, you know that. Yale hushed it all up because Daddy stepped in and threw money at the problem. If she'd been an eighteen-year-old black kid from New Haven, she'd be in jail still, and where's the fairness in that?"

All three men had been watching the Williams family for quite some time. Charlotte surely would have been embarrassed if she knew how much both of these men knew about her life. Including her love life.

She stood as Scarsford approached her. It was a pity he was the devil—he was actually nice looking.

"Can we go now?"

When she stood close to him, he realized she wasn't as tall as he'd first thought. He'd been seeing pictures of her day after day for the last several years, and he'd been prepared for her prettiness. What he hadn't been ready for was the intoxicating mix of reserve and heat she gave out. Very controlled, very elegant, very stylish. But she moved like a cat, and her face was so expressive. He wished for a moment he could take her to bed, really find out what made her smile, what made her eyes close in delight, what made her curl up inside. But that was never going to happen, because he was going to put her father in jail, and that tended to be a dating no-no. Smiling wryly at himself on the inside, he maintained his cool and simply nodded.

ONE OF THE things an expensive Upper East Side education gave you, supposedly, was the ability to make polite conversation with anyone. You might run into a diplomat one day and a king of some small country the next, and a properly educated young woman should easily be able to discuss a variety of neutral topics. But it turned out that riding downtown in a car with a man responsible for arresting your parent was a tough situation to chat your way through.

"Music?" As soon as he said it, he kicked himself.

Charlotte simply turned and looked at him, one perfectly arched eyebrow lifted. "What would you suggest? 'Folsom Prison Blues'? 'Jailhouse Rock'?"

Silence. He'd graduated first from his class at Columbia Law, slaved as a junior associate at a white-shoe firm, learning the ins and outs of securities litigation, and joined the SEC determined to bring big business and fat cats to task for cheating the common man. Instead, he'd spent most of the previous half-decade watching rich people get richer while getting away with crimes poorer people would have rotted in jail for. He wanted to feel nothing for Charlotte Williams and her ilk, the protected offspring of the wealthy. But she was hot and smart and apparently had a sense of humor even now.

"Sorry, you're right. Not appropriate."

More silence. They were crawling down Fifth, and he cut across the park, joining traffic that was moving a little faster. She gazed out, seeing familiar buildings sliding by, filled with people who presumably had worries of their own. Piles of stubborn black snow clung to the corners here and there. *Sometimes the puddles in the intersections got so deep they'd go over her boots when she and Daddy were walking to the park, jumping and squealing, even though he'd gotten her the boots with the string at the top, even though his strong arms held her up when she jumped, even though.*

Scarsford looked over. She was looking out the window, her profile still. He'd seen many people in trouble, and some weeks, those were the only people he talked to. Usually, they were chatty, trying to win you over, trying to make things easier by making a connection, hoping you would overlook whatever the hell it was they'd done. Not this one, not this girl. She couldn't care less about him. She was probably thinking about what to wear to dinner.

Sometimes they'd go to ride Charlotte's pony, and he would walk alongside her, talking about the trees and the birds, making up stories about what the pony was thinking, about how he dreamed of her all week, waiting for her to come and ride him, and his head would be level with hers almost, because the pony was very small and he was very tall, Daddy was.

She sighed. Scarsford sneaked a look again, nearly rear-ending a cab. The sudden stop made her jump, disturbing whatever shopping spree she was dreaming of. Charlotte turned to him, her eyes full of tears. She looked at him for a long moment, her face the prettiest and saddest thing he'd ever seen, and then the traffic moved again, and so did they, and he lost her to her dreams once more.

Then they were there.

THE METAL DETECTOR was interesting. Scarsford went first, pulling a gun from inside his jacket (Charlotte had been surprised to see it, short and ugly and lying like a toy in the plastic tray), then a wallet, a watch, a class ring.

Then it was her turn. She removed her watch (IWC), a tennis bracelet (Tiffany's, a present from her dad), a ring (emerald, vintage, Alexander's), and a collar pin (also emerald, vintage, Alexander's, of course). All told, it represented more than the annual salary of the woman working the metal detector, but she couldn't have cared less. She'd worked there for nearly two decades, and honey, she'd seen it all.

"Shoes?" Charlotte looked at Scarsford, but he shook his head.

"Not here."

"Jacket?"

This time, he nodded. She slipped it off, revealing a simple lawn chemise, sleeveless, utterly see-through, La Perla underwear clearly visible. She stepped over the metal threshold, but it beeped. She frowned, stepped back, tried again. Another beep.

Scarsford was waiting on the other side as the woman stepped forward with the wand, and he let himself follow its path up and down her slender body. Clean all the way down, clean all the way up, but then it beeped at her head. She had been frowning, slightly embarrassed to be holding up the line to be scrutinized by strangers, but now her face cleared.

"My clip."

She reached up to the back of her neck, pulling the transparent cotton tight across her breasts for an instant, making Scarsford start to get hard, despite his best efforts to think of the tax code. He was lost a second later, though, when her long hair tumbled down, just reaching her breasts, the diamond clip dropping into another tray, and then she was next to him, no beep, just the scent of her hair as she moved past him, the soft curve of her shoulder close enough to touch. What the hell was wrong with him?

She was struggling with her watch, and he stepped forward to help, aching to touch her smooth skin.

"No, thank you. I've got it."

Her cool voice made him feel twelve again, and he stepped back.

She fastened the watch, the jewelry, the pin. Then she turned her back on him and twisted her hair, her long, thin fingers gathering it into a knot, revealing the soft nape of her neck. A click. She turned again, once more covered and under control.

"Shall we go?"

Scarsford just nodded, not trusting his voice, and headed to the elevators.

After taking a deep breath, she followed.

Chapter
NINE

Jacob looked at his daughter across the table, a cold cup of coffee the only thing on its chipped Formica surface.

"You look lovely, Charlotte."

It had been his first thought when she walked in. Sun filtered down a mine shaft, illuminating what seemed like impenetrable darkness only seconds before. It had been a gray blur, the men in nice suits taking him from his office, the ashen face of his secretary, the ink on his fingertips. It was a nightmare, but now Charlotte was there, and he would hold on to that.

"You look like your mother."

She sat and reached for his hands, so cold. "Have you eaten anything?"

He shook his head.

Charlotte looked around the room. Cinder-block walls with no paint. Painted cement floors, like an old school. Mysterious dark spots on the walls suggested blood and violence. Under it all, a smell of fear and confined sweat. Suppressing an urge to run as far away as possible, she stood again and went to the wide mirror on one wall.

Raising her voice, she spoke to her own reflection. "Scarsford, I've watched *Law and Order*. I know you're in there. If you don't bring him some food immediately, I am leaving. He's an old man. He has a medical condition. If I have to call for a doctor, you can be sure the press will hear of it."

She sat back down and smiled tightly at her dad. She had been shocked to see him when she walked in, and the lost look on his face had frozen her own fear in place, forced her to pull it together. She was getting quite an education in her own strength today.

"I'm not old. Nor do I have a medical condition." His quavering voice made it a lie.

"You're not old, Dad, but you aren't young, either, and this must be horrible for you. I know it is for me, and Greta and Davis look as if they could fall apart at any minute. And the medical condition? They don't know that." *Besides,* she thought to herself, *I might have a coronary any minute, just from the pressure of not losing it completely.* But on the outside, she was cool, and among the men watching them through the one-way mirror, only Scarsford had any idea how much pain she was in.

The door opened, and a young man came in, carrying a fresh cup of coffee and some sandwiches. He put them down without a word.

"Eat," instructed Charlotte. "Then we'll talk." She looked away, trying to give him some privacy. She read a poster about her rights that was translated into four languages, none of them giving her the right to take her dad and leave, which was the only one she wanted to exercise.

The first bites of food nearly choked him, but gradually Jacob felt better, some color returning to his face. He drained the coffee cup, tucking it under the older one, neat and tidy.

"What shall we talk about, honey?"

Charlotte paused. For a second, she wondered if he'd lost his mind. His voice was just like normal, but it shouldn't have been. Everything he'd built, everything he'd worked for, was under threat. Why wasn't he storming around? Why wasn't he angry?

"I don't know, Dad. How about you getting arrested for fraud? Seems current, anyway."

He frowned at her. "You're mad at me."

"No, just confused. Why do they think you did this?"

He shrugged.

"Are they listening to us? Can they hear what we're saying?"

He shrugged again. "I expect so, but I don't want to talk about it, anyway. I want to talk about your mother."

She paused. "Why?"

"Because we've never talked about her, have you noticed?"

Fantastic, thought Charlotte. *Years of silence on this pivotal topic, and now all of a sudden, he wants to talk about it, now that we're sitting in front of a hostile audience.* A lump started to form in her throat.

"Dad, I think we need to focus on how to get you out of here, all right? We can talk about Mom later on, at home."

"There won't be a later on, honey. They're never going to let me out. I know the SEC intimately. They don't tend to act unless they're sure, because it's their own hand in the drawer, if you follow me."

"OK, but they're wrong, aren't they?" In the distance, she heard a man yelling, his anger abruptly cut short by a door slamming. The hair on the back of her neck stood up.

Jacob sighed. "Did you know your mother had two miscarriages before she had you?"

Tears of frustration sprang to Charlotte's eyes. "Why are you telling me this now, Dad? We need to get you out of here. Don't you realize how much trouble you're in?"

He nodded. "I do. But maybe now that I'm here, I can focus on what's important, which is telling you about your mother and how much she loved you. We tried for a long time to have children, you know. All she wanted was children, to be a mommy. We planned to have lots and lots of kids and go live on an island far away from this one. You and your brothers and sisters were going to run around barefoot all day, swimming in the ocean, wearing just flowers in your hair. It wasn't supposed to end this way."

"Dad—"

"Don't interrupt, honey. She was pregnant again, finally, when the car accident happened. No one knew but me. We were going to tell everyone that weekend, but she didn't make it. And the baby was so small there was no chance. Your brother or sister." He sighed. "All gone."

Charlotte took a shuddering breath. Clearly, she needed some help here.

Jacob just kept going. "And then Miss Millie came, and she took such good care of you, and Greta, of course, and work just didn't make any sense anymore. What was the point, without her? I took advantage of something. A loophole. A small thing. I just didn't care anymore, if they saw me do it. But they didn't see me, so I did it again. It took on a life of its own, rolled on like a snowball, and years passed before I started to feel anything again. When I did, when I saw that if Jackie were here, she would hate what I had become, it was too late. I was lost."

Charlotte gazed at him in horror. Was he confessing? "Shh, Dad, never mind. It doesn't matter now. Let me get Arthur, we can talk when he gets here, OK?"

She suddenly realized that if they were listening to this, which presumably they were, then without Arthur present, they could use it against her father, as evidence. Right? She stood and banged on the mirror.

"Mr. Scarsford, my father would like his lawyer, please."

A pause.

Jacob was still talking, as if she were still sitting across from him. "Your mother just wanted a simple life, Charlotte. She just wanted to be happy and quiet with her children. She would be so proud of you, of what you've become."

"And what's that, Dad? A spoiled young woman?"

He laughed.

Scarsford came in. "Mr. Bedford is on his way, Miss Williams. The more your father can tell us, the more we can help him."

Charlotte snorted. "Mr. Scarsford, please."

Jacob looked up at them. "You're not spoiled, Charlotte. There's still time for you to have the life you want to have, that your mother would have wanted you to have. You should leave Manhattan, though. It's not a very easy place to keep things simple. Things have a way of getting out of hand."

"Things like what, Mr. Williams? Things like the fund?" Scarsford had moved into the room.

"Don't answer that, Dad. Mr. Scarsford, please leave the room. I have asked for counsel, and this conversation is over."

"It seemed like a small thing at the beginning, Charlie. Just a quick thing that didn't seem to hurt anyone."

Charlotte was starting to cry, her body shaking uncontrollably. Where was Arthur? "Shh, Daddy, don't talk now. We're waiting for Arthur, OK?"

Jacob smiled up at her, just as he always had. "Honey, it's too late for Arthur. It's not his fault." He reached up and stroked the side of her face. "You look like your mom, did I tell you that?"

Charlotte sobbed. "Yes, Daddy, you told me that."

And then she took his head in her arms and held him tightly, as he started to sob himself. "It was just a small thing, Jackie, just a small thing. I'm so sorry, Jackie."

Charlotte held on tight and waited for the lawyer.

Chapter
TEN

After that, things got even worse. Jacob had cried for a while and then fallen silent and sullen, refusing to talk even to Charlotte. Arthur had ordered the investigators from the room.

"I think it's clear your father is in shock, Charlotte. I think we should have him looked at by a doctor."

Charlotte felt as if she herself could use some medical attention, or at least a Xanax or three, but she pushed it down. "Will it be someone we know or someone they bring?"

Arthur frowned. "I'm not sure."

In the end, the investigators allowed Jacob's own doctor to attend him, and once Dr. Levinger was finished, they allowed him to transport Jacob to a hospital for further evaluation.

Mallory was brusque. "Mr. Bedford, if this is your client's attempt to escape prosecution by feigning illness, then you should advise him that it hasn't worked for organized crime, and it won't work for him."

Arthur was starting to get his confidence back, now that his own shock was receding. He looked down his nose at the policeman.

"Good grief, Detective, there's no need to be rude. Mr. Williams has suffered a great shock, and the doctor merely wishes to ensure that there isn't anything else going on. If he collapses while in your care, it wouldn't look very good for you, would it?"

Mallory said nothing for a moment, then, "I'm not sure you realize how angry people are about this. If I let him leave the building unguarded, he might not make it to the sidewalk."

Charlotte went pale. "What are you talking about? What people?"

"The people whose money he stole, Miss Williams. Did you think it was all faceless corporations and big banks? No, he took the life savings of couples who'd planned to retire, who'd worked all their lives and were finally about to be able to rest. He took the nest eggs of families with children. He took whatever he wanted, Miss Williams, and people tend to look askance at that kind of greed."

"You're wrong about him," Charlotte said, although inside she was feeling less sure. Her father had seemed so happy and normal and confident only the other night. Was it possible that everything she took for granted, everything she thought was certain, was actually a total lie? She'd have broken down if she'd had any tears left.

WHEN THEY LEFT the building, her father in a wheelchair, his doctor at his side, she saw firsthand what Mallory had been talking about.

"There he is, there's Williams!" A small crowd surged forward, their faces twisted with rage. "You thief!"

Charlotte made eye contact with one woman, a normal-looking woman in her early forties maybe.

"You bitch!" the woman cried. "Your father stole everything I ever worked for. He's a fucking thief, and I hope he dies in jail, and you, too, you whore!"

Charlotte faltered a little, feeling as if she'd been physically assaulted. As she paused, she felt a hand on her elbow, guiding her, and she managed to keep going. As she passed the woman, she felt wetness on her face—the woman had spat on her. Charlotte stumbled, but the hand on her elbow was strong and kept her going.

"Don't stop, Charlotte. I've got you." The voice was low in her ear, but she kept going.

Someone threw something at her father, and he ducked his head. It smashed on the ground, a bottle.

Suddenly, the police formed a barrier between their small group and the larger crowd, and they got to the ambulance. As the doors slammed and it pulled away, Charlotte was propelled to another waiting car, and she turned to see who was helping her.

Scarsford. He didn't let go until she was in the car, and when he did, her arm felt suddenly cold.

Faces pressed up against the window, struggling with the police, fingers pointing, rage, anger, and . . . loss. She could see sadness and panic on these faces and suddenly realized what her father stood accused of. And she realized in the same moment that he was guilty and that life was never going to be the same again.

THE SCENE WAS similar in front of her apartment building, although there were fewer police to protect her. Scarsford kept his arm around her shoulder, and she ducked her head, but she could still hear the insults and threats people were throwing.

Not to mention the photographers.

"Come on, gorgeous, they're going to love you in jail. Give us a smile."

"Over here, bitch, over here."

"Look up, Charlotte. Let's see you."

They wanted something to put on TV, just as Emily had said, and she was damned if she was going to give it to them.

And then someone said, "I hear you fuck your father for money, Charlie."

She looked up, enraged and horrified, and a million flash bulbs went off. That was the shot the tabloids would run of her. She looked terrible: furious, scared, but still hot as hell. Editors ate it up all over the country. It was a shot that would haunt her forever.

Scarsford yelled at the photographers to get back, and they got close enough to her building for the doormen to step in. Suddenly, she was in the lobby, safe.

Scarsford took out a handkerchief and wiped her face. It came away red.

"Am I bleeding?" Charlotte was surprised.

A brief smile flickered across his face. "No, more traditional. Tomato. Someone threw one, I guess, and splattered you."

She looked down at her suit. Oh, yeah. All over her. "Just as well I picked navy."

Scarsford's phone rang, and he stepped away to answer it. When he looked back a few moments later, she was gone, the distant chime of the elevator the only trace of her. The lobby guard was watching him expressionlessly, and after failing to come up with a legitimate reason to go after her, Scarsford left.

———

THE ANSWERING MACHINE was full, but the apartment was empty.

Greta and Davis had left, presumably to go home, but Greta had left her enough food for three dinners, and Davis had left a big note on her bed with his cell number and an exhortation not to go anywhere without calling him first.

Charlotte was glad to be alone. She needed to think.

She wandered upstairs and took a long shower, trying to relax and get rid of the smell of the downtown jail. Operating almost on auto pilot, she hot-oiled her hair and wrapped it in a warmed towel, then covered herself with pure shea butter warmed in her palms. A floor-length Turkish toweling robe and slippers made her feel almost cozy, and she curled up in her dad's chair in the den, flicking on the plasma and curling her fingers around a fresh cup of hot chocolate.

She flicked from channel to channel for a while but couldn't help herself. She turned to CNN. She spilled her cocoa.

Emily was on the screen, apparently standing in front of her building. The subtitle said, "Family Friend," but Emily didn't sound all that friendly.

"Yes, Mr. Williams was always at work. We hardly ever saw him. Charlotte was basically raised by the servants."

Servants? Davis and Greta weren't going to like that at all.

"It really isn't surprising that Charlotte went off the rails like she did."

Charlotte's jaw dropped. Emily disappeared, replaced by the horrific shot of her from earlier. Great. She looked like that Munch painting. The announcer was talking about her.

"Jacob Williams has a daughter, of course, the socialite Charlotte Williams, who was nearly expelled from Yale a year ago for allegedly burning down a building in a lovers' spat." Then they showed a variety of party shots of her, a few of them quite risqué. Where had those come from? Surely Emily wouldn't have—

"At this time, Miss Williams is not a suspect in the fraud, but the authorities might well have questions going forward."

Charlotte turned it off. Somewhere in the apartment, her phone was ringing. Then the house phone started. Her phone stopped, then started again. Charlotte realized there was no one in the world she wanted to talk to. No one except her dad, and he wasn't taking calls right now. Unless it was him calling? She leaped up but didn't make it in time. Standing there, she hit the play button on the answering machine.

Many of the messages were people yelling, which made her wonder how they'd gotten the number, but then she realized that they were her dad's investors, and he'd presumably given out the number himself. *Note to self: Change the number.*

Suddenly, a friendly voice came out of the machine, making her gasp.

"Miss Charlotte, it's Miss Millie here. I saw the news about your daddy, and I just wanted to remind you that God loves you, and so do I, and that you're special and good, and whatever happens, you need to remember that, do ya hear? I think of y'all all the time and pray for you every night. Give my love to Miss Greta and Davis and, of course, to your lovely self. Come to New Orleans if you need to. We'll be here! 'Bye now."

Other messages weren't so nice.

"Charlotte, this is Michael Marshall." Her dad's partner had surfaced at last. Charlotte went to pick up the phone, forgetting for the moment that it was just a message. Marshall had paused, but then he continued. "I . . . uh . . . I'll try you again later." *Click.*

She called him back.

"Michael, it's Charlotte. Are you all right?"

He sighed.

It was a funny thing. When Michael Marshall had joined her father's firm, it looked as if his daughter, Becky, and she were going to be friends. They were the same age, went to similar schools, had similar hobbies. For the first few months, the two families hung out together quite a bit: dinners here and there, a trip to the beach. And then, just as suddenly as it had started, it stopped. Becky didn't return her calls, ignored her texts, unfriended her online. She'd been upset and tried for a while to get her to explain what had happened. Eventually, she'd given up. Now she had the sinking feeling she knew what had happened. Maybe.

"I'm fine, Charlotte. How are you? Were you able to see your dad?"

"Yes. He's pretty confused, I think. Did they question you, too?"

There was a long pause. "Charlotte, I have to tell you something." He sounded very old, and almost close to tears. "Your father was very good to me, and in many ways, he's one of the most honorable men I've ever known. But he was breaking the law, Charlotte, and I knew it. For a while, I kept quiet, hoping it would stop or blow over or change in some way so I could leave with my conscience intact. But it didn't. And I couldn't look my own children in the eyes anymore, because I was involved."

Charlotte's blood grew cold. "So you turned on him to protect yourself?" Her voice was soft.

"They were catching on to us, anyway, Charlotte, I could see it was just a matter of time."

"So you threw him to the wolves and presumably cut some kind of deal. That's nice, Michael. Loyal. My father would be impressed."

"Your father is a criminal."

"You would know."

"Yes, I would know. I was there, and I should have done something to stop it right away. I'm going to have to live with that forever."

"Well, that's comforting. At least you'll get to live with it somewhere nice and sunny, where getting raped in the shower isn't
business as usual."

Michael's voice broke. "I'm sorry, Charlotte. I didn't feel I had a
choice. He destroyed hundreds of people, maybe thousands."

"And you destroyed only one. Yes, I can see how that's much
better."

Charlotte hung up and sank slowly onto the stairs. This was not
the best day ever, by a long shot. The phone rang again.

"Yes, Michael? Thought of something else?"

"Who's Michael?"

Not Michael. Another voice, unfamiliar.

"Who's this?"

"This, Charlotte Williams, is the man who's going to kill you."

"I beg your pardon?" She looked at the number. Blocked.

"I'm going to kill you, Charlotte Williams, to show your dad
how easily something precious can be taken away. He took everything I have, and I'm going to do the same to him. I doubt he cares
about money, he has so much." The man laughed. "But he has only
one of you, pretty girl, which is ironic, because you're going to be
the easiest thing of all to take away."

Charlotte was shocked. His tone was almost friendly, conversa-
tional, and yet he then began describing in horribly graphic detail
how he was going to kill her. One thing was for sure. It wasn't
going to be quick.

———

SCARSFORD WASN'T THE first to arrive, but it was close.
She'd been smart enough to call the police from the house phone,
in the hopes that they could trace the call on her cell, and somehow
he'd heard about it. Maybe they'd bugged the phone.

"Are you stalking me, Mr. Scarsford?"

She looked much younger now, still wearing her bathrobe. She'd washed the oil out of her hair as soon as she wasn't alone in the house, and it was still wet, darker from the water. The technicians had taken her phone, and a nice policewoman had taken her statement. She hadn't been expecting that, the sympathy. It was almost harder to bear than the cold efficiency the other policemen displayed.

"No. I'm just watching my case."

"And that includes me."

He nodded. "Did you recognize anything about the voice? Had you ever heard it before?"

He sat down across from her, looking tired. She'd never met a man like him before—he couldn't have been more different from the boys she grew up with. He was young, probably not much more than thirty, but he had an air of capability and strength that was very attractive. If he hadn't been using his skills to destroy her, she'd probably have wondered about his personal life. But now she had to trust him.

She shook her head. "No. At first, I thought it was Michael, because we'd just been talking. But this man's voice was much deeper."

"Michael Marshall?"

"I guess you know him already."

"He's been helpful, yes."

"Amazing what a cornered animal will do to protect itself."

Scarsford said nothing. Charlotte's bravado faded as quickly as it had appeared.

"Do you think that man is really going to kill me?"

A single tear rolled down her cheek, and he willed himself not to lean forward and brush it away.

"No. We're not going to let him."

"Why do you care, anyway? I'm a criminal's kid—all those people today hated my guts, and they don't even know me." She laughed suddenly, slightly hysterically. "Although knowing me probably wouldn't help."

"I think it would." He bit his tongue. But her claws were in.

"Thank you." She closed her eyes briefly. "You know, this day started out pretty well, but it's really been a downhill slide ever since breakfast."

He smiled at her, a real smile, and for a second, things seemed brighter. "Maybe tomorrow will be better."

But it wasn't. In fact, it was a hell of a lot worse.

Chapter
ELEVEN

Emily had the balls to call in the morning. You had to hand it to her, she was fearless.

"Hey, Charlotte, did you see me on TV? Did you know your phone is going straight to voice mail? Do you have to go to jail to see your dad today, or do you want to have brunch?"

Charlotte had woken up feeling much better and had decided to tackle things head-on today. Accordingly, she was dressing carefully and was in the middle of creating a low, braided knot at the back of her head when the house phone had rung. After spitting a hairpin out onto the bathroom counter, she spoke firmly to her friend on speaker.

"Emily, you have some fucking nerve calling me as if appearing on CNN and essentially calling me a spoiled bitch wasn't a bit, oh, I don't know, totally uncool and messed up."

Emily sounded shocked. "Charlotte! I never said you were a bitch."

"You said I was raised by servants."

"Which is true. So was I. So was everyone we know."

"And you said I went off the rails."

"Which is also true. So did I. So did everyone we know. Come on, Charlotte, I came over to give you moral support, and you weren't there. The CNN guy was super-hot and told me I was really photogenic, and I decided to go with it." She sighed. "My parents weren't too pleased with me, either, if it's any consolation."

"It isn't."

"I won't do it again. Promise."

"Did you give them those photos?"

"I might have. Look, just think of all the ones I could have given them."

Charlotte looked at herself. She'd gone Ralph Lauren today. Wide slacks, tightish man's shirt, blazer. Simple makeup, elaborate hair, no jewelry. It would make a nice counterpoint to the seminaked and completely drunken photos Emily could release if she decided to. Well, live by the sword, die by the sword.

"Emily, I'll have to call you back once I know what I'm going to be doing today, OK? I have to call Dad's lawyer."

"OK, babe, call me back."

Emily disconnected, and Charlotte hit the hang-up button. She immediately hit it again and dialed Bedford, picked up the phone, and carried it downstairs. Enough hiding in the bathroom. Time to face the world.

GRETA LOOKED AS if she'd been crying, and Davis didn't look much better. Both of them avoided her eyes when she walked in, and once she was finished talking to Bedford, she called them on it.

"Hey, guys, what's going on? You both look mad. I realize this is terrible, but we'll get through it, OK?"

Davis looked at Greta, who shook her head almost imperceptibly.

He grimaced, then spoke. "Miss Charlotte, Greta thinks I shouldn't ask you this, but I have to."

"Don't."

Charlotte raised her hand. "It's OK, Greta. We can't have secrets from one another now. Please, say what's on your mind."

Charlotte sat down at the breakfast table, and her two employees slowly joined her. She realized suddenly that they were her employees; with her dad not there, she was in charge of everything. She didn't even know where her dad kept the checkbook. Or if they even had a checkbook.

Davis cleared his throat. "Miss Charlotte, both Greta and I invested money with your father, and it appears that it, too, is gone. Neither of us can access our accounts, and when we call the office, we're just told the fund is under investigation."

Charlotte's stomach turned. How could her father have done this? "Was it a lot of money?"

Greta hung her head, a tear plopping off the end of her nose. Davis nodded.

Charlotte got to her feet. "I'll write you a check right now." She walked to her dad's office and then realized it was useless to do so. There was nothing there. She didn't even know if there was money in their bank account. For a second, she panicked, her hand on the study door. But then she pulled herself together.

"Davis." She entered the kitchen with a lot more gravitas than she actually felt. "I need to work out exactly what is going on with our finances. Do you have the number for Dad's banker?"

He nodded, and while he went to get it, Charlotte gave Greta a hug.

"Don't worry, I'm going to sort it all out, OK? I know Dad didn't mean to hurt anyone."

Greta looked so old and so broken-hearted. "Do you think so,

Charlotte? I didn't want to invest my money, but he persuaded me it would be better if I did. If he didn't mean to take it, why didn't he leave me alone?"

Charlotte wanted to cry but bit her lip until it bled instead. "I don't know, Greta, but we're going to push on, OK?"

Davis came back with the number.

Charlotte stood. "On second thought, Davis, why don't you just drive me downtown? I'll call on the way."

CHARLOTTE RECOGNIZED THE bank as she entered the marble lobby, but it must have been years since she'd been there. It had been designed by Reed and Stern, the architects for Grand Central Station, and it had the same cavernous feeling. Very intimidating. At the age of eighteen she had come into some money her mother had left her and had been brought there then to set up accounts or sign documents or whatever it was. She kicked herself for not paying more attention. What on earth had she been doing for the past few years? She felt as if everything she'd learned until now was utterly useless in this situation. She was starting to feel as duped as everyone else, even though she knew her dad loved her.

Her dad's personal banker came forward as she entered. Mr. Edelstein was older than God and apparently had bounced a Rockefeller on his knee or something, because he knew everyone and everything about the rich in Manhattan.

He greeted her warmly and then led her to a private room. Davis hesitated as they entered, and he chose to remain outside. She wanted him to come with her, wanted him, in fact, to hold her hand, because she was petrified, but she covered it up well and merely sat down and waited for Mr. Edelstein to speak.

He sighed heavily. "This is a sad business, Miss Williams. I am shocked beyond belief."

"As are we all, Mr. Edelstein. While my father is awaiting trial, I have to keep going, though, and I realized this morning that I have no idea of our finances or what the investigation means for us. Do you understand it at all?"

He looked at her and felt pity he couldn't show. Usually, it was wives who sat like this. Abandoned by their husbands, realizing they knew nothing about their own money, they came to him to find out if they could fly to Antibes while the divorce came through or if they had to go get a job at Starbucks. Too often, it was the latter.

"Well, Miss Williams, it's somewhat complicated."

She sighed. "I imagined it would be. Many things are turning out to be harder than I anticipated."

He smiled briefly. "There is some good news, though. You have money of your own, money that is entirely separate from your father's. Your mother's will basically left all of her money, money she'd earned in her lifetime, to you in trust. When you turned eighteen it became legally yours—you might remember signing documents?"

She nodded.

"Well, that money has basically been left untouched, quietly growing thanks to the miracle of compound interest, and now amounts to a little more than ten million dollars."

Charlotte's heart lifted. She could pay Greta and Davis back, at least.

"However, the investigators have frozen all of the accounts your father had access to. I was planning on calling them today to remind them officially that your account should not have been included, as your father does not have access to it, but they are proving intransigent." He sighed again. "The FBI and the SEC both can be difficult if they want to be."

Charlotte swallowed. "So I have no money at all?"

"You have money. You just can't get it."

"And how long will that be the case?"

He shrugged gently. "I am working on it."

Charlotte put her hands on the table. "And can you give me a loan? I need money to live on. Presumably, they can't prevent you from doing that?"

For the first time, Edelstein looked embarrassed. "I can speak to my fellow bank officers."

She frowned. "Once the case is over, I presume they will be just as happy to keep our money for us? They, of all people, know I'm good for it."

He wouldn't meet her eye. "Yes, Miss Williams. But many of our other customers have invested money with your father, and it is unclear at this time how much this situation is going to cost the bank. It would not be prudent for us to . . . uh . . . "

"Help me while your other customers are so angry." She understood. "Will you keep bothering the FBI and SEC, please, and I will call you at the end of business today to see if you've made any progress." She'd pulled her mask down, and he would never see her vulnerable again. She stood. "I believe I have some jewelry in a safety deposit box, yes? Am I able to access that?"

He coughed as he stood. "Yes, Miss Williams. The investigation overlooked that or, rather, didn't care about it. You have your mother's diamonds, of course, and a rather valuable pearl necklace."

As she followed him down to the vault, Charlotte found herself growing hard inside. She realized that if she was going to get out of this situation, she was going to have to be resourceful. Creative. Bold.

But first? Shopping.

DOES IT REALLY *count as shopping if you're selling things?* Charlotte wondered. Probably not, but it was a fine distinction. Squashing the horror she felt at doing it, she'd taken her mother's diamonds, the pearl necklace, and half a dozen other pieces from her Chinese chest and carried them to Mr. Geller.

Mr. Geller's was a name that, among the rich of the tristate area, had become synonymous with a certain kind of trouble. "She's gone to see Geller" is all you needed to say to convey that so-and-so was having a little financial difficulty. Charlotte had actually already been to see Geller, when she was eighteen, in order to pay off a foolish bet she'd made with a friend which she'd been too embarrassed to ask her father about.

Mr. Geller was an expert in fine jewelry and discretion, equally important areas of expertise for someone in his position. He worked out of an office in the Flatiron Building, with simply his name on the door, and you never ran into anyone else there. You had the feeling he'd just been sitting there waiting for you, and only you, and that after you left, he would go back to sleep until you returned to reclaim your valuables.

Charlotte had called him as she left the bank, and it was as if he'd been expecting her call. And he might have been, if he watched the news like everyone else.

Davis had made no comment when she gave him the address, although he must have known its significance. Geller had been as gracious and charming as ever and brought her an excellent cup of coffee as they sat in his office.

"I am so happy to see you, Miss Williams. It has been quite a while since you were here last."

He smiled with every apparent sincerity. He was a dapper gentleman of uncertain age. He could have been forty. He could have been sixty. The gossip was that he spoke many languages fluently and traveled the world extensively helping the wealthy liquidate their assets. He had reputedly never been robbed, leading people to speculate that maybe he also assisted those connected to organized crime, who would hate to lose Grandma's emeralds while they were under his protection. His office was richly carpeted and incredibly comfortable, with a slowly ticking grandfather clock in the corner. It all looked a bit like Freud's treatment room in turn-of-the-century Vienna.

Charlotte cleared her throat. "I find myself in a somewhat unusual position."

Geller inclined his head ever so slightly. "It is not at all unusual, Miss Williams. I have seen many old friends lately, with the economy so difficult. I am always happy to take care of things as best I can."

She smiled at him. Geller's gift was in taking the shame away from pawnbroking. You knew he would hold on to your items until you either claimed them back or told him he could keep them, at which time he would dispose of them in such a way that you wouldn't see them around the neck of a friend two weeks later. He made you feel that you were simply doing the sensible thing.

Charlotte got down to business. "I wanted to show you some items that were my mother's."

As always, Geller raised his eyebrows in delight. "Really? How lovely. May I take them to my workroom?"

She handed over the black velvet case and drank her coffee as he took it next door. After only a few moments, he returned.

"Miss Williams, I am so honored to see your mother's diamonds. They are famous, of course, but I had never seen them in person. The pearls are incomparable and the jade highly collectible. Your father has always had exquisite taste in vintage jewelry."

"I'm glad you think so. Do you have any thoughts about what they might fetch at auction?"

"I would think a conservative estimate would be around one hundred fifty thousand dollars for the diamonds and maybe another sixty or seventy thousand for the other pieces. You chose very well from your collection, Miss Williams."

"Please call me Charlotte."

"Thank you. I would be pleased to." There was a delicate pause. "You know, I would be happy to hold these items for you—on consignment, so to speak."

Charlotte wondered how many people had gone through this elegant and elaborate charade with Geller. There was never any discussion of "pawning," never any tickets or claim checks. Just the helpful holding of items, the preparation of them for "auction."

"That would be enormously kind of you, Mr. Geller, and I would appreciate it. May I leave them with you today?"

She had heard that he kept a million dollars in cold, hard cash in his workroom, but it was polite to give him the option of extra time to have the money ready for you. She was in luck.

"That would be lovely. I shall clean the pieces, of course, and when you come to take them back, they will be exactly as you left them."

"Of course."

Ten minutes later, she got back into the car with more than two hundred thousand dollars in her pocket.

"Let's go home, Davis. We've got some things to take care of."

"Very good, Miss."

Geller, watching from the window, saw the long, low car slide away from the curb and wondered how long it would be before he saw the rest of her collection. He also pondered the fact that several of Jacob Williams's former clients were coming to see him that day and sighed. There are always those for whom bad business is good business, and today Geller's business was booming.

Chapter
TWELVE

Charlotte didn't actually make it home. Her phone rang just as they were approaching the park.

"Mr. Bedford, good morning. How is my father today?" She caught Davis's eye in the rearview, but he dropped his gaze.

A minute later, she hung up. "Davis, we need to go downtown. Center Street. Daddy's being arraigned at eleven."

"Didn't that happen yesterday?"

Charlotte started to sweat and wished she'd worn darker clothing. "Yes, but apparently, he wishes to change his plea." This time, his eyes held in the rearview, and she shrugged.

THE STEPS OF the Criminal Court Building were thronged with reporters and camera people who were there for something exciting.

It turned out she was the excitement, as her father had already gone in and been heckled.

"Charlotte, Charlotte, do you have anything to say?"

"Is he pleading guilty?"

"Is he pleading insanity?"

"Where's the money, Charlotte?"

Charlotte just tucked her head down and pushed through, glad she'd locked all of that cash in the glove box. Suddenly, a woman pushed through the throng of photographers and hit her on the shoulder, hard, spinning her around.

"Hey, bitch," said the woman, spitting with fury. "You're not going to be so pretty when I'm done with you." And she swung her fist directly at Charlotte's face. Charlotte ducked, and the woman's fist grazed her cheek, knocking her to the ground. The woman jumped on her and managed to get in a few hard slaps, despite Charlotte's covering her face with her arms. It seemed like forever before the police pulled her off, still screaming obscenities. Through streaming tears, Charlotte could see the TV cameras still running, their red lights like a dozen staring eyes. No wonder no one had helped her. They had shots to get, careers to protect.

One camera-less reporter helped her to her feet, and as she went to thank him, she recognized him from the park. That seemed like days ago, but it was just yesterday.

"Miss Williams." He smiled gently. "Are you OK?"

"Mr. Robinson." Amazingly, she remembered his name. "I am, thank you." She looked at her hands, which were shaking. She could hardly feel her face. "Does it look really bad?"

Robinson was pale, though his eyes were very bright. "Um . . . "

"It hurts," she said, and then everything went dark, and down she went again. As the photographers realized she'd fainted, they pushed in, surrounding her like the vultures they so closely resembled. The only movement was Scarsford, who was running down the wide marble steps of the court building.

And the woman who'd attacked her, who was sobbing uncontrollably, handcuffed to a policeman.

"IT'S NOTHING AT all, honestly. I really need to get back to Center Street."

Charlotte was sitting on the edge of a gurney, wearing a gray hospital gown with Beth Israel logos all over it, her face swollen, her nose still a little bloody.

The doctor peered over the chart at her.

"You can go wherever the heck you want once I'm done here, but if you pass out again, go to a different ER, OK? They dock my pay every time I release someone and they come back within the hour."

She looked at his name tag. "Dr. Waxman, you said yourself nothing was broken."

He ignored her, completing his work before responding. Scarsford was standing there, as was a female police officer and a very pale Davis.

Finally, he looked up. "OK, look, here's the thing. Yes, nothing's broken, but she walloped you pretty good. It's lucky she didn't break your nose. No plastic surgery in the world would have stood up to that."

She narrowed her eyes at him. "Yeah, that's lucky. It's also my real nose."

He shrugged. "Whatever you say. It's up to you, Miss Williams. You might have some delayed shock, you're going to have some minor bruising, but yeah, you can leave now." He looked at Davis. "She should rest, but I get the impression she basically does her own thing."

Davis nodded. He looked as if he should be admitted himself, and the doctor paused.

"Are you all right?"

Davis nodded.

Waxman looked at him a moment longer but apparently decided he would live. He left, barking at a nurse to complete the paperwork to release them, and eventually they were able to leave.

IN THE CAR on the way back to Center Street, Scarsford filled her in.

"Your father pleaded guilty and basically hasn't said a word since."

She frowned. "Why would he do that?"

"If he's not guilty?"

"No, why not talk?"

Scarsford looked out the window, not wanting to meet her eye. "Maybe he's protecting someone. Now that his plea is entered, we go straight to sentencing. There's no need for further investigation, no need for him to say anything if he doesn't want to." He looked back. "I mean, he can cooperate with our investigation if he wants to, and God knows we would like him to, but the law cannot compel him to do anything else."

"Whom would he be protecting? Marshall is already cooperating. Sheila?" Her dad's secretary.

A quick shake of the head. "Nope, Sheila doesn't really get involved in much more than basic office stuff. She's in the clear."

She was silent for a moment. Then she got it. "You mean me, don't you? You think he's protecting me."

"You're all he has left."

"Does he know someone walloped me?"

Davis answered that one. "I spoke to Mr. Bedford on the way to the hospital, to assure him you were fine. I didn't want your father to hear you'd been attacked but not know you were all right."

"I don't know anything about his business." She looked at Scarsford firmly. "I have no idea about any of it, and I'm still not convinced Dad did anything wrong."

"You don't take his word for it? What's the matter, don't you trust him?"

She tightened her lips and turned away.

"I DID IT, Charlotte. I'm sorry, but there it is." Jacob looked a lot better than he had the previous day. Calmer. Healthier. Wearing an orange jumpsuit. He looked around the visitors' room, which was old and gray, with surprisingly beautiful high, tall windows cut into the thick walls. Ironic, seeing as no one there wanted to be reminded of the beauty of outside. "I can't say I like the dress code, but I doubt there's anything I can do about it."

Charlotte felt stunned. She hadn't mentioned the bruising on her face, but she'd expected her dad to be all freaked out. Instead, he hadn't said word one about it. He was almost relaxed, leaning his elbows on the red Formica of the table.

"You know," he leaned forward. "It's strange, but I actually feel enormously relieved that it's all over. It was very hard to maintain, you know."

Charlotte frowned. "Really? I expect that will be nice for the people to know. The people whose money you took."

Jacob's smile faded. "Yes, that part isn't so good, is it?"

"What about Davis and Greta? You took their money, too."

He looked at his hands. "Yes. That was a mistake. I was hoping to cash them out and just never got around to it."

Charlotte regarded him steadily. Her face hurt, the painkillers were wearing off, and she was starting to feel more than a little bit annoyed. Why had she never noticed how selfish her father was?

Maybe she was too selfish herself to pay attention to him. A sobering thought.

"I did mean what I said yesterday, though. I didn't anticipate it turning into the problem it did. I found a loophole, and it was more like a game than a plan."

That she understood. Many times, she'd started things just for fun and ended up in bed with people she didn't really want to be with or said hurtful things to other girls or ruined situations without intending to. Mind you, those things were a little different from embezzling billions of dollars, but she guessed it was a question of scale.

"Mr. Bedford says they're probably going to seize the apartment in the next day or so. They've already frozen our bank accounts."

Her father frowned. "Do you have money?"

"I pawned some jewelry."

He said nothing for a moment. "Well, that's a little embarrassing. Geller was polite, I assume?"

She nodded. "He's an honest man." She meant it to sting a little, but there was no sign on her father's face that he felt it.

"So you're all right for money?"

She shrugged. "I have some money. I can go and get a job."

He nodded. "Of course you can. You're a very capable young woman."

She was surprised. "I am? I'm not sure I feel very capable, but thanks for the vote of confidence."

He had already moved back to his favorite topic. "So, Bedford tells me I will probably be sent to a federal prison with some very frightening individuals. He's going to try to get me moved to a minimum-security place. Who knows, I might get some reading done."

"That's a positive way to look at it." She was clearly angry with him, and he finally picked up on it.

"You're annoyed. Is it the apartment? The jewelry?"

"Dad, you stole millions of dollars. You've ruined our lives. I've got no place to live. A woman I've never met was so angry with me she tried to break my nose."

He was surprised, finally. "That's not very polite, is it?"

"She didn't manage it, though."

"Well, that's good. Did they arrest her?"

She shook her head. "Yes, but I didn't press charges. I decided we'd hurt her enough."

"That's nice of you." He considered. "Maybe you should take a vacation."

"On our yacht?"

A quick smile. "No, I think the FBI might be using that now. But maybe you should take a trip." Something occurred to him suddenly. "Did you say they're shutting you out of the apartment?" She nodded. "Listen, this is very important. In your mother's dressing table, there is a key. The key is for a chest in the green guest room. Are you following me?"

"Yes, of course. But what on earth are you talking about?"

"Listen to me. Go to the chest and take out a red box. I intended to give it to you on your wedding day, but I want you to take it now. It's very important, very important indeed, that you take everything that's in that box. Do you understand me?" He looked like the old Dad for a moment, intelligence and force in his eyes, focus and passion. No wonder people had trusted him with everything.

She had.

She leaned forward and took his hands.

"No touching," barked the guard.

"Daddy, why did you do it? We had plenty of money. We had each other. We could have left New York and done what you and Mom planned, run away to some island."

"Really?" His face was blank. "What about your friends? Your schooling? Your clothes and toys and ponies and cars? That all seemed very important to you."

Her eyes grew hot with unshed tears. "Compared to you? Compared to watching you go to jail? That's not fair, Dad. If you started this soon after Mom died, then I was only a little kid. I didn't know the difference between rich and poor. We could have gone away then and just hung out. It would have been heaven." Now she was just letting the tears come. "Instead, you chose money, and I lost you. You were always at work when I was a kid, and now that I'm starting out in the world, you're going to jail. Why did you make that choice?"

Her heart was breaking, but her father seemed strangely unmoved. He just looked at her silently as she put her head down on the table and sobbed. Slowly, he reached out a hand and stroked her shaking head.

"No touching," said the guard.

Chapter THIRTEEN

The apartment had strangers in it. Labeling things. Taking things.

She called Greta and Davis to her room and locked the door behind them. After falling apart with her father, she had come to the conclusion that the going was tough, and she'd better toughen up and get going. Her jaw was set, and her hands had stopped shaking as the taxi passed Grand Central, heading uptown.

"OK, they're going to take the apartment. There's nothing we can do about it. Dad has fucked us all over, so to speak, but the first thing I'm going to do is pay you two back the money you lost. I'm not going to apologize for him, because I sincerely hope he will apologize himself, but I'm sure you know how I feel."

They were silent, but Greta took her hand and squeezed it.

"So, how much are we talking about. Davis? You can round it up."

"Seventy-five thousand."

She didn't blink. She peeled notes off her pile, shuffled them together, and handed them over. "Davis, you have been a rock in my life ever since I can remember. I cannot tell you how much I love you and appreciate your loyalty and support."

He looked at the money and started to hand it back. "I can't take this, Charlotte. What are you going to live on?"

She shrugged. "Oh, there's plenty of money where that came from, don't you worry. Besides, I have lots of friends who'll help me. Greta? How much did that dickhead take from you?"

"A hundred."

"Thousand, I assume?" She counted it out. Who knew Greta had a hundred grand to lose?

She felt good, having paid them back, and it made what she had to do next a little easier.

"You realize, I guess, that there isn't going to be a job here any-more."

They nodded. Davis spoke. "I can stay, though. You can't be here alone. It isn't safe."

She smiled and stood. She went to her closet and pulled out her handsome leather suitcase. "I won't be here, Davis."

They were concerned. "Where will you go?"

"I'm going to the one place where I know I can trust people." She turned to look at Greta, who she knew would understand. "I'm going to New Orleans to find Miss Millie."

SHE DIDN'T LIKE creeping about in her own house, but neither did she want to draw the attention of the investigators. So, after stepping out of her shoes, she padded along the upper hallway to her parents' room.

Her mother's dresser was just as she had left it. Opening her drawers released the faint scent of her perfume, light, cucumbers and lemons, natural and sweet. She wondered if it was really there or if she was just imagining it. She was also coming to realize that her mother wasn't exactly as the public thought. Chanel No. 5 for going out, lemons for staying in. Regal queen on the runway, sweet young woman in private. Maybe everyone had at least two faces. She certainly did. Charlotte rummaged through the underwear drawer, finding the cool hardness of the key right away.

The guest room was rarely used, but Greta kept it immaculate, of course. Looking around, Charlotte couldn't see a chest, and she frowned. She finally found it under the bed. She paused, hearing voices in the hall. They passed. She breathed and then opened the chest.

Three things lay inside: a flat jewelry box, a ring box, and a flash drive on a silver chain.

Back in her own room, she flipped open the boxes. In the first lay a magnificent agate and diamond collar with matching earrings. She caught her breath. A famous *Vogue* cover of Jackie wearing this very necklace hung above the fireplace in her father's study, Jackie's arms folded across her bare chest, her eyes closed, her hair smoothed back from her forehead. She hadn't been much older than Charlotte was now. The ring box contained a simple gold band, Jackie's wedding ring. Charlotte turned it over—the inscription inside merely said "J & J & J & J . . . " all the way around. Nice. If only things had stayed that simple.

The tiny zip drive lay in her palm. Was he asking her to hide something from the investigators? She decided to think about it later and hung it around her neck, where it hung almost down to her belly button. *Hmm.* Maybe her father had worn it. She almost took it off to give to the authorities right away, but as her hand closed over it, she changed her mind. What good could it do? He'd already confessed to the crime; they didn't need any more evidence.

And he'd said it was for her, for her wedding day, and why would he give her criminal evidence as a wedding present?

GRETA RUMMAGED IN her purse. "I do have it. Hang on." She pulled out a battered red notebook.

"Greta, didn't I give you an iPhone for Christmas? You shouldn't keep all your addresses in that old thing."

Greta shrugged. "I only just worked out how to make the phone play music. Anything else would be beyond me. This little red book works just fine, Charlotte." She flipped through it. "Here it is. Do you have a pencil?"

Charlotte was holding her phone and merely raised her eyebrows.

"OK. Millie Pearl, 1778 Robideaux Avenue, New Orleans." She frowned. "I'm sorry, I don't have a phone number."

Charlotte closed her phone. "S'OK. I got it when she called the other day. Besides, I'm just going to show up and surprise her."

Greta turned away and carried on going through kitchen drawers. Charlotte had told her she could take what she wanted, and she was gathering her favorite tools. It looked like a pile of wooden spoons to Charlotte, but she knew better than to question Greta.

"Be careful, Charlotte." The older woman turned suddenly and pointed a spatula at her. "Not everyone knows you the way she and I do, and people are going to judge you badly because of what your father has done. Protect yourself."

"I don't care what people think of me."

"I know you think that, Charlotte. But it still hurts. Someone attacked you yesterday, and you're pretending this is all OK and it really isn't." Her voice faltered. "It really isn't OK at all."

THE PHONE RANG through from the front desk. "Clara Acker-
man is here to see you, Miss Williams. Shall I send her up?"

Charlotte frowned. Clara was the last person she expected to
see. "Of course, thank you."

Charlotte met Clara at the elevator. When the doors opened,
Clara looked worried, but her face lit up when she saw Charlotte.

"Oh, I'm so glad to see you! When we saw you on the news,
that you'd been attacked, we were all so worried." She gave her a
big hug. She was wearing a winter white cashmere coat with a red
fake fox collar and looked wonderfully elegant and together.

"We?" Charlotte suddenly had visions of all of her school
friends getting together in a bar to witness her downfall. *Take a
shot every time someone calls Charlotte a party girl!*

"My family." Clara looked around. "Why are all these people
here? What are they doing with your things?"

Charlotte made a face. "They're taking them. For some reason
I don't fully understand, the investigation has seized the apartment."

"You're joking."

"Sadly, I'm not."

"Well, come and stay with us, then. As long as you like." She
tugged off her leather gloves and cashmere cloche hat, stuffing
them all in her pocket.

Charlotte was a little bit stunned. She and Clara had gone to
school together and moved in the same circles, but they had never
been close. Her closer friends had either not called her at all or had
gone on TV, the way Emily had.

"Uh . . . that's very nice of you, Clara, but I doubt your parents
would like the daughter of a suspected felon staying in their guest

room. Or a horde of paparazzi outside at all hours." Even all the way up there, they could hear the baying of the hounds.

Clara smiled. "My mother told me to tell you not to let the bastards get you down." She giggled. "I think it shocked her to say the word, to be honest, but she was brave about it. Our family doesn't like the press, you know."

Charlotte shook her head. "Why not? I see your parents in the society pages all the time."

Clara shrugged. "It's older than us. I think it must be on account of the whores."

There was a pause.

"What horse?"

"Not horse. Whores. Prostitutes. You know, women of easy virtue."

Charlotte laughed. "I know what a whore is, Clara, I've just lost the thread of the conversation."

An investigator was pulling books off the shelves and riffling their pages, apparently looking for very thin bars of gold bullion.

Clara looked at her and dropped her voice. "All our money was made a long time ago, right?" She turned up her palms and grinned. "The Ackermans brought a shipload of women from Holland and set up a floating brothel in New York Harbor. We did very well. So well that we repeated the pattern in harbors all over the eastern seaboard. It was the first recorded example of an offshore corporation." She laughed. "We're tax dodgers from way back."

Charlotte was shocked. "How is it possible that no one knows this?"

"Lots of people do know it, so I always assume everyone does. Apparently, my great-great-great-grandfather wanted to run for office back in the day, and the newspapers of the time made a big fuss about the whores, and he couldn't run. We've never forgiven the press, so we're totally on your side."

Charlotte was touched. "Even if my dad is guilty?"

Clara nodded. "Yes, why not? You didn't do anything. Everyone makes mistakes." She grinned. "Besides, have you looked in the mirror lately? You look terrible. It's just as well no one is inviting you anywhere."

Charlotte laughed despite herself. She went over and sat next to Clara, giving her a hug. "You are the only person who has come to see me, did you know that?" Clara shook her head. "I cannot tell you how much it means to me. I was really starting to feel alone."

Clara squeezed her hand. "Well, you're not. And you're welcome to come and stay with us if you need to. We have a lovely guest suite, and we'll take very good care of you."

"I know. But I've decided to get out of Dodge for a while instead."

Charlotte told Clara her plan to go to New Orleans. Clara remembered Miss Millie, of course, and understood that part.

"But why go now? Surely you're safer here? I mean, no one knows you in New Orleans."

"And that," Charlotte said, smiling, "is exactly the point."

SCARSFORD WAS MORE blunt. "You're insane."

Charlotte had gone to catch a cab to the airport just as Scarsford was pulling up.

She turned to look out the window. He had offered to drive her, apparently so he could talk her out of leaving.

"We can protect you here. Someone punched out your lights, remember?"

"Of course I remember. I've got a big fat swollen nose, OK?"

"New Orleans is a wild town. I've been there."

"For Mardi Gras, I presume. Did you show everyone your tits?"

He made a face at her. "Seriously, you can't leave town. You're under investigation."

"Actually, I can definitely leave town, and I'm not under investigation."

She was confident on this point, because she'd spent an hour on the phone with Arthur Bedford. He'd tried to talk her out of leaving, too, but she'd been firm. He'd also taken the last of her money, more or less, in payment for his legal services for her father. She still owed him the gross domestic product of a small nation, but she was sure he would manage to protect at least his own fee from the ravages of the government. Lawyers and accountants had a way of making sure they got paid, even if no one else did. Now she had a little less than five thousand dollars in her purse, and they weren't going to let her fly for free.

Strangely, it was exhilarating. But now Scarsford was raining on her parade.

He made a frustrated noise. "You could get hurt there."

"I got punched here. I can't live my life in fear, Mr. Scarsford. My dad is going to be in jail here for a while waiting to get sentenced, and every time I see him, it upsets me a little bit more. I need some time to think things through."

"Where will you stay?"

"With friends."

"You have friends here."

She sighed. "Look, Mr. Scarsford, I'm going to New Orleans. I'm going to get myself together and work out what I'm going to do with the rest of my life."

They pulled up at the terminal and got out, Scarsford showing his badge to the cop on the curb. He offered to carry her bag, but she shook her head. Time to carry her own shit.

He stayed with her all the way to security.

"Charlotte . . . " She turned and smiled at him. "Please be careful."

"I will, Mr. Scarsford."

"Please call me Jim."

"OK, Jim."

She stretched up on her toes and kissed him on the cheek. He could smell her light perfume, cucumbers and lemons, and for a moment, her body brushed his. He watched as she put her suitcase on the conveyor belt, stepping out of her shoes, unclipping her watch, removing her jewelry. As the first gray plastic tray rattled into the X-ray machine, she suddenly remembered something and reached for another. She pulled a necklace from around her neck and dropped it into the tray. He saw it and frowned.

"Good-bye for now, Jim. I'll be back for sentencing, and my mobile number is the same." She smiled a brilliant smile at him, turning and making her way through the scanner.

He stood there, motionless, and watched her gather her belongings. She didn't look back; she'd already forgotten him. What was wrong? Why was he feeling angry?

And then suddenly, he realized what he'd seen dropping into the tray. A zip drive. Just like the one they'd taken from Jacob's office. No wonder she'd been happy! She was getting away with evidence.

He stepped forward, but the TSA guard held up his hand. Scarsford started to reach for his badge but stopped.

She'd swindled him, just as her dad had swindled everyone else. So pretty, so charming, so vulnerable. But apparently capable of taking valuable evidence and walking off with it. Having the balls to kiss him as she did so.

You fool, Jim. You total fucking idiot. He turned on his heel, white-hot anger clearing his brain wonderfully. *Time to get back on the case, Charlotte. I'll be seeing you sooner than you think.*

Chapter
FOURTEEN

It turned out that flying coach wasn't much fun. No hot towels. No complimentary alcohol. No handsome movie actors in the seat next to you. No ensuing Mile-High Club experience. Charlotte smiled to herself as she looked out the window. That had been just the one time, to be fair. You couldn't expect an airline to come up trumps every time. The old lady sitting next to her continued to empty her purse into the seat pocket in front of her. Magazines, check. Mints, check. Book of word searches, check.

The old lady turned to her. "Young lady, might I use your pocket? Mine is full and I need somewhere to put my water bottle."

Charlotte smiled and nodded. Unfortunately, the old lady took this to mean that they were BFFs, and by the time the plane began to bank down over Louis Armstrong Airport, Charlotte knew all about Maude's three daughters, her bunions, her flatulence, and, surprisingly enough, her secret love of opera. Maude had been happy to talk about farting at great length and volume, but she dropped her voice for the Wagner.

Charlotte had been to New Orleans before, once, for Mardi

Gras, but she'd been with a group of friends and hadn't really been paying attention. For the first time, she noticed there was jazz playing over the airport address system and paused to look at a huge mural of jazz musicians on the way out. She liked jazz well enough but couldn't help associating it with older people, a previous time.

She waited in line for a cab, another new experience. What did people do when it rained? The weather was mild, warmer than New York. She folded her heavy coat over her arm, wishing she had someone to hand it to.

Like every other city she'd visited, New Orleans had built its airport where there was room—the middle of nowhere. Getting to the city involved driving through some pretty desolate areas, and the effects of Hurricane Katrina were still clearly seen. She frowned. It had been years; surely someone could have cleaned up all this mess by now?

Miss Millie's house, however, was immaculate. The older parts of the city, those built on higher ground, had survived Katrina more or less intact, but Millie's house was especially neat. She remembered Millie telling her about it.

"My grandma bought our house for twenty dollars at the turn of the century, back when that was a lot. She and my granddad cleaned it up and worked on it every spare moment they had. It's a shotgun house. Do you know what that is?"

Charlotte had shaken her head, and Millie had laughed.

"What does that fancy school teach you, anyway? A shotgun is a house that has all the rooms in a row, one behind the other. They said you could fire a shotgun in the front door and hit someone out back."

Now, looking up at the beautiful house, its Victorian gingerbread trim painted a soft yellow, its wooden shutters a pale blue,

Charlotte paused. Was this an enormous mistake? She sighed, squared her shoulders, and knocked.

Nothing. Silence.

The cab had already pulled away, and the warm night air was thick but empty. Distant music, maybe a footstep or two, a sudden laugh somewhere close making her jump. But from the house in front of her, nothing.

"Looking for someone, boo?"

She whirled around, and for a moment, time stood still as she gazed at the woman who had been the closest thing to a mother she'd ever known. She'd taught her to ride a bike. Encouraged her to take singing lessons. Explained the facts of life when she got her first period. Held her hand waiting to cross the street. All of these images and memories crowded in, a rush of childhood emotions. It had been horrible, to be honest, losing her mom, and Millie had been the rock she'd clung to as the storm raged around her. And here she was, tossed out by another storm.

"Miss Millie!"

"Charlotte!" Millie's face lit up, and it was such a relief for someone to be pleased to see her that Charlotte felt a lump in her throat. Both of them were a little tearful as they hugged, Miss Millie as much with surprise as anything else.

Millie hugged her tightly. "I hoped you'd come to see me, baby. I'm so glad you did."

As Charlotte pulled back to smile at her friend, she noticed for the first time the tall, handsome young man standing just a little way away. Miss Millie followed her gaze.

"Y'all lost your tongue, Jackson? This here is Miss Charlotte Williams."

"I gathered that." He inclined his head maybe half an inch, unsmiling.

There was a pause, and then Millie laughed. "Ignore him, boo. He's just cranky." She fished for keys in her purse and opened the door. "I'm so glad we came home just now, so you didn't wander off." She looked over her shoulder. "I was praying you'd come down, but I didn't want to pressure you. I know how independent you are."

Charlotte followed her into the house, suddenly aware of how tired she was, how tightly she'd been holding on. Was *independent* another way of saying *alone*? The events of the last several days filled her head, and a half-sob escaped her.

Miss Millie turned just as Charlotte went pale and calmly said, "Catch her, Jackson," as the young woman crumpled and fell.

———

AS HE LOOKED down at Charlotte, lying on the battered old couch in his living room, Jackson Pearl was surprised. She looked like a regular girl. A pretty girl, sure, but New Orleans had more than its fair share of those. And a well-dressed girl, too. But still, just a girl.

For years, Jackson had hated Charlotte Williams. His mom had gone away to look after her, leaving him in the tender care of his grandmother, who, admittedly, had doted on him and his sisters and spoiled them rotten. But he'd still resented Charlotte, and even after his mother came back home—once he'd made her pay for her absence by cold-shouldering her for a month or two—he hadn't bothered to let that resentment go. Now, looking at her pale face and, in his opinion, underfed frame, he realized how silly it was.

He felt his mother watching him, and turned to her. "Don't these people eat?"

She arched an elegant eyebrow at him. Millie Pearl had been

a beauty in her youth and was still, in her fifties, an attractive and elegant woman. Her skin was the color of creamy coffee, her eyes almost black. Her son had darker skin, and his eyes were copper, startling and bright like pennies. The resemblance—and the connection—between them was very strong.

The front door opened, and one of his sisters came in. Camille was a year older than Jackson and was carrying a sleeping toddler on her shoulder.

"Momma, can I put Charles down somewhere? He fell asleep at dinner, and I'm waiting for Jimmy to bring the car around to get us." She had already been whispering, so when she entered the living room and saw the apparently sleeping girl, she just kept her voice low. "Do we know this child, or is she one of Jackson's many fans, overcome by proximity?"

Her mother grinned. "You can put Charles on my bed, hon."

"It's Charlotte Williams." Jackson kept his tone neutral, but his sister narrowed her eyes at him. She knew how he felt about the Williams family, and over the previous few days, the news about Jacob Williams had freshened old wounds.

Charlotte started to stir, and Camille went to put down her sleeping son. Jackson turned on his heel and went into the kitchen, leaving Millie and Charlotte alone together.

Charlotte opened her eyes, feeling disoriented.

"Are you all right, honey? Do you feel sick at all?"

Charlotte propped herself up on her elbow, and the room swam. "Miss Millie?" she whispered.

The older woman knelt quickly and easily by her side, reaching out her hand to smooth back the young woman's hair. Millie found herself strangely touched to see Charlotte, an ache in her chest reminding her of the bond they'd once shared. Taking care of any child connects you to that child, and Millie had taken care of Charlotte for more than five years. When they'd first met, Charlotte had been deeply wounded by her mother's death, and it had taken a few weeks for her even to look Millie in the face. Once she trusted her, though, they became inseparable. Millie wondered anew how much damage her leaving Charlotte had done. At the time, she'd had no choice. Jackson was starting to get in trouble at school, and she had to choose her own child over the child who felt so much her own yet wasn't. Now she looked into Charlotte's eyes, and it was as if they'd never been apart.

Those eyes filled with tears, as Charlotte saw Millie looking at her with such affection. "I've missed you so much," she whispered, and then broke down completely. Millie sat on the sofa and put her arm around Charlotte's shoulder, shushing her over and over, tucking her hair back over her ears to keep it out of her face.

Jackson watched from the kitchen door, a cup of tea growing cold in his hand. He wasn't sure what he felt, apart from pity.

Camille stepped up behind him. "You made me a cup of tea? Jackson, you are just so sweet." She took the cup over to the kitchen table and sat down. He joined her.

"You know what that means, don't you?" She nodded toward the living room. He shook his head. "Trouble."

He frowned at her. "Why? Mom can take care of herself."

Camille laughed. "Not for Mom. Mom's made of steel. No, sugar. Trouble for you."

Then she raised the cup of tea in a toast and drained it.

Chapter
FIFTEEN

When Charlotte woke up, she found she was not alone. A large ginger cat was standing very close, watching her with thoughtful eyes. For a moment, they blinked at each other, then the cat turned and stalked off, apparently satisfied.

"You're approved of, it would seem."

Charlotte sat up, pulling the blanket up as she did so. Jackson was sitting in an armchair across the room, drinking a cup of coffee and reading the *New York Times*.

"How would I have known if he didn't approve of me?"

Jackson smiled briefly. "You would never have known. You just wouldn't have woken up."

Charlotte raised her eyebrows. "Really? He didn't look that tough to me."

Jackson turned back to his paper. "Appearances are deceptive."

Millie came in, bustling. "How did you sleep, sweetness? I'm afraid it's no Park Avenue apartment, and the sofa's all we got."

Charlotte stretched happily. Jackson had looked up as his mother came in and watched the young girl as the blanket fell away, revealing her silky camisole and long, smooth arms, lovely despite her bruised face. Frowning, he disappeared behind his paper again.

"It was really comfortable, and I slept like a log. Thank you so much for putting up with my surprise visit." She blushed. "And my falling apart like that."

Millie hugged her tightly. "Honey, anyone would have fallen apart after what you've been through. I was just happy to see you in one piece. I saw on the news that some crazy lady jumped you."

Charlotte shrugged. "As you can see, I'm battered but OK."

"You were lucky."

"And so was everyone around you," Jackson said, hidden in his paper. "She could have had a gun. She could have killed a totally innocent person."

There was a silence. His implication was clear, and Charlotte suddenly felt uncomfortable.

Millie's mouth twitched. "You'll have to forgive my son, Charlotte. I raised a proud black man who remembers his heritage, his history, his debt of gratitude to those who went before, and his responsibility to those who will come next. However, he totally forgets his manners." She balled up a tissue and threw it at his paper. She had good aim.

"I didn't say anything impolite," he protested, folding his newspaper and getting to his feet. He was taller than Charlotte remembered and wider at the shoulders. She dropped her gaze. "I just said the truth." He walked out of the room, leaving the atmosphere somewhat depressed.

Millie patted Charlotte. "Ignore him. He's always been feisty. I imagine you would like to take a shower and get dressed. What's your plan?"

Charlotte pulled some clothes from her bag. "I was thinking of getting a job."

Millie's eyebrows went up, but she smiled. "OK. Shower's down the hall, baby. I'll see you when you're all ready."

Charlotte smiled but caught sight of Jackson putting on his jacket to leave. She wondered what he did, what was in the heavy bag he picked up by the door. He didn't say good-bye, and when she turned back to Millie, the woman was looking at her with a strange expression. She smiled, though, and pointed down the hall.

CHARLOTTE GOT DRESSED carefully, glad to see the swelling on her face was starting to go down, although there were still some interesting bruises. A light cotton Armani shift, a TSE cashmere sweater loosely belted, ballet flats, and one-carat sapphire solitaires at her throat and ears. She looked at herself and smiled, thinking how fun it was to dress down for a change.

It wasn't far to the French Quarter, which was the only part of New Orleans Charlotte knew anything about. It had been packed to the walls the last time she'd been there, midnight Mardi Gras, and it turned out to be elegant and beautiful in the soft morning light. A lingering smell of last night's party was getting hosed off the sidewalks, gradually being replaced with the scents of toasted pecans, brown sugar, and chicory. A few young men still sat numbly on the cracked and broken sidewalks, looking as if they weren't sure which way was up, but the locals were stepping over and around them without missing a beat.

Taking a seat at a sidewalk café, one of many, Charlotte ordered coffee and beignets, which seemed to be the traditional thing to do. She looked around, trying to get her bearings. The streets were narrow, with delicate wrought-iron balconies on the second levels of all the houses. There weren't many cars or vehicles, but people swooped about on bicycles, managing to avoid the worst of the

potholes, which were positively New Yorkian in their depth. It
wasn't much past nine but it was already warming up, and Charlotte loosened her sweater.

The waiter was young, and Charlotte watched him going about
his work. She thought she could probably manage to be a waitress;
it didn't look that hard. Smile, write things down, carry things,
check. She thought about other working people she was familiar
with. Maids seemed to work pretty hard, so that was out. Chauf-
feurs needed to know the city, so that was impossible. Hostessing
in a good restaurant was probably doable; they only seemed to be
hired for their looks. That would be worth a shot. She reflected
that she didn't really have many marketable skills. Being able to
speak French was definitely going to be helpful there; she could
hear French everywhere. Heavily accented French but French
nonetheless. It was just as well she'd burned down that stupid
building. See? Her dad was right; every cloud had a silver lining.
She wondered how long it would take him to reframe jail as a
positive step. She'd always considered his ability to see the bright
side a strength, but now she wondered if it was just a delusion.
What to him was only "a small thing" had destroyed hundreds
of lives. She wasn't sure if he really understood the magnitude of
what he'd done, even now.

Feeling depressed, she paid for her breakfast and went to find
a guidebook.

———————

IT TURNED OUT that in the French Quarter alone, there were
dozens of restaurants with three stars or more. Charlotte visited
twenty-seven of them before lunch, and none of them wanted a
hostess with no experience. At most of them, she was swiftly turned
away, but at one, the hostess took two minutes to speak with her.

"Listen, hon. Being a hostess is harder than it looks. You run the reservations, which can be easy or hard, depending on the night and the folks, neither of which you can control. Most hostesses have a degree in restaurant or hotel management." The hostess looked at Charlotte with some sympathy. "I expect you thought we were hired for our looks, right?" She herself was tall and gorgeous, with long, dark red hair braided in a thick rope down her back. "Well, looks help, but they aren't the point. Go get a waitressing job. It's hard, but you'll catch on." She grinned. "We all got to start somewhere, right?"

Charlotte managed to smile, but her feet hurt.

Eating lunch, she felt glum. The food helped, though. She'd ordered gumbo, trying to get a sense of typical New Orleans food, and it was delicious. Warm and strongly scented, with lumps of sausage and vegetables cooked to perfection. She looked around and watched the people wandering by. So many different skin colors, so many different styles of dress, but all somewhat relaxed and everyone happy. Was it possible that no one in New Orleans was cranky? Where were the sullen teenagers dressed in black? Lurking in corners, maybe.

She brushed off her dress and went to do battle again, pasting on a warm smile and trying to keep her head up.

MILLIE PEARL HEARD the front door open and leaned back from the kitchen counter, where she was cutting up a squash.

"That you, Camille?"

She heard a bag hit the floor. "No, Millie, it's Charlotte."

Millie wiped her hands on a dish cloth. "Well, come on through and tell me your impressions of our beautiful city! I want to hear all about it."

Charlotte came in, looking as if she'd been smacked about the head with a dead fish. Millie laughed out loud. "My Lord, child, you look just about all beat down. What happened?"

Charlotte threw herself into a chair. "Nothing, which is the problem. Amazingly, no one wanted to hire a young woman with no experience whatsoever and a swollen nose."

Millie frowned. "No one?"

Charlotte laughed bitterly. "Well, not as a waitress, anyway. I got two stripper offers and one straight hooker opportunity, but I turned those down."

"This is all in the Quarter, right?" Millie pursed her lips. "You might have better luck uptown, maybe, or even over in the Garden District. I'll ask around and see if I can help."

Charlotte put her head down on the smooth wood of the kitchen table. Her voice was muffled. "I don't know why I thought it would be easy. Everything seemed easy until a few days ago."

Millie sat down, chuckling. "You're not remembering right. I was there, too, remember? You had a very hard time when your mom had just died; that wasn't easy. And it took you several weeks to learn to ride a bike. I was starting to think maybe you were a little retarded."

Charlotte laughed, and Millie joined her. It felt good to be together again. To be with someone who knew her from before the evening news.

"Look, not everyone gets the whole bike-riding thing right away, OK? I was always good at singing."

Millie sighed. "That's true. I remember when I first heard you sing, I marched straight into your father's study and told him you had to start taking lessons."

"And he said yes, I presume."

"Of course. He was scared of me, I guess." Millie's face clouded slightly. "And, to be fair, he was still a little out of it from losing your mother. It broke him inside, I think. Not that I knew him before." She stood and returned to her dinner preparations. "Are you going to have a rest before dinner?"

Charlotte shook her head. "I was wondering if there was somewhere I could plug in my laptop. I wanted to check my e-mail and all that good stuff."

Millie showed her where, signed her on to the network, and left her in peace. The peace didn't last for long.

She'd intended just to check her mail, but she couldn't help checking the news. Her dad was still making headlines, this time simply for being transferred from one jail to another. She was mentioned, with "sources" saying she'd left the city in disgrace. She frowned. It wasn't really in disgrace, it was more like . . . OK, it was disgrace. Then she made a big mistake and scrolled down to the comments area following the article. People were not being very kind.

"People like this should be sent to the electric chair. Now all our tax dollars will be used to keep this scumbag alive and well, while those he swindled will just have to suck it up. No wonder his bitch spawn ran away, she probably feared for her life. AND SHE SHOULD."

Charlotte swallowed.

"Jacob Williams is a parasite, and his ugly socialite daughter is just as bad. Fake tits, fake ass, fake smile, and no brains at all. And clearly no remorse as she's run off to find a new party town to fuck her way around in. These people are disgusting. My heart goes out to those who've lost everything."

And her favorite!

"I knew Charlotte Williams in high school and she had no morals or conscience then. She was such a bitch and never failed to make fun of anyone who wasn't wearing the right clothes or shoes. I hated

her then and I am GLAD her life is ruined. She's probably still doing
better than the people her criminal father ripped off. I hope she rots
in hell."

The really sad thing, she realized, was how true much of it was.
She had been a bitch in high school. She had made fun of what
other, less well-off kids were wearing. It had been her favorite
sport. She couldn't help thinking there was something fair about
the pleasure other people were taking in her downfall now. Even
if it hurt like hell to see herself trashed on the screen.

Jackson walked into the house, dropped his heavy bag, and
called out to his mother.

She came out and met him in the hall, giving him a big hug.
"How was work?"

He shrugged. "Same as ever. Most of the houses down there are
unsalvageable. We do what we can, but it's not much." He spotted
Charlotte sitting at the computer. "Looking for things on Ama-
zon?"

She narrowed her eyes at him, but his mom poked him hard
in the chest. "Will you quit baiting her?" She turned to Charlotte.
"Jackson is spending his days in the lower Ninth Ward, helping
to rebuild some of those houses down there—the ones that have
anything left to build on, anyway."

"That's very noble of you." Charlotte wasn't in the mood to be
made fun of.

He raised his eyebrows. "It's called supporting the community.
Google it."

"I already did. Right after I Googled 'superiority complex.'"

Millie laughed. "You two are silly. You know, Jackson has a
band, Charlotte. You two have a love of music in common. I've
told him all about your voice, of course."

"About a million times."

"Really?" Charlotte was still feeling bitchy. "I haven't heard of your band at all."

"That doesn't surprise me. You don't really get out of the Upper East Side all that much, do you?"

Millie threw up her hands. "I'm going to leave you two children to it. Dinner in half an hour."

Once she'd left the room, they just stared at each for a moment, and then Jackson snorted a laugh and headed down the hall to change.

THE NEXT MORNING, Charlotte woke up in a practical mood. She needed more clothes, and it didn't look as if she was going to get a job as quickly as she'd thought. She needed to maximize every penny. She flipped through her guidebook to the shopping section and soon found what she was looking for. Encouraged, she carefully packed up another of her linen shift dresses and a Chanel suit it was already too hot to wear and headed out the door.

Magazine Street wasn't as famous as Rodeo Drive or Fifth Avenue, but it contained almost as many couture stores and designer houses as both of them. Charlotte didn't pause, though, just walked fast, heading for the end of the street.

Noblesse N'oubliez billed itself as a vintage couture store, and as soon as Charlotte stepped through the door, she knew she'd come to the right place. The walls were painted peacock blue, and Louis XIV chairs were covered in pink fake fur and arranged around an Eames table. Clothing was arranged by color and subdivided by piece. It reminded Charlotte of her closet, and she turned impulsively to the girl behind the counter.

"Why by color?"

The girl looked up from her magazine, utterly unfazed by the question. "Because it's Tuesday. Because it's January. Because I felt like it. Sometimes I do it by piece, all the skirts together, sometimes I do it by designer, all the Lagerfeld together."

"Chronologically, though, right?"

The girl looked scandalized. "Of course. How else could I find things?" She tipped her neat little head to one side. "Are you looking for something in particular?"

Charlotte was a tiny bit embarrassed. "I wondered if you did trade."

The girl looked interested. "Sure. For couture only, though. What do you have?"

"Armani and Chanel. A shift and a suit." She opened her bag and took them out. The girl touched the garments knowledgeably, fingering the seams, examining them closely.

"The Armani is 2008, right?"

"Yes."

"I heard they had problems with the buttons in that collection."

"I hadn't noticed."

"I'll give you five hundred dollars in trade."

"It cost twelve hundred."

"That's nice to know."

Charlotte laughed, feeling as if it had been too long. "And the Chanel?"

The girl smiled at her. "It's lovely. Do you wear it much?"

Charlotte put the most recent time out of her head. "Not very. And it's a little formal for down here."

"Oh, you'd be surprised. But it'll fly off my racks, so I'll give you eight hundred for it." Charlotte opened her mouth to complain that it had cost four times that, but the girl held up her hand. "I already have three just like it, so that's the best I can do."

"A thousand."

"Nine hundred."

"Deal. Can I take the money in the form of clothing? Assuming I find something I like?"

Now it was the other girl's turn to laugh. "You can leave that part to me. I know you better than you know yourself. It's my job." She held out her hand. "Kat Karraby."

"Charlotte Williams."

"Pleased to meetcha, Charlotte."

Kat had a sleek Mary Quant bob, the two points of which met nearly under her chin and were dyed red to match her lipstick. She had large blue eyes and a cheeky expression. She was dressed in head-to-toe mid-'60s couture, presumably to go with the hairdo, and Charlotte would have traded her car for just the boots. They had goldfish in the heels.

Kat walked over to the racks and stood for a moment, thinking. "Are you wanting to stick with high couture, or can I experiment a little?"

Charlotte shrugged. "I'm trying to get a job, so nothing too out there."

"OK." Kat leaned forward and pulled a cream trouser suit off the rack. Even on the hanger, it was awesome.

"More Armani? Too dressy and too easily wrinkled."

Kat laughed. "You're right. How about this?"

"Early Gaultier? Too '80s."

"This?"

"Katherine Hamnett. Mid-'80s, still. Mind you, she did some nice things before the big T-shirts."

Kat looked at her strangely and then reached for something else. Charlotte smiled.

"Ah, early '90s Calvin Klein. Simple but a little boxy for me, maybe. I'm too small-chested. How about—"

Kat beat her to it. "Donna Karan. Why didn't I go there first?" She held up a deceptively simple pale green jersey dress, and her eyes sparkled. "This is going to look great, and it's only two hundred dollars."

Charlotte leaped up to try on the dress. Silk jersey. Lined. Beautiful. Easy to wear, up or down. She smiled at Kat as she went by. "You really do know your stuff. Your boss must love you."

"She does." Kat laughed. "She's me."

SIXTEEN

Kat's story was an interesting one. Her family was New Orleans royalty. Her mother had been the Komus Queen, which meant nothing to Charlotte but was apparently the crowning achievement, so to speak, for a young New Orleanian of a certain class. Her father owned one of the oldest restaurants in the city, and Kat had led as pampered and spoiled a life as Charlotte had. They were the same age, too, and Charlotte couldn't help wondering if they'd have been friends in New York. Kat's older sister had followed in her mother's footsteps, doing the whole debutante deal, as Kat described it with rolling eyes, but Kat had always gone her own way. She'd opened her store when she was just eighteen, using a loan from her daddy that she'd long since paid back.

Charlotte told her about her mother's clothing collection, and Kat nearly choked on her coffee.

"Zandra Rhodes, really? Ozzie Clark? That stuff was already vintage when she was working."

It was always funny to Charlotte when strangers knew who her mother was, but for once she appreciated it. She liked this girl, and wanted to be liked by her. It was a novel experience, caring about someone else's opinion.

"I think she was like us. She got into modeling because she got into fashion first, as a stylist."

Kat sighed. "That's my dream job. I get a chance every so often down here, but there aren't that many styling jobs for left-of-center stylists in New Orleans. The rich play it pretty straight, and the hipsters aren't so interested in high couture." She thought of something. "I did get a mention in *Vogue,* though." She went behind the counter and pulled out a very dog-eared copy. "After Katrina, everyone came here for a while, to support the city and all that good stuff, and I got a picture!" She flipped through and handed it to Charlotte.

The shot was actually Kat herself, although at first Charlotte wasn't sure. Kat was working a Jean Seberg boy cut, blond, wearing a '50s beach dress with a Mardi Gras print, rope-soled sandals, and a fabulous straw beach bag with a sombrero-wearing donkey embroidered on it. A little accompanying blurb mentioned the store and referred to it as a mecca for vintage couture.

"The dress is Hartnell, right? I love the bag. Who is it?"

Kat laughed. "Target." She pronounced it with a French accent.

Charlotte frowned. "I don't know them."

Kat thought she was joking and roared. When Charlotte just looked perplexed, she laughed even harder. "You have a lot to learn, Charlotte. Lucky for you I've got plenty of free time." She got to her feet. "All right, let's go get you a job. I've got to get changed, though."

"Why? You look awesome."

Kat grinned. "Why, thank you, darlin'. But we're going to go see my daddy, and he likes me a little more ladylike."

WHEN CHARLOTTE AND Kat walked into the restaurant an hour or so later, a large man looked out through the kitchen door and shouted.

"Katherine Karraby, don't you look a picture!"

"Hey, Daddy. How y'all doing in here today?"

Kat was wearing an original Laura Ashley tea dress from the early '70s, long enough to cover the Dr. Martens underneath. Charlotte had grinned to see them, but Kat pointed out that one could only sell out so far.

"Daddy likes me to wear a dress, but he's never noticed shoes in his life."

Her father, David Karraby III, was as tall as Charlotte's father but a great deal larger in every other respect. He was easily as charismatic, though, and made Charlotte feel immediately at ease.

"Charlotte, you say? Of the North Carolina Charlottes?" He roared with laughter and gave her a friendly hug. Behind his back, Kat rolled her eyes in apology. "Why, there's nothing at all of you, nothing but the frame you came with." He turned toward the kitchen. "Louis, we need beignets out here, and lay on the sugar with a heavy hand, man." He pulled out chairs for them both, and they sat, as if they were all old friends.

David Karraby managed somehow to make Charlotte feel like the center of attention while at the same time greeting absolutely everyone who walked in, some of them by name. At one point, he got up to hug a party of about two dozen people, and Kat leaned over to explain.

"The Karrabys have been in New Orleans since before it was American. We're Creoles, ya know? As far as my family is concerned, the *vieux carré* is the only *carré,* baby, though even we moved out when the tourists moved in."

Charlotte laughed but didn't really understand. Like most New Yorkers, she took little interest in the history of other cities. All she knew was that for some reason, New Orleans felt good to her, reminded her of Paris, and these friendly Karrabys were part of it.

"Even though many of our customers are from out of town, most are locals or frequent visitors, and my father prides himself on never forgetting a name or face." She watched her dad working, with affection. "He loves it, really, wouldn't want to be anywhere but here. After Katrina, we were one of the first places open."

David Karraby sat back down, having grabbed yet more food from somewhere. He pressed it on them. "Eat, Charlotte, eat. You'll need stamina to make it through the humidity of our summers." He sat back and regarded her thoughtfully. "You know, when you walked in, I thought you looked familiar, but I assumed it was because you were a friend of Kat's. But I just put it together—you're Jacob Williams's daughter, aren't you?"

There was a silence. Charlotte carefully put down her beignet and dusted off her fingers. She looked at Kat, who just smiled.

"Daddy, you're getting slow in your old age. I recognized her as soon as she walked into my store, but I was raised with more gentility than you, it would seem."

Charlotte stood. "I'll leave. I'm sorry."

Kat and David were horrified. "Oh, sit down, darlin', sit down!" he said. "The goings on in New York couldn't matter less of a whit down here, for one thing, and secondly, if we were all held liable for the sins of our poppas, the Louisiana jails would be even fuller than they are." Karraby looked sorry that he'd worried her, but his eyes were still as sparkly as his daughter's. "New

Orleans is a sanctuary for many, and you are welcome to our fair city, Charlotte Williams."

Kat leaned forward. "She needs a job, Daddy."

He smiled. "Can you wait a table, sugar?"

Charlotte tried to look confident. "I can try."

He laughed. "Well, if you can't, you can always wash dishes. That would be novel for you, I'll wager. You can start tomorrow night."

Another crowd came in, and he bounded to his feet.

"Mr. Mayor! *Bonjour!*" He launched into a charming, laughter-filled mix of French and English, clasping everyone by the hand and greeting them as if they'd been on a desert island for a decade.

Kat watched her daddy at work and grinned. "You'd never think the mayor was at our house just this past weekend, would you?"

Charlotte was curious. "Do you still live at home?"

Kat shook her head. "I have a place in the Marigny, but my mother would just about die if she didn't see me every weekend. She worries I'll become too bohemian if I don't get rinsed off in the Garden District from time to time." She looked at her daddy, who was still very much engaged. "We should get back to the store. Do you have simple clothes and comfortable shoes for working in?"

Charlotte shook her head. "I don't know, really."

"OK, then, honey, I am going to show you the time of your life. We are going to take a few hundred bucks of your credit and go get you a complete working wardrobe."

"Where? Heaven?"

Kat laughed. "One better. Target."

Chapter SEVENTEEN

Three hours later, they threw themselves through the door of the store and dropped their bags with a flourish.

"Well, that was the most fun I've had in ages—on my own, at least." Charlotte laughed.

Kat pouted. "Hey, I was there!"

Charlotte looked at her new friend and grinned. "True, and it never would have happened without you. Are you hungry?"

"Sure, let's dress up and go eat."

Charlotte frowned. "I don't want to get anything on my new dress. "

Kat extended her arms and turned in a slow circle. "Think of this as the biggest dress-up box ever. Most of it will fit you, and you can think of it as an ad for the store. We'll go out to dinner, then to a club, and when everyone comes up and asks you where you got your amazing clothes, you can name-check the store. It's marketing, baby!"

After much discussion, they decided to go with a '40s jazz club style. Kat pulled dresses with that classic New Look silhouette—

wide shoulders, tight waists, mid-calf length. And Charlotte did their hair in low, rolled chignons. Bright red lipstick, liquid eyeliner, powder—when they were ready, they looked like latter-day Lena Horne or Lauren Bacall, all curves and sass and style.

Kat was tickled pink. "I never had a wing man before," she crowed. "My sister is just too proper to wear clothes that someone else owned first. She doesn't get it at all."

Charlotte fingered the rose-colored silk of her dress. It had been the haute couture of its day, and every button, seam, and fold was of the highest quality. "The woman who originally bought this dress knew she was making an investment, and she was right. It's still as gorgeous today as it ever was."

"And you, my friend, look amazing in it." Kat tipped her head. "I don't suppose you like to sing, do you?"

Charlotte was surprised but nodded. "I actually always wanted to be a singer, professionally, but everyone persuaded me to go to Yale instead."

"And they don't have music at Yale?" Kat was sarcastic.

Charlotte blushed. "No, of course they do, but I guess I have the wrong sort of voice or something. I tried out for a couple of rock bands, but they just said I had a good look but no thanks. Eventually, one of the musicians told me I sounded like Norah Jones, which was apparently not a good thing."

"But she's very successful."

"Sure, but not as a rock singer." Charlotte shrugged. "I've tried to sing differently, and it doesn't work. It's a funny thing, but when I'm singing, I feel as if that's actually me. Do you know what I mean? And I've decided that there's not going to be any more changing of me. I've done that too much in my life, and those days are done."

Kat laughed. "Yay! *Viva la revolution!* Anyway, I have the perfect place for us to go; they love Norah Jones there. Don't forget, jazz was born right here in New Orleans."

"I don't really think of myself as a jazz singer. I just have that kind of bluesy voice, apparently."

Kat frowned at her. "Child, this is the Big Easy. We don't believe in labels, OK? It's all just music to us."

"Well, that's easy for you to say. You had the balls to follow your dreams when you were only eighteen. I just did what I was told." She sighed. "Until now, that is."

Kat squeezed her hand. "Look, if I can do it, you can do it. And let's face it, there's nothing I like more than a makeover." She looked down at the vintage clothes they were wearing. "Or, in this case, makeunder."

And with that, she grabbed some evening bags from the enormous collection on the wall of the store, and they headed out into the scented evening air.

THE CLUB WAS deep in the heart of the French Quarter, and at first, Charlotte thought she'd traveled in time. The sounds of a big band wafted out into the street, and the people milling about were all dressed as they were, although some had veered forward into the '50s. They worked their way through the crowd until the bouncer saw them, and once he'd spotted Kat they were whisked inside in no time. Inside, a girl wearing fishnet tights and carrying a tray of cigarettes around her neck directed them to a table. Everything inside was deco—mother of pearl and red leather banquettes, twinkling lights on the dance floor, elegant cocktails in period glasses. It was a dreamland.

Kat leaned forward to yell over the music. "I have a friend who runs this club. It's newish. Before this, he did a whole '70s disco thing, over at another location. He likes to do the period thing, you know, and we all just kind of go along with it. It's fun!"

Charlotte grinned. "I have a friend like that. You'll have to come to New York and meet him one day."

"I expect I will, once you're tired of the Big Easy."

The band struck up a tune, and couples took to the dance floor, all of them accomplished swing dancers. It was amazing to watch, and after a couple of cocktails, even Charlotte's toes were tapping. The band had an enormous sound and swung hard, like the Ray Charles Big Band or even the Quincy Jones Orchestra—highly syncopated rhythms and brilliant orchestration and arrangements. Janet had taught her to listen properly to music, and she could really appreciate the mastery of this band.

"I'm going to dance, OK?" Kat got up and wandered over to a nearby table, pulling a handsome guy to his feet and giving him a hug. Kat clearly knew a lot of people, and in many ways, she reminded Charlotte of herself. Herself but nicer.

Kat and the guy danced well together, and Charlotte watched happily, feeling safe and relaxed for the first time in a while. Being in a new city was uncomfortable, but a nightclub was familiar territory. And oh, the music. She found herself singing along under her breath, unable to stop herself.

The song ended, and a white spotlight found the bandleader. Charlotte was looking elsewhere, but when he started talking, she turned at the familiar voice.

It was Jackson.

She looked more carefully at the band. "Jackie Pearl and the Pearly Kings" was written on their music stands. *Huh.* Millie had said he had a band. Charlotte just hadn't realized she meant an orchestra.

"Ladies and gentlemen, my good friend Kat Karraby informs me we have a visiting musician in our midst."

Charlotte's heart sank. *Oh, no, she didn't.* But she had. Was there anyone Kat didn't know?

"Can Kat's mystery friend please join us on the bandstand? The Club du Quarante has a tradition of singers sitting in, and we might as well invite the Americans to join us, why not?" The audience laughed.

Kat showed up at the table, her eyes twinkling. "Come on, Charlotte, don't keep them waiting."

"You're kidding. I can't stand up there and sing."

Kat frowned. "Why not? You said you could sing, right?"

"Yes, of course. But that doesn't mean I'm ready to do it right now."

"Oh, come on, this is New Orleans. The normal rules of time simply don't apply."

Jackson spoke from the podium, unable to see through the spotlight. "Is it possible that a Karraby has lost the powers of persuasion we all thought they'd traded their souls for?" More laughter.

Kat lowered her voice. "Charlotte, my reputation is formidable in this city. If you knew who you were dealing with, you'd be too scared to sit there." She grinned. "Besides, you owe me, I got you a job."

Suddenly, Charlotte grinned back and tossed down the rest of her cocktail. She got to her feet and tugged her dress into perfect alignment.

"I have a feeling you're a force of nature, Kat Karraby."

"Hurricane Kat, that's me."

Charlotte let the applause wash over her as she crossed the dance floor, the bright spotlight making it impossible for her actually to see anyone. Jackson reached down to help her onto the stage, and as she stepped into the spotlight he hesitated, just briefly.

"Well, hello again," he said softly. "I guess you and I are going to jam together whether we like it or not."

Charlotte felt the effects of the cocktail and smiled broadly at him, making him raise his eyebrows.

"Jackson, let's bury the hatchet for one song, OK? Your band is awesome, and I promise I won't embarrass you."

Suddenly, he grinned back. "All right. What do you fancy? We have to stay in period, so pick something you know."

"How about 'I've Got News for You'?"

"Ray Charles?"

She nodded. It was a classic blues song, and the lyrics struck her as particularly appropriate for that night. Jackson shrugged and turned to face his band, baton raised.

Vamping chords, then a wailing sax introduced the song.

"You said before we met," Charlotte crooned into the vintage radio mic, starting low, her voice like velvet, *"that your life was awful tame. Well, I took you to a nightclub and the whole band knew your name."* The audience burst out laughing, and Jackson got into the spirit of the thing, slowly turning and fixing her with a glare. Swinging gently at the mic, she sang the song to him. *"Well, baby, baby, baby, I've got news for you, somehow your story don't ring true. Well, I've got news for you."*

With each verse, she turned up the volume and the ache in her voice, and soon her passion and love of the music infected everyone in the club. It was an amazing moment, with hundreds of people all listening intently, smiling, swaying to the blues, and watching this tiny white girl lay into the song as if she'd been born to it. The band caught it, too, and the solos were inspired, the sax player in particular loving it. While the musicians played, she danced slowly with her mic stand, her eyes closed, her beautiful face looking relaxed, occasionally adding some harmonies.

Jackson was thrilled to hear her sing, not that his face showed any emotion at all. A big band like his worked superbly with a featured singer, and he'd been looking for the perfect voice. How ironic that it would belong to someone he didn't particularly respect, and a northerner at that.

When the song was over, the room exploded. Whistles, cheers, stomps, and yells filled the air, and Charlotte beamed. Jackson shook her hand sedately. Charlotte leaned into the mic.

"Thanks for the chance, guys, and if you're looking for the perfect dress for next time, Noblesse N'oubliez has just the thing."

Kat was still laughing when she got to the table. "OK, now we're quits for the job. That was awesome! You're amazing!!"

Charlotte shrugged. "I love singing, I really do. I wish I could do it for a living, but there just aren't that many jobs out there, you know."

Kat pointed at her. "Hey, let's have a positive attitude, OK? If there's any city in the world where music is as accessible as water, it's this one. Let's finish getting drunk, and we'll put together a plan for world domination."

Charlotte nodded and signaled the waitress for more Manhattans.

Silence.

"Thanks for letting me sit in."

He shrugged. "You sing well."

More silence.

"OK, well, I'm going to bed now. I'm starting work tomorrow."

"You got a job already?"

She nodded. "Waiting tables at Kat's dad's restaurant."

His mouth twisted a little. "Proving yet again that being connected is all you need in life, right? Well, good for you." His tone was sour. "I'm off to bed, too." He paused at the door and turned back, looking reluctant. "Maybe tomorrow if we run into each other, we could talk about more gigs."

She frowned. "Gigs?"

"Yeah, well, the band really liked you, and clubs love a singer, and well . . . " He trailed off.

"Are you asking if I want to sing with your band sometime?" Her tone was neutral. She didn't want to piss him off, and truth be told, she was overcome with excitement at the thought of getting to perform again.

He nodded.

"Well, sure, that would be great. We'll talk tomorrow, OK?"

He nodded again and walked off. She stood for a moment until she heard his door close, and then she let out a quiet cheer. Two days in New Orleans, and she had a friend, a job, and now a chance to sing with an amazing band. She pulled off her clothes and climbed under the blanket on the sofa, hugging herself and smiling as she fell asleep.

Maybe things were starting to look up for her.

Or maybe not.

AFTER A RESTLESS night and a slightly hungover day wandering the city, Charlotte got ready to go to work for the late-afternoon and evening shift at the restaurant. Simple black pants, a white shirt, and the ugliest yet most comfortable shoes she'd ever owned. She pulled her hair back into a long braid, her one concession to her own style being vintage barrettes with black pearl butterflies. Simple makeup and clear nail polish, and she was just like every other young girl heading into the Quarter to wait tables. She had nearly a thousand dollars' worth of French silk underwear on, but no one would see that. She smiled, despite her nerves. It was exciting having a job.

Jackson was in the kitchen, looking tired. "Hi there," he said softly. "Off to work?"

She nodded. "I'm nervous."

"Your first time?"

"Yes. Silly, right?"

He shrugged, pushing his chair back and starting to make himself a cup of coffee. "I was nervous the first job I had. I think everybody is. It would be kind of weird not to be, actually."

"What was your first job?"

He smiled as he spooned sugar into his cup. "Fill-in piano player for the Quincy Jones Orchestra."

"Holy shit."

"Yeah. I think I lost three pounds that night, just from sweating. But it was fine."

"Did he invite you to join the band?"

Jackson snorted. "Are you joking? He never even spoke to me. There was another orchestra runner, the lead sax, who hired me for the one night, paid me after, and never even remembered my name. Quincy Jones is a god, though. It was an amazing honor just following his baton." He peered over the rim of his cup at her. "You're really a good singer."

She smiled. "Thanks. You're really an amazing bandleader."

"You need to loosen up a bit, though."

A pause.

"How do you mean?" She leaned against the doorframe to look nonchalant, but actually her heart was racing.

"Well, you've got a very bluesy voice, particularly for a Northern white chick with classical training, but you might want to relax a bit, stylistically."

"I was singing the blues and knocking it out of the park, I thought."

He shrugged. "Look, don't get all freaky. All I'm saying is you're a good singer, but you could be great. It's hard to really sing the blues and mean it if the worst thing that ever happened to you was Barneys running out of size two."

Her eyes narrowed. "I'm a zero."

"That's not what I'm saying."

"A size zero, you idiot."

"How can you be a size zero? Does that mean you don't exist on a physical plane?"

"We were talking about music, remember?"

He stood up. "Look, crazy lady, I have to go get ready for work, and you're going to be late for your first shift."

She looked at her watch and cursed, grabbing her bag, which immediately tipped over, dumping the contents on the floor. Jackson knelt to help her, and for a moment, they were very close together. He put his hand on hers.

"Look, Charlotte, really, you're a great singer, and you're going to be amazing. I'll help you, OK?"

She frowned at him. "I'm not a charity case, thanks."

He grinned at her. "OK, princess, keep your hair on. Have a good time at work, ya hear?"

She snorted at him and left.

Standing there, thinking carefully, Jackson heard a phone ring somewhere near his feet. Looking around, he finally spotted it. Charlotte's cell phone, under the chair. It must have dropped from her bag.

"Hello?"

"Hello there, you whore."

"I'm sorry, what did you say?"

The voice on the other end laughed. "Sorry, asshole, I was looking for your girlfriend. Fuck her while you can, dude, because I'm going to cut her heart out and watch her bleed to death."

As Jackson snapped the phone shut, he could hear the guy still laughing, and as he grabbed his jacket and raced out the door, he was just glad she'd told him where she was working.

———

AS IT HAPPENED, Agent Scarsford had arrived in New Orleans that morning, and he was sitting at a café across from Captain's House, waiting for Charlotte. As he waited, he flipped through the FBI field reports on Kat Karraby and the Pearl family. The Pearls were totally clean legally, but Kat Karraby's file was thicker. How likely was it that these two had just met? Was it possibly just coincidence, or was their connection much older? Kat's grandfather had . . . wait, there was Charlotte now. Scarsford lowered the brim on his baseball hat, keeping a low profile. He'd been surprised to learn she'd gotten a job. He strongly suspected she had access to the money Jacob had stolen, but maybe it was all part of her cover. It wasn't as if she didn't realize she was being watched; she could hardly buy herself a Maserati. Assuming she could even drive, he doubted she'd ever needed to.

Scarsford was still angry, with himself and with her. But as he watched her following another waitress around, learning the ropes, smiling and doing her best, he felt a little touched. Maybe she wasn't involved. Maybe she was innocent. She looked young and fresh in her simple white shirt, and if he wanted nothing more than to take it off her, then that was his problem to deal with.

IN THE RESTAURANT, Charlotte was doing her best. She'd been warmly welcomed at the restaurant, and Kat's dad made sure everyone knew she was to get all the help she needed to pick up the job. On the one hand, that was great, because God knew she really needed the help, but on the other hand it seemed she was never going to get treated as a normal person. Maybe she just wasn't one.

She'd been placed in the tender care of Sam King, a waitress with dark wavy hair and intelligent eyes, who was to show her the ropes. A Northern Californian by birth, Sam was full of insight and humor about the New Orleans way of life and, in particular, how to make people feel they were really experiencing it.

"A good percentage of our customers are from out of town, because the restaurant is rightly famous for its Creole cuisine. But at the same time, this place is very popular among the locals or those people who come to New Orleans a lot. Our job is to make all of them real welcome, in the Southern tradition, flirt a little, keep the drinks coming, smile a lot, and make sure they leave happy." They watched an older gentleman help his slightly inebriated wife out of the restaurant, colliding with the hostess stand as they did so. "She might be borderline too happy, but she's walking." Sam lowered her voice. "You have to make sure if they're getting too drunk, you tell the barkeep so he can mix their drinks a little more gently. The goal is to have them vomit away from the restaurant."

Charlotte laughed, but Sam was serious.

"Drinking is a major part of New Orleans life, always has been. You can walk around with a drink in your hand, you can even drive around with a drink in your hand, as long as it's frozen."

"The hand?" Charlotte grinned.

"The drink, silly. You haven't seen the drive-through frozen daiquiri stands? You will."

Charlotte shook her head. "I'm not a big drinker, to be honest."

Sam looked approvingly at her. "Smart girl. It will only get you in trouble here, that's for sure. Customers will try to buy you drinks all the time. Just tell them it's company policy not to accept. Eventually, they feel bad and just give you a bigger tip." She frowned. "Hey . . . that's Jackson Pearl. What's he doing here?"

Charlotte whirled around. Jackson was standing at the door, talking with the maitre d'. "You know him?"

Sam nodded. "Of course, everyone does. His band is one of the hottest in town right now, standing room only when they play. Besides, he's hella cute."

The maitre d' was looking around and found Charlotte. He beckoned her over.

Sam raised her eyebrows. "You know him, too?"

"Kind of. Be right back." Charlotte squared her shoulders and walked over, trying to frown at Jackson and smile at the maitre d' at the same time.

Jackson lowered his voice. "Charlotte, some creepy guy called you on your cell phone. It must have dropped in the kitchen when . . . you were at home . . . " Jackson looked slightly abashed but genuinely concerned.

"What did he say?"

"I'd rather not say in here. But I think we should call the police."

Charlotte shook her head. "I'll do it after I finish working, OK? He's in New York. The police already know about him."

David Karraby came over. "Everything all right, Charlotte?" He nodded at Jackson. "Good evening, young man. Please pass on my best to your mother."

Jackson nodded and smiled a little.

"Yes, Mr. Karraby, everything's OK." She frowned at Jackson. "Let's talk about this later." She was worried she would lose her job, and she hadn't even worked an hour yet.

Jackson turned to David Karraby. "Charlotte got a threatening phone call, and she got attacked in New York, you know. I think she should call the police."

Charlotte was furious. "I'm quite capable of making that decision for myself."

Karraby didn't blink. "Charlotte, my darlin', my first responsibility is to my patrons and staff. I'm sure you understand. I'm going to call the police now, and when you've sorted all this stuff out, you'll be welcome back at work, OK?" He reached for the phone.

Charlotte nodded, tears of frustration prickling in her eyes. Within a minute, the police pulled up, and people started to gather. You were never far from a show in the French Quarter, and tonight she was apparently it. Charlotte heard her name being muttered, passed around like a note in class. Great, people were recognizing her. So much for starting over. All she wanted was to be left in peace. A week ago, she'd been in Paris, happily eating croissants and watching the boys, and now she was in a strange city, trying to do a job she never in a million years thought she would have to do, and some crazy guy was fucking up her first night at work. It was bullshit, and she was getting more than a little overwhelmed by it. What she would give to see a friendly face.

"Charlotte."

She looked up and saw Scarsford crossing the street. He'd stayed hidden until the police pulled up, and then he'd headed toward her without even thinking about it. Now, as he pushed through the watching crowd, she pulled away and ran toward him, throwing herself into his arms.

Chapter
NINETEEN

Scarsford had managed to get a quiet room at the police station, away from the roaring drunks and shrill whores who'd apparently set up shop in the detectives division.

"We're not in Kansas anymore, right?" He smiled tightly at Charlotte. He'd been so taken aback when she'd run to him, so overwhelmed with the urge to protect her, to take her away somewhere safe and keep her close, that for the moment he'd forgotten his suspicions. He was back under control now, though, he reminded himself, back on the job.

For her part, Charlotte had been glad to see him. She wasn't sure why—it wasn't as if he was even on her side, so to speak—but she trusted him.

The New Orleans police had wanted to put her in a squad car, but Scarsford had flashed his badge and brought her down to the station himself. They had driven Jackson to the station and commandeered her phone—she was starting to think she'd give up on cell phones forever—and still had him in the squad room, asking him questions about the call. She'd been shocked to hear what the caller had said and felt very vulnerable, even though he was

presumably back in New York. The New Orleans cops had been
stony-faced and unmoved. New Orleans had a horrific crime rate,
and they'd seen it all. Having said that, they recognized a potential
shit storm when they saw it, and the last thing they wanted was the
daughter of a major criminal getting publicly murdered in their
city. They were just getting the tourists back after Katrina. They
were more than happy to hand Charlotte over to the SEC agent,
and soon the local FBI agent would show up, and they would be
able to wash their hands of Jackson, too.

Scarsford was on the phone, and Charlotte watched him. He
was handsomer than she'd first thought, and somehow the casual
jeans and T-shirt were sexier than the suit had been. He was more
muscular than she'd suspected, and his arms were taut and tanned,
and suddenly she felt a tightness in her stomach that surprised her.
He walked over to the small window and looked out at the city,
unintentionally giving her the chance to admire his broad shoulders, the sense of coiled power and control that was so alien to her.
He turned suddenly, and she saw he was angry, presumably with
whomever he was talking to.

"No, I don't think that's going to work. She needs to be in custody." He paused, looking at her but not really seeing her. His
mouth was tight, his eyes narrowed, and she shuddered. She didn't
want him ever to be that angry with her. She wanted, she realized,
to curl up in his arms and stay there until all of this was over.

"Fuck." He snapped his phone shut and glared at her. She was
looking up at him like a puppy, those big eyes wide in her beautiful
face, seeming smaller than ever sitting in this strange room. *Damn her.*

"What's the matter?" Even her voice was soft.

"You're the matter. I don't want you to get killed, but seeing as
you're not actually in anyone's custody, it's proving hard for me to
get you officially protected. You're not a witness, because your father

has confessed, and hardly anybody thinks you're involved, anyway, so until this guy actually makes a move on you, we're in limbo."

There was a pause as she thought over what he'd said. "Hardly anybody? You said hardly anybody—does that mean somebody thinks I'm involved? Involved in what, anyway, my dad's stuff?"

He nodded. "It's still possible you have information that could help us."

"Do you think so?"

He was silent for a moment, looking at the floor. Then he looked up, directly into her eyes. "What's on the zip drive, Charlotte?"

She looked surprised. "What?"

He was tired, and he rubbed the side of his face with his palm. "The zip drive. I saw you drop it into the tray at the airport. It wasn't with the other computer equipment you turned over, and it should have been."

"That's why you're here?" Suddenly, the attraction she felt for him receded, replaced by self-righteous anger. "You're here because you suspect me, not because you want to protect me."

"I just want to know what's on it, Charlotte. If it's totally unimportant, then you presumably won't have any problem sharing it."

Her anger was increasing. "I have no idea what's on it, you asshole. My father left it for me, along with some other very personal things, and I haven't even looked at it."

She was flushed and had never looked sexier to him. His body ached for her, but his mind was definitely in control.

"So let's look at it together."

"Fine. Let's." She folded her arms on the table and glared at him. "Where is it?"

"In my luggage, back at Millie's house." She sighed. "Look, Scarsford, I've told you before, and I'm telling you again. I know nothing at all about the bullshit my dad was up to, and I have no idea what's on the zip drive. It could be music, for all I know. Or it could be details of his Swiss bank accounts and offshore companies, in which case you're welcome to it. You're welcome to the music, too, if you want it. Take what you want: everyone else does."

"Don't tell me you're feeling sorry for yourself."

"Fuck you."

Scarsford left the room without bothering to reply, and several minutes passed. Charlotte looked around, slightly amazed that rooms this ugly existed. Beige walls, dark green hairy carpet tiles, furniture of the type found in crappy public schools—and yet no doubt all manner of human drama and excitement had played out against the bland background. Murderers confessed, victims cried, mothers turned against sons, and sons lied for mothers. How many other sweaty palms had rested on this tabletop? How many other lonely people had watched the second hand sweep around that clock face?

"Come on, we're moving." Scarsford's voice startled her.

Walking through the police station, she saw Jackson, still tiredly answering questions.

"Why is he still here?" She tugged on Scarsford's sleeve. "He was helping me. Why are they keeping him?"

Scarsford didn't even look around. "Who knows? Who cares?"

Charlotte stopped. "I do."

"Why?" Scarsford sighed but went over to talk to the cop with Jackson. He came back quickly, walking past her and gesturing for her to keep up. "He's fine. He's waiting to sign his statement, and then he's free to go. You can catch up with him tomorrow."

"Not tonight?" Charlotte had long legs and walked fast as a general rule, but she was having a hard time keeping up with Scarsford, who appeared to be on a schedule.

"No. Tonight you're with me."

She slowed, but he didn't miss a step.

Chapter

TWENTY

Scarsford's hotel room was as nondescript as the interrogation room had been, despite the carpet being a different shade of green. Two large beds faced the obligatory plasma TV, and the desk was covered with paperwork and two laptop computers. Scarsford cleared the paperwork and was still hooking up the laptops when a cop knocked on the door to deliver Charlotte's luggage.

"Do you want to do the honors?" Scarsford had put the suitcase on the bed and was about to flip it open when he apparently remembered his manners.

Charlotte shrugged. "Aren't you supposed to have a warrant or something?"

"Do I need one? I thought you wanted to show me."

"I don't want to show you anything. But I don't see that I have much choice."

"Of course you do. You don't have to give me anything you don't want to give me, Charlotte."

She looked at him for a long moment. What she really wanted to give him, right at that moment, was a swift kick in the nuts, but that probably wouldn't be wise. She thought he liked her. Thought he trusted her. She flipped the locks on the case and threw back the lid.

When she hooked up the zip drive, nothing happened right away. Clicking on a document called "Index," she and Scarsford both held their breath. They weren't sure what they wanted to see, but neither of them expected what popped open.

"Who's that?" said Scarsford after a moment.

Charlotte was silent. She swallowed as music filled the room. "It's my mother. And me."

The zip drive contained home movies. Judging by the index, there were hours of them. Jackie pregnant, laughing, in Central Park. Jackie holding a baby in her arms, sleepy in bed, lit by a small bedside lamp, as beautiful as it's possible for a woman to be.

And there was sound.

First her father's voice. "Who do we have here, Jack?"

Her mother laughed. "This is Charlotte Louise Williams, age four days." She looked down at the baby, who gurgled back. "She has your nose, sweetheart."

A laugh, off-camera. "We can fix that later. As long as she has your sweet disposition, we'll be fine."

"She seems pretty mellow, not that I have anything to compare her to, just yet."

"Is she getting sleepy?"

Jackie looked down, the corners of her mouth deepening in a smile. "She is, the little strudel."

"Sing to her, darling."

Jackie looked up at Charlotte's dad, behind the camera, and started singing a lullaby. It was as much to him as to the child, and the melody and lyrics were very personal.

"My love, my sweet, my dove . . ." Charlotte gasped. Her mother's voice was gorgeous. Deep, warm, strong, just like hers. "You fly in my heart, a bird from above . . . "

And suddenly, Charlotte remembered the song, the lyrics and melody flying back into her mind with the certainty of years. "Wing in wing, hand in hand . . . Sleep as you fly, surrounded by love . . . "

Jackie smiled down at baby Charlotte, humming the tune, as the grown-up Charlotte sobbed, the sudden memory of her mother's voice too much for her to bear. How could her father never have told her where her voice came from? Why did he never play these movies for her before? But as she watched the movie, tears streaming down her face, she realized why. Being reminded of what you lost hurts. She knew this because it hurt her now.

Turning to Scarsford, she tried to speak through her tears. "Satisfied now? Not secret codes, just old movies."

She turned back to the screen, watching footage of her mother running with her as a toddler, crossing the great lawn in Central Park. He put his hand on her shoulder, wanting to comfort her, and suddenly she turned to him, stumbling up from her chair, needing to be held.

For a while, they just stood there, holding each other, as Charlotte's crying slowly subsided. Then his arms tightened around her, and when she turned her face up to his, he bent to kiss her gently.

"I'm sorry . . . " he started to say, but she pulled his head down again and kissed him herself, less gently. Her tongue stole into his mouth, tracing the edge of his lower lip, and he stepped back and sat on the bed, pulling her onto his lap. For a moment, they kissed passionately, then he pulled back and lifted her off, setting her back on her feet effortlessly.

"Charlotte, I think you can see that I find you incredibly attractive. I have from the first moment I saw you. But we can't do this."

She frowned, stepping forward to straddle him again. She needed to take control, needed to be in charge for just this moment. She reached up behind herself and loosened her hair, unwinding her long braid. The smell of her hair filled the room, and the memory of the court building in New York overwhelmed him. She could see the effect she had on him, how much the sight and smell of her turned him on. But he stood up and walked to the window.

"There are lots of reasons it would be a terrible idea for us to sleep together. I'm investigating your father's crime, for one. I could lose my job or my ability to stay focused." He turned and looked at her, her hair tousled, her face flushed. He couldn't believe he was able to keep his hands to himself.

Charlotte was frustrated and angry. "Are you suggesting I want to sleep with you because I'm trying to distract you from your investigation? Isn't it possible I just want you?" She slowly unbuttoned her shirt, dropping it to the ground, the slight curves of her body glimmering in the light from the computer screen, her delicate underwear concealing and revealing. "Look at me, Jim. Don't you want me? Why can't we forget all of this stuff just for one night?"

Scarsford was only human. Two steps took him to her, and he pulled her into his arms, bending her slender waist as he kissed her deeply. His hands traced her curves, lightly, briefly, then he stepped away once more.

"Charlotte, believe me, you're gorgeous, and there's nothing I'd like to do better than take you to bed. But not like this."

Tears of loneliness filled her eyes. "You know what?"

He took her chin, and tipped her face up. "What, Charlotte?"

"You suck."

Then she walked into the bathroom and slammed the door.

Chapter
TWENTY-ONE

Sunday morning in New Orleans, particularly in the older parts of the city, had a weird magic all its own. On the one hand, you have your hungover frat boys, slumped at café tables, still a little drunk and more than a little nauseated, and on the other, you have the freshly in love, just met the night before, couples sharing breakfast for the first time. *You like toast? I like toast!* Table A, spoonheads with their hats on the right way for once, the brims shading their aching eyes, silently contemplating death. Table B, stubble-burned chins and gleaming eyes, long silences and intertwined fingers, sudden calling for the check.

Charlotte regarded all this over the rim of her café au lait, trying to ignore the fact that Scarsford was digging into deep-fried French toast at her side. Finally, she couldn't bear it.

"That stuff will kill you, you know."

He looked up. "French toast? I doubt it. It might make me fat, but it won't kill me."

"Sugar is a silent killer."

"Really?" He made yum-yum noises, smacking his lips. "It's not all that silent, is it? Sounds delicious to me." He was actually exhausted, having spent the night in the hotel lobby, dozing in an uncomfortable chair, watching the doors, while Charlotte slept alone in his room upstairs. When she'd come out of the bathroom, he'd been gone. He needed some sugar and caffeine to get going.

He signaled the waitress for more coffee, and as she took his cup, she caught Charlotte's eye and made the universal face for "hot guy, nice work." Charlotte sighed inwardly.

"What's the plan?" she asked Scarsford, who was wiping his mouth and sitting back, looking a lot better than he had earlier.

"There isn't a plan." He shrugged. "I can't get you into protective custody, because the guy's only made phone calls, and you have a job to go to, anyway, remember?"

"If they still want me." Charlotte was worried that David Karraby would rather avoid waitresses with stalkers, and who would blame him? "I should go find Jackson and see how he's doing. I feel bad he ended up at the police station for so long."

Scarsford paid the check and got up. "I'm going to go shower and get it together, OK? Why don't you go sort things out with Jackson and meet me later?"

"Why?"

There was a pause.

"Uh, to talk. I want to teach you a little about stalkers, about self-defense, about being watchful. This guy probably won't ever do anything beyond picking up the phone, but you never know." He smiled at her. "It would be a pity if you got all bruised up again, now that your nose is back to its normal size."

THE HOUSE WAS quiet when she walked in, but she could tell Jackson was home. She went to the kitchen and started a pot of coffee, carefully keeping the noise to a minimum. Maybe it was because she was being so careful that she didn't hear him get up, and when she turned and saw him leaning on the doorframe, she nearly shrieked. She definitely jumped. Unexpectedly, he laughed, and after a second, so did she.

He was just wearing jeans, which hung pretty low, and it seemed likely that was all he was wearing. He was very tall but not skinny, just slender and well muscled. He wasn't like the boys back home—his muscles looked earned rather than crafted, and his smooth brown skin gleamed with health rather than product. She thought he was gorgeous, and by the time he'd finished laughing, she had turned away to get the coffee, trying to hide her blush.

"Well, Charlotte Williams, you don't go quietly, do you?"

She handed him his coffee, frowning. "What do you mean?"

"I mean, you've been here three days and already got a job, made a friend, and spent the night at the police station." He stirred in sugar and cream, licking the spoon. "Most visitors take at least four days to do all that."

"I'm really sorry about the police station. I didn't expect them to keep you there."

He shrugged. "Most of those guys are friends of mine, anyway, so it was cool. It's not like I was a suspect or anything." He raised his eyebrows at her. "Although your boyfriend gave me one or two suspicious looks."

"Scarsford?"

"I don't know his name, sugar, all I know is he wasn't very friendly."

She looked down at her hands. "He's an SEC agent investigating my dad. I think he thinks I know something."

Jackson drank his coffee thoughtfully. "And do you?"

She met his eyes squarely. "Not a thing. I led a completely oblivious life, I'm afraid."

"Why afraid?"

"Because the farther I get from it, the more it looks shallow and pointless. My dad went off to work. I never really cared what he did. All I cared about was my charge account at Barneys, my parties, my clothes, my whatever . . . " She shook herself. "Self-centered. Self-obsessed. Embarrassing."

Jackson wasn't sure what to say. "But you came here, right? You had the balls to leave town."

"Is that balls? Isn't it just running away?"

He shrugged. "It depends, I guess, on what you intend to do now that you're here."

"My plan was to work, to start over. Although . . . I guess I was also running away. I was, and am, so angry with my dad and so confused about it all. I thought he loved me."

"And what makes you think he doesn't?"

She raised her eyebrows at him. "If he loved me, wouldn't he have avoided going to jail?"

Jackson laughed at her. "He did avoid going to jail, Charlotte. According to the reports, at least, he avoided it for more than a decade. If you were being logical, you'd be angry with the FBI and the SEC, not your dad."

"I am angry with them. But what he did was wrong, and they're just doing their job."

"Does that include sleeping with you? Is that part of the job?" His face was hard to read. "Nice work if you can get it."

"I didn't sleep with him." Not from a lack of trying on her part, but she pushed that thought to the back of her mind. Jackson just stood up to get more coffee, offering to get her a cup, too. She shook her head. She could tell he didn't believe her. Did it matter?

"When is your mom back?"

"Tonight. Why?"

"Because I found some video of my mom with me when I was a baby, and I thought she'd like to see it. I want to show it to her."

He looked interested. "Found it?"

"Well, my dad gave it to me, sort of. I think he'd been saving it for a special occasion, not sure why. But anyway, he told me where it was, and I watched it last night. I think she'd like it because my mom sings . . . she sounds like me. Or rather, I sound like her. You know, it was your mom who encouraged me to pursue music in the first place. She heard me singing to my dolls or whatever and told me I was good, that people would like to listen to me." Her eyes got shiny. "I know you don't like me, Jackson, but whatever you think, I think your mother is a wonderful person. I would never do anything to hurt her, and I'm sorry I didn't stay in touch the way I should have."

It was surprising, Jackson realized, how easily old prejudices could slip away. Looking at this young woman across the table he saw how hard she was trying to do the right thing. She continued talking about his mom.

"You know, she and Greta were my moms, and they taught me everything that I'm needing to know right now. To be honest. To work hard. To get up and try again when you fall." Charlotte's tone was serious. "Once she left, I kind of forgot it. My dad might have loved me, maybe you're right, but he didn't teach me any of the important stuff. He didn't even tell me about my mom, never even mentioned her until just a few days ago." She sighed, feeling suddenly exhausted. "I owe your mom a lot." She looked at him. "And you. You had to do without her, right? That's why you hate me."

He nodded. "Yeah. But I don't hate you. Not anymore. I did when I was younger, because I didn't understand why she wasn't there when I needed her."

"Why did she come to New York to work?"

He laughed. "Why do you think? Money. She had no husband and three kids. We lived at my grandmother's house. She had a degree in education and would have taken her master's if she could have afforded it. Your father paid her twice the going rate for teachers in Louisiana."

"How did he find her?"

He shrugged. "Greta found her, she said. You'd have to ask her."

"How old were you when she left?"

"Six. The same age you were, right?"

She nodded.

"So, in a way, we both lost our mothers at the same time."

She smiled bitterly. "Yes, but you got yours back."

"Once you were done with her."

There was a pause.

"You still hated me when I got here. What changed?"

"I met you. It's hard to hate someone in person, don't you think?" *Especially when they look like you,* he thought to himself, *and when they're in trouble.*

She thought about the woman outside the courthouse and the man on the phone. "Apparently not. Plenty of people hate me right now."

"They don't know you." He stood up and stretched. "I'm going to throw on a shirt, and then we're going to play some music. We've got a gig in two days, and I'd like you to sing with us, if you're not working."

She nodded. "I think I got fired, but I'm not sure." But he didn't seem to hear her.

He wandered down the hall, and maybe he could feel her eyes on him as he did so, or maybe not. But he was back quickly, wearing an old Crescent City Brewery T-shirt.

"Nice shirt."

"Local brewery. Got to support the native talent, right?"

He sat down at the old piano and played a few chords. She watched his strong hands and felt a shiver go over her. She'd always been a sucker for good hands. He vamped a little, then turned to her.

"OK, Charlie, what do you fancy? Standards?"

She nodded. "Your mom used to play me old jazz discs all the time. Nina Simone. Dinah Washington. Julie London. More recent stuff, too. Diana Krall, stuff like that."

"My mom is a traditionalist, that's for sure." He played the opening to "Girl Talk," a bluesy standard made famous by Julie London. "Let's hear it, baby."

Suddenly, Charlotte wanted to sing. She thought of her mom, holding her so tenderly, her voice as much an expression of love as anything could be. She began to sing. It was a lighthearted tune, with lyrics that are basically about gossip, and it took on new meaning now that people were talking about her. She gave it a sarcastic edge, drawing out the words, bending the notes, and Jackson matched her interpretation easily.

He was surprised. At the nightclub, she'd done a great job with the blues, but she was handling this lighter song just as well. That a skinny little girl from Manhattan could produce as full and rounded a sound as this was simply proof that God enjoyed music as much as the next man.

"OK, let's see how well she educated you."

He switched songs, but she kept pace. He moved through several jazz standards: "Love for Sale," "Summertime," "How High the Moon," and she made each one her own, revealing and reveling in her wide range. He sneaked a glance at her, swinging gently next to him, her eyes closed, an expression of real happiness on her face. He smiled himself to see her and joined in with some harmonies. Then he started playing some newer stuff, some Norah Jones, even some Fiona Apple. She knew it all and simply added more or less edge to her voice as the song required.

After nearly an hour, Jackson suddenly stopped and got to his feet. "Hey, do you want to learn something new? I have something I wrote that I've been doing at occasional gigs, but I want to hear you do it."

He almost ran down the hall, and she leaned against the piano and grinned. It was wonderful to sing, wonderful to be with another musician, and even though she was still a little nervous with Jackson, she realized how good a pianist he was. In many ways, it was like making love, learning each other's styles, feeling out what worked and what didn't, anticipating what would make your partner smile. He was back, and she put those naughty thoughts out of her head and turned her attention to the music.

AFTER A COUPLE of hours, Charlotte headed back to the hotel to meet Scarsford. When she spotted him, he looked just about ready to murder someone. He grabbed her by the arm in the hotel lobby and bent his head to her ear.

"Don't say anything, just follow me to the elevator, OK?"

She nodded and waited until the doors closed. Then she pulled her arm free and turned to frown at him. His fingers had left marks on her soft skin, and she rubbed them angrily.

"What the fuck, Tarzan?"

Scarsford watched the floor numbers tick by. "We're being watched. Or, rather, you're being watched, and I'm along for the ride."

"You're talking crap. Of course I'm being watched—you're watching me."

He shook his head impatiently, rushing off the elevator and striding toward his room. She had to quicken her pace to keep up, her heels catching on the carpet. Damn Louboutins.

"You're all over the Web. Someone's following you, and if it isn't your phone stalker, then it won't be long before he works out where you are and follows you down here."

Charlotte dropped her bag on the bed and came to stand next to Scarsford, who was clicking keys on his computer. He straightened and stepped back.

"See?"

She bent to look and sucked in her breath. *Holy shit.*

At www.charlottewilliamssucks.com, there were pictures of her from yesterday. Under the headline "Charlotte Williams Turns Tricks in the Big Easy," there was a shot of her and Scarsford entering the hotel lobby, and the words underneath were even less flattering than the headline.

"Now that Charlotte Williams has to do without Daddy's millions—which weren't his in the first place—she's reverted to type and is selling the only thing she owns, her own ass. I guess there wasn't anyone left in New York she hadn't slept with already, so she ran off to New Orleans to ply her trade. I guess once you've been fucked by Katrina, it's easy to get blown by Charlotte!"

Below that was another shot, of her and Jackson standing at the restaurant. The caption to this one was insulting to both of them.

"Good to know Charlotte is an equal opportunity whore—she'll take money from anyone, black or white."

And finally, there was a shot of her and Kat entering the nightclub two nights before, all dressed up. It was actually a great photo; she and Kat both looked gorgeous and were laughing and happy. The caption was cruel.

"Looks like Charlotte found another friend to ruin. Here local rich girl Kat Karraby gets all slutted up for a night on the streets. Watch out, Kat, you're hanging with the wrong crowd now."

Tears stung Charlotte's eyes. "That's so unfair. Who's doing it? Are they allowed to say those things about me?"

Scarsford was grim. "He just signs himself 'The Bitch Watcher,' and the site is registered anonymously through one of the big URL houses." He shrugged. "It'll be hard to get a warrant to find out the registered owner—he or she isn't doing anything illegal."

Charlotte sank onto the chair. "But isn't it libel or something?"

"No. It's free speech. The online world is still pretty much the Wild West, and any good lawyer would argue that this person is just expressing a personal opinion. Besides, it would take months to get this to court, and in the meantime, they'll just keep posting."

He was gazing down at the streets below, thronged with tourists, all carrying cameras, cell phones, tiny video cameras. A thousand prying eyes per block.

"Unfortunately, we have another problem, or at least I do. When my bosses see that photo of us together, they'll probably take me off the case."

Charlotte felt her stomach sink. "Why? You could just have been questioning me, right?"

He still hadn't turned around. "Alone? At night? At my hotel? At the very least it's bad judgment, and at worst, it's collusion with a suspect."

"And what are we supposed to be colluding about?"

"Money. What if you secretly know where all the millions are hidden and we're sleeping together and are planning to share the money?" Now he turned, and his face was as hard and cold as she'd ever seen. "I could lose my job, and even if I don't, I've endangered the investigation and given your father's lawyer some-thing to bring up in court to distract the jury."

"Well, if it's any consolation, I don't know where any money is. I don't even know if there is any money. For all I know, he's been giving it away."

Scarsford laughed suddenly. "You're amazing, you know that? You're living in a dream world. What, you think he's been feeding orphans and widows with the money?"

She shook her head, getting angry. "No, clearly. But he could easily have been paying for the apartment and everything else with just his salary. He made millions every year."

Scarsford just snorted, and Charlotte eventually gave up and walked away.

Chapter
TWENTY-TWO

Sunday morning had stretched into afternoon, but the atmosphere at the Karraby restaurant was timeless. Just walking in made Charlotte feel better, and when she saw Kat sitting with her dad, she broke into a wide smile. *Fuck the world, let them say what they want.*

Kat and her dad looked happy to see her, and when she sat down it became clear that they had been talking about her.

David Karraby leaned back and pointed his finger at her. "You know what it is, Charlotte Williams? You're in a piece of trouble right now, and it seems to be a Karraby trait to attract trouble."

"I'm sorry, Mr. Karraby. I thought I'd left it behind in New York, but I guess the world is a smaller place than I thought."

Kat laughed. "We're not in the middle of nowhere, you know. We've even heard of the Internet down here."

Charlotte blushed. "I'm sorry, I didn't mean to sound like that. Speaking of the Internet, I don't suppose you saw the stuff online? I'm really sorry, Kat."

They both frowned, and Charlotte bit her lip. Kat pulled out her laptop, and Charlotte silently navigated them to the offending

Web site. Kat went pale when she saw herself online and pushed the laptop over to her dad.

There was a pause as David Karraby read the page, and a small line appeared between his brows. He looked at his daughter.

"Well, honey, it's up to you. I can fire her, and you can walk away if you like."

Kat was shocked. "Daddy! How can you even suggest such a thing?"

Charlotte's stomach was turning, and tears came to her eyes.

Surprisingly, David Karraby laughed. Loudly. "I'm joking, honey. The Karrabys aren't cowards. It's online, it's out there, and probably by now, many people we know have seen it. So what? A little gossip never hurt anyone, particularly in New Orleans." His voice dropped a little. "You know that already, sugar." He turned to Charlotte. "Look here, young lady. I don't want my guests disturbed by photographers or other bullshit like that, so if you want to keep working, you can work in the kitchen for a while, OK? Same money, same hours, different level of privacy."

Charlotte was enormously relieved. "That would be great, Mr. Karraby. Thank you so much."

"I don't suppose you speak French, do you?"

She nodded. "I do, actually."

He sucked in his breath. "Oh, Lord. Well, bring some cotton wool to work, then; otherwise, your ears might burn right off."

AFTER DAVID KARRABY had left them alone, Charlotte asked Kat what her dad had meant. "He said you already knew about scandal—what was that about?"

Kat sighed, and signaled for more coffee.

"Well, as you might have noticed, I have a particular sense of fashion."

Charlotte smiled at her. Today Kat was wearing a '70s outfit—a cream pantsuit with a dark brown ribbed wife beater underneath, a thin orange man's tie loose around her neck. Ali McGraw with red hair.

"Now, New Orleans is a place of wild music and wild women and all that jazz, well, particularly jazz, but high school is high school, right? The girls wore the right kind of shoes, the right kind of pants, the right kind of whatever. I couldn't have cared less about what was current. All I cared about was what I liked, and they didn't like that at all." She stirred her coffee. "I wasn't completely alone, I had some other freaks to hang out with, but you know, high school can be hell." She looked up. "Right?"

Charlotte nodded, but she knew the truth. She had been one of those girls. Policing everyone else. Leading the pack. Looking down on kids who didn't have the right phone, the right car, the right labels. She was too ashamed to admit it to Kat, though.

"They couldn't physically touch me, because my daddy knows everyone, and the Karrabys are powerful people in the city. But they could ignore me and whisper about me, and they did that in spades. There were weeks at school when I didn't hear a friendly word, or any word, from anyone at all. It was as if I was utterly invisible. Well, not even, because the kids would all move away from me as I walked down the hall, but no one smiled or waved or even looked at me. It was agony. Anyway, it all came to a head at the prom, in true movie style. I went alone, because no one was brave enough to ask me to go with them." She raised her eyebrows. "Anyway, they were all in fluffy, flouncy prom dresses, and I wasn't, and it was totally miserable."

"What were you wearing?"

"Floor-length 1973 Halston. Goddess style. Fiery red."

"Nice."

"I thought so. Anyway, they all cut me dead, and then I came home and swallowed a bottle of my mother's sleeping pills."

The sounds of the café receded. Charlotte gazed at her new friend in horror. "Oh, my God, what happened?"

Kat shrugged. "A surprising thing. My sister Jane came in to talk to me. You know, I mentioned her before, she was the Mardi Gras queen, blah blah. She's always fit in, always had loads of friends, all that stuff. She and I didn't always see eye-to-eye, but you know, there's four years between us, which is a lot when you're a teenager, right? She was already in college at this point, having made it out of high school alive."

Kat pulled out her purse and flipped through a wallet of photos. "This is Janey." The picture showed a classic beauty, smiling sweetly for the camera. She looked every inch a prom queen.

"Anyway, she came in and sat on my bed in the dark and asked me about the prom. She'd watched me leave; she knew I'd decided to go dressed as myself, if you follow me. I told her about it, how nobody had spoken to me all night, how I'd sat at the side alone." Kat's face had grown dreamy, remembering. "She didn't say anything for a while, then she kind of gave a big sigh and leaned over and hugged me. She said, 'Kitty Kat, fuck them. In ten years, they'll be fat and frumpy, looking like each other and crying at night over their cellulite and their cheating husbands and their bratty little kids. You will be as elegant and beautiful and unique as you always have been, and they will look at you and know that they caged a rare bird instead of learning to fly themselves. Their loss, cherry pie, and your gain.'"

Kat had tears in her eyes, and Charlotte was deeply touched.

She obviously remembered the scene all too clearly, even after several years.

"And I told her what I had done, and she called me an idiot and told my dad, and we went to the hospital, and they pumped my stomach." Kat opened her eyes wide and looked squarely at Charlotte. "Listen, girl. You cannot let the words of other people enter your brain as if they were truth. They're not. They're just meaningless gossip and pointless opinion, and if you lose sight of that, they've won." She waved her hand at the laptop. "Someone's bothering to follow you around and take pictures and then scurrying home to upload them, spending hours on it? What kind of life is that?" She got to her feet. "Come on, I'll take you back to the kitchen and introduce you to the guys. Trust me, they don't give a shit who you are. All they care about is how cute your ass is and how fast you wash a dish. We can talk about the guy with the camera later."

Charlotte followed her to the back of the restaurant, thinking about what she'd just heard. Kat was awesome, and she felt lucky to have met her. But she wasn't sure she had the strength this Southern girl had. She felt very much alone and unsure of who exactly she was. She'd been one of those bitches, and she wasn't sure she knew who she was if she wasn't comparing herself favorably with some loser. What if she didn't have enough substance to stand alone? If she gave up being a rich girl with a bad attitude, what did that leave her with?

Then she stepped into the steamy maelstrom that was the kitchen and started to find out.

Chapter TWENTY-THREE

The first one to notice her was a short guy who was spraying water from an overhead faucet onto a pan that seemed almost big enough for him to climb into.

"Yo, Kat brought a friend—*une amie . . . jouer . . .*"

Kat laughed. "Not to play, Ronnie, to work. This is Charlotte. She's going to show you guys how to do it back here."

A handsome black guy leaned back from the grill and looked Charlotte carefully up and down. "I'd like to see how she does it. Go ahead and show us, baby."

Charlotte smiled and said nothing.

The man looked around the kitchen. *"Elle est toute petite, elle sera inutile."* The Creole was heavily accented, but Charlotte could grasp it: "She's very small, she's going to be useless." She kept her smile in place.

Another chimed in. *"Ouais, mais des petits mains ferraient paraître ta bite plus grosse."* OK, this one was easy: "Yeah, but her tiny hands might make your dick look bigger."

And a third, *"Je lui donnerais bien un truc à sucer."* Apparently, this one wanted to give her something to suck on.

OK, enough was enough. Charlotte cleared her throat. *"Je doute que tu me proposes quoi que ce soit d'appétissant, mon chéri, mais tu peux peut être travailler de nouvelles recettes,* eh?" Roughly translated, she'd responded that she doubted they had anything she'd find appetizing, but perhaps she could teach them some new recipes.

There was a moment of shocked silence and then a roar of laughter. A good-looking girl who spoke dirty French? Bonus!

"Bravo, baby." Ronnie wiped his hands dry. "Now that we've got the traditional sexist bullshit out of the way, let's put you to work."

IT WAS INTERESTING to see how long a manicure lasted in a busy restaurant kitchen. Hers was destroyed immediately, because Ronnie made her cut her nails, put on long rubber gloves, and tie her hair back under a hairnet. He handed it to her and sent her into the bathroom. With Kat's help, she turned it into a Rosie the Riveter kind of '40s chignon. However, when she came back out, he just barked out a laugh and pulled the net over the front of her hair, too.

"The idea, *chérie,* is to cover all your hair so it doesn't drop into the food, get it? This is a kitchen, not a fashion show." He turned to Kat. "How come you don't give your pretty friend a job in the store?"

Kat shrugged. "Because I don't need any help in the store, and I have no money to pay her with. Apart from that, it's an awesome idea." Clearly, she and Ronnie were old friends.

"And why isn't she out front? Too clumsy to wait tables?" He was obviously smart and inquisitive, and after a brief nod from Charlotte, Kat gave him the 411.

He sighed. "Well, *cocotte,* you'll be well hidden back here, and you'll earn your money." He looked around at the other guys, who were larking around and playing with knives. "If anyone asks, just say you have a jealous boyfriend and you don't want anyone to get hurt. They should leave you alone." He looked her up and down again. "I myself am immune to your charms, because my heart belongs to Kat."

Kat threw a slice of red pepper at him.

Once Ronnie had introduced her to the excitements of the dish-washing station—scalding water! industrial soap!—Kat leaned against the wall to watch her tackle her first stack of sauté pans.

"Charlotte, do you want to come and stay at my place for a bit? Until you get settled?"

Charlotte was surprised. She'd assumed she was going to stay at Millie's for a while, especially as she and Jackson appeared to have signed a peace treaty that morning, but that didn't mean she was totally cool with it. He was very attractive . . . and the sofa wasn't all that comfortable.

She smiled at Kat. "Why are you being so incredibly nice to me? We just met, and you've found me a job, gotten dragged into an online gutter, and, most importantly, been a friend. Do I seem that pathetic?"

"Yes," said Kat seriously. "Utterly pathetic." She waited a beat, then giggled. "No, you don't seem pathetic at all, but I live alone, I have a spare room, and I thought it might be fun. I'll make you pay rent once you get paid, don't worry. It's not charity, it's sensible."

Charlotte was thrilled. "I would love to come live with you. That would be totally awesome." A thought occurred to her. "However, it might mean more trouble for you, with whatever wacko is following me. And it might get worse, I have no idea."

Kat laughed. "Well, let's just try it and see what happens, OK?

If I wake up and find a horse's head in my bed we can reconsider."

Charlotte frowned.

"You have seen *The Godfather,* right?" Kat looked horrified. Charlotte shook her head. "OK, well, then that's what we'll do tonight after your shift. Here." She scribbled on a notepad. "Here's my address, it's not very far. Call me when you're done, and I'll walk from my house as you set out from here. We'll meet in the middle."

"I don't have my stuff. It's at the Excelsior Hotel."

"Oh, that's right, where you were turning tricks." Kat grinned. "We can pick it up on the way later."

Charlotte was overwhelmed with gratitude. "You are so awesome, Kat. I can't thank you enough."

"Oh, I expect I'll think of some way for you to pay me back," her friend replied airily. "Besides, I'm planning on going through your bag looking for nice clothes to steal."

Charlotte laughed. "There's a 1972 Pucci clutch you can have if you like."

"Right, then, I'm leaving." Kat mimed a running start and gave Charlotte a quick hug. "Have fun with the lads. They're harmless really."

"I hope so," Charlotte replied. "And if all else fails, I'll blow them away with my high-power water cannon." She waved the hot-water jet threateningly and laughed.

AS KAT WALKED out of the restaurant, the man snapped a few shots and then clicked the lid on his camera. She wasn't his main target, but she was nice local color. He hooked his camera to his laptop, downloaded and then uploaded the shots, and added them to his site, all while sipping his latte. Thank God for the Internet. He settled back and ordered a muffuletta with three kinds of meat. It was hungry work, ruining someone's life.

CHARLOTTE'S SHIFT DIDN'T end until nearly midnight, and she was dead on her feet by the time Ronnie said she could leave. But she was proud of herself. She hadn't complained once, nor had she taken a break or slowed down at all. Ronnie and the other guys had noticed.

"You know, *nana,* you look as if the heaviest thing you've ever lifted is a charge card, but you're strong, doll. You worked like a guy." Ronnie slapped her on the shoulder, hard. "We'll see you tomorrow, OK?"

She nodded and smiled tiredly. "Thanks, Ronnie."

She called Kat from the bathroom as she pulled off her hairnet. "Oh, God."

"What?" Kat had answered just in time to hear Charlotte's shocked exclamation.

"My hair. It's stuck to my head. Apart from this one piece in the back that's sticking up like Alfalfa. I don't know that I've ever looked this bad in my life."

Kat laughed at her. "You might be revealing hidden rivers of vanity, Charlotte. Haven't you ever worked hard before? Don't you sweat?"

"Well, of course, but usually something more interesting is going on than just washing dishes."

Her friend just snorted. "Stop looking at yourself in the mirror, princess, and head out on Main Street. I'll meet you halfway, OK?"

"Are you sure it's going to be safe? It's after midnight. What if no one is around?"

More laughter, then Kat hung up. Charlotte frowned, shrugged on her jacket, and headed out the kitchen door, down an alley alongside the restaurant. Two steps out, and she saw why Kat had laughed.

There were more people in the French Quarter at 12:15 at night than there had been during the day. It was swarming with people, and music of all kinds competed for airspace on the streets. Girls who were either hookers or just really bad dressers were cat-calling and hollering at the groups of men wandering aimlessly down every block, and the smell of beer and pot permeated the air. Everyone seemed to be laughing and having a great time, and once Charlotte got over the shock of it, she felt herself starting to smile, too. It was like the world's biggest block party, and as Charlotte walked along, someone handed her a martini glass, to go. Well, why not?

After a minute or so, she met up with Kat, and the two of them walked along companionably.

"Do you get used to it if you live here?"

"What?"

"The constant partying."

Kat laughed. "You're from Manhattan, right? Well, aren't there parts of Manhattan that are buzzy like the French Quarter?"

Charlotte looked doubtful. "Well, sometimes, but never like that all the time. It's Sunday night, no special event, and it's like a parade back there."

"New Orleans is all about parades, but yeah, I guess it is a little unusual. The French Quarter is a special place. But New Orleans is much more than just that part. You'll see. And yes, you get used to it, especially if, like me, your family business is in the Quarter. I just allow time to get from one end to the other, especially if it's after ten A.M., or the weekend or, heaven forbid, Mardi Gras."

They had left the French Quarter and were in what Charlotte recognized as the Garden District. Wrought-iron fences just managed to keep the lush greenery of the gardens in check, and large, elegant houses could be seen set well back from the street. Some were floodlit, some still had all their lights on, and others were silent and dark.

"Here's us." Kat turned into one of the larger gardens.

"What? This is your 'little place'?"

Kat giggled. "No, dumbass, I have the back house." She led the way through the garden, onto a brick path that ran alongside the house. Tucked in the back was a smaller, one-story building. Wisteria covered the front, and the red brick façade was punctuated with small white windows.

Charlotte sucked in her breath. "Oh, my God, I'm going to have a cute attack. Everything's going dark."

Kat laughed. "I know, adorable, right? When my dad said he had a friend who had somewhere for me to stay, I had visions of a cellar or something." She shrugged as she fished in her purse for the key. "What can I say? I'm the pampered favorite child of a rich southern gentleman. I cannot change who I am."

She pushed open the door, and Charlotte stepped in. And fell in love.

THE BACK HOUSE had originally been for servants, but they must have been pretty appreciated servants, for the main room stretched maybe thirty feet from side to side. A large fireplace anchored one end, while French doors lined the walls on both sides.

"You need to be able to open the whole thing up in the summer, because it's so hot and humid. A breezeway was the only air conditioning they had back then." Kat pointed out the other features of her obviously much-loved home. "A fireplace was necessary for heating water and because occasionally the nights get cool."

Charlotte looked around. "Is it just this one room? Where do you sleep?"

Instead of answering, Kat led the way around the corner. Tucked in an ell was a small kitchen with a charming skylight and a short hallway leading to two small bedrooms. Wide plank floors and deep windows showed how old the building was, and the simple furnishings were in keeping with the period.

"Wow, you should be an interior decorator, dude. This place is awesome."

Kat grinned. "Thanks. It's all part of my urge to style every-thing. I love this place. I couldn't be happier. I'm glad you like it, too." She sighed. "Now, let's have a drink. Allow me to introduce you to the Sazerac, a local specialty."

When Charlotte eventually fell into bed, her head spinning, she realized she hadn't thought about her father all day. She wondered if he was thinking of her.

Chapter
TWENTY-FOUR

Charlotte didn't need to be at the restaurant until mid-morning, so the next day she accompanied Kat to her store. They split some coffee cake and opened up Kat's laptop, checking the horrible Web site.

Charlotte shivered. "OK, that's creepy. And slightly embarrassing."

The front-page picture on the site was her emerging from the alley behind the restaurant. A high-powered lens had obviously been used, because every detail of her greasy hair was highlighted, and in case you'd missed it, the commentary was acerbic.

"How the mighty have fallen! The former socialite Charlotte Williams has turned to working in a kitchen to make ends meet (guess no one wanted to pay to fuck her anymore), and it's not the best look she's ever offered us. Nice hair, Charlotte! It must be quite a shock, ladies and gentlemen, to have to work for a living instead of living off stolen money. Meanwhile, Bitch Watcher hears that Jacob Williams was attacked in jail yesterday and had to be taken to the infirmary. How nice to see two fat cats finally get what they deserve!"

Charlotte was already dialing her father's lawyer.

"It's true, I'm afraid." Bedford seemed a little distant on the phone, but maybe she was imagining it. "Someone pushed into him in some line or other and stuck him with a shiv, or a skiv, or whatever it is they call it. A sharp instrument of some kind." He rolled over Charlotte's nervous questions. "He's fine, Charlotte, and probably safer in the infirmary than he is in the general population."

Charlotte took a breath. "I thought you were going to try to get him moved to a minimum-security facility, Arthur."

The lawyer sighed. "This *is* the minimum-security facility, Charlotte. It's still jail, you know. I can hardly request that he serve his time in Turks and Caicos, can I?"

IT TOOK A while for Charlotte to calm down, but eventually, she pulled it together.

"I'm so tempted to go back to New York, to be nearer to him."

"Well, unless you pretend to be a guy, get arrested for something, and somehow get sent to the same jail, you're not going to be able to help him," Kat said. "I'm not making light of it. I realize how awful this must be for you, but I'll be blunt. He broke the law, right?"

Charlotte nodded sadly.

"Well, as my schoolteachers would have said, and probably did, if you can't do the time, don't do the crime."

"My teachers said that, too."

"Well, there you go then. If you want, I can help you drag up, and I'll drive a getaway car very slowly so you'll get caught."

Charlotte imagined the scene and started to laugh. "I got lucky meeting you. There aren't many people who would offer to be a

really inefficient criminal sidekick after less than a week of knowing someone."

Kat smiled. "Well, maybe they lack imagination. I'm doing a
whole mental review of the wardrobe in *Bonnie and Clyde*. That
cream beret she wore almost makes jail worth it."

Charlotte wandered around the store, flipping through the
clothes. "You have a commitment to fashion that is awe-inspiring."

"Why, thank you."

She changed the subject, wanting to stop talking about her
father. "What is your sister doing now? Is she in college still?"

Kat shook her head, "No, she's in medical school. She's a high
achiever, is Janey. She has her whole life planned out: doctor
by thirty, married by thirty-three, kids at thirty-six and thirty-
eight, move to private practice . . . I'm not sure I remember much
beyond that. It's weird. I barely know what I'm going to have for
lunch."

Charlotte was intrigued. "I wish I had a sister. Even if she was
super-anal and organized."

Kat started folding vintage T-shirts, and Charlotte stepped
over to help. "Well, as I said, seeing as she basically saved my life, I
can hardly complain, but I wish she'd relax." She sighed. "Mostly,
I wish she'd come visit."

"What about your mom? You haven't mentioned her very
much."

Kat was quiet for a moment. "My mom is . . . challenging.
You'll see. I expect she'll request your presence soon, and seeing as
neither my dad nor I can refuse her anything, you'll have to come
along and be inspected."

"Well, that sounds scary."

"Don't worry. You've been questioned by the FBI; it was probably good preparation. Did they torture you at all?"

"Only mildly."

"Well, then, you'll be fine."

When Charlotte stepped out of the store a little while later, she was surprised to see a familiar face.

"Mr . . . uh . . . Robinson, isn't it?"

The reporter from New York smiled. "It's amazing what a good memory you have, Ms. Williams."

"What are you doing here?"

He nodded. "I'm afraid I heard about your latest adventures online, and my editor sent me down to see if you'd agree to an actual interview. When I went to the restaurant, a waitress said you might be here."

She started walking toward the French Quarter, and the reporter fell in alongside her.

"I don't think I want to be interviewed, I'm afraid. For one thing, I don't have anything newsworthy to say. My father has been jailed, and I'm trying to make a new life for myself."

"Well, that's exactly what would be interesting to our readers. How does a wealthy young woman start over? Are you really working in a kitchen?"

She nodded, subtly quickening her pace. He might be polite, but he was still the enemy, right?

"And how does it feel to be doing such demeaning work? How do the men in the kitchen treat you?"

She stopped and turned to face him. "Mr. Robinson, my colleagues are not animals. They treat me with respect, because we're all in the same boat, trying to earn a living. Unlike the people I grew up with, they judge my ability to work, not my ability to pay. Sadly, being rich and good at shopping doesn't really qualify you for very much except more of the same. I'm just grateful they've given me an opportunity to earn some money. Now, I need to get to work. I really don't have anything else to say. I'm sorry you came all this way for nothing."

And with that, she turned away and set off at a brisk pace, leaving the reporter standing there, looking after her with a thoughtful expression. Then he grinned.

––––––––––

ANOTHER FRIENDLY FACE was waiting for her at the restaurant: Millie Pearl.

Charlotte ran up and hugged her, and Millie beamed.

"You look better already, girl. The Crescent City works its magic once again, I guess."

"How was your sister? Did you have a nice visit?"

"I did." Millie sat down, and, after checking that it was OK with David Karraby, Charlotte joined her.

"I can't sit for long, I have to get to work in the kitchen."

Millie laughed out loud. "I can remember Greta making you wash dishes at home. Do you recall?"

Charlotte laughed. "I didn't until you mentioned it, but now it comes back to me. You both were very insistent that I should clean up after myself. I used to bitch about it all the time, I certainly remember that."

"Yes, you really did. You were pretty spoiled when I got there and not much less when I left. Your dad denied you nothing." Millie's expression was indulgent, though. "He meant well."

Charlotte looked at her curiously. "Do you think he's a bad man? Did you leave because of what he was doing?"

Millie looked shocked. "Do you honestly think that if I knew what he was doing, I wouldn't have reported him to the police? Lord, child, he embezzled millions of dollars!" She sighed. "Having said that, though, I don't know that I think he is a bad man. I think he did a bad thing, but I don't think he did it to hurt people. I think he just did it because he could. But I don't really know, and probably no one does. All I know for sure is that he missed your momma terribly, and he loved you very much. Maybe those two things combined to make him feel it was OK to steal. Who knows?" She looked at Charlotte. "Jackson told me you found some film of your mother? Is that true?"

Charlotte smiled. "Yes. My dad must have been keeping it for me or something. Millie, she has the same voice as mine! That's where it came from!"

Millie gestured for the check. "Well, it came from God, Charlotte, but if your momma had the same voice, then I guess he liked you both. Do you want to come over for dinner tonight after work? You can show me the film, and I can show you some Creole cooking that is more down home than this fancy joint."

"I'd love that. Can I bring my friend Kat?"

"Kat Karraby? Surely. She was in my seventh-grade history class. It will be fun to see her again."

"So you became a teacher when you came back?"

Millie nodded. "I needed to keep a close eye on Jackson and his sisters, and the best way to do it was to teach high school. Thanks to your dad, I had enough money to get my master's at the same time." She stood up and swung a large and obviously heavy bag onto her shoulder. "And now that my kids are done with school, I'm teaching teachers at the university."

"That's so cool." Charlotte looked at her wrist and jumped. "Shit, I have to run."

Millie gave her a quick hug. "Yes, run along, work hard, and I'll see you and Kat tonight, OK? Around eight or nine?"

Charlotte headed toward the kitchen, nodding and waving over her shoulder.

SCARSFORD WAS GONE. Her phone had beeped while she was working, and she'd had to ignore it, seeing as she was up to her elbows in hot, greasy water. Now, walking toward Millie's house with Kat, she checked her messages.

"Back to NY. Will be in touch." Chatty as ever.

She wasn't sure what she was feeling. On the one hand, she felt anxious that he was gone, because his being there meant someone was looking out for her. On the other hand, she was relieved. His being there reminded her of her dad, not that she was trying to forget him, exactly, and he also made her behave badly. On the whole, she was glad she hadn't slept with him. She would have regretted it.

And God knew she had plenty of regrets already.

Chapter
TWENTY-FIVE

They knocked on the door just after nine, but it sounded as if the party was in full swing.

When Jackson opened the door, he smiled broadly. "Kat Karraby!"

Ah, not smiling at her, then, Charlotte thought. Not that she cared, of course.

"Jackson! Hey!" They hugged, and Kat led the way into the house, chatting nineteen to the dozen.

Jackson looked over his shoulder at Charlotte. "We were in biology together!"

"Super."

She wasn't jealous. That would be ridiculous. And she was glad Kat looked especially gorgeous tonight, in a see-through man's shirt from the '40s over Katharine Hepburn–style wide-legged pants. What did it matter that her own hair was stuck to her head or that she had a faint line across her forehead from the hairnet or that her plain white T-shirt had a tomato sauce stain the shape of Rhode Island on it? It didn't matter, apparently, because nobody was looking at her.

The kitchen seemed almost too full to enter. Millie was standing over a huge pot, a pot that usually held gumbo, Charlotte had learned, and her children were milling around. Jackson and Kat were getting beers, Lilianne and Camille were laughing over photos on the back of a camera, and through the door she could see Camille's toddler asleep on the sofa. She was impressed with his ability to sleep through all the noise, but maybe New Orleans kids got used to it.

Surprisingly, it was Bob Marley blasting, rather than the jazz she had come to expect from Millie.

Jackson brought her a beer. "Hard day at work?"

At first, she thought he was laughing at her, but she searched his face and found he was just asking. She decided to get over herself and nodded.

"Yeah, I know it sounds wimpy, but my back is killing me. The pots are heavy, and the water is way above my head." She made a rueful face. "It turns out that an hour at the gym three times a week just isn't good preparation for anything except getting a tan."

He laughed. "You'll get used to it. I know when I started working construction, I was as stiff as a board for days. Now I hardly notice it."

"Is that what you do when you're not playing music?"

He laughed again. "No, music is what I do when I'm not working construction. I wish I could play music all the time, but there's not really a living in it, you know? I like doing something physical, so I started after Katrina, rebuilding houses. They taught me everything on the job, so now I can pretty much do anything in that line." He looked proud. "It's silly, but I love taking a broken-down, mud-caked house and turning it back into a home. People lost everything, and we give something back."

Charlotte remembered the footage from Katrina. The bodies

covered with sheets. The whole lower part of the city underwater. The stories. The days it took for help to come. She'd given money. Everyone had. And then she'd forgotten all about it, more or less. But here it was, years later, and the work continued.

Jackson was still talking. "There are whole neighborhoods that no one returned to. It's sad, because they were once full of people, generations of families all within blocks of one another. But I guess they set up elsewhere and started over."

"Like me."

"Yeah, like you. They lost everything; you lost everything."

"Not everything. I still have some money. I still have some friends."

He took her hand suddenly and squeezed it. "And you still have your talent."

She frowned, not getting it at first. "My voice?"

He raised his eyebrows. "You're very blasé about it. Your voice is incredible. If I had half that much of a gift, I'd be doing everything I could to get out there and get famous."

Kat wandered over. "Get famous? Isn't she famous enough already?"

Charlotte laughed. "I'm not sure infamous and famous are the same thing."

She told the assembled company about the Charlotte Williams Sucks Web site, and of course they all wanted to see.

"Oh, crap. There's Mom."

Millie whirled around to where her children were huddled around the kitchen table, Jackson's laptop open to the Web site. For a long second, she just looked, reading the evil caption that mentioned her being an "ex-servant." Then she grinned.

"I look so skinny! I should run out and buy another pair of those pants, who knew I looked so good in them?" Then she turned back to the gumbo, singing along with Bob under her breath.

Her kids all laughed, but Charlotte was impressed. Maybe she should try to be that cool about it. She was finding it hard.

Kat broke into her thoughts. "But what were you saying, Jackson, about Charlotte's voice? The other night at the club, she was amazing."

"I know. She and I worked yesterday on some of my songs, and I think she agreed to sing with my band."

"I did." Charlotte blushed. "But I have to check with Mr. Karraby."

"Watch out, Charlotte." Camille, Jackson's sister, looked sternly at him. "It starts off as fun, and then, before you know it, he's got you touring the diviest bars in Louisiana, playing for nickels and generally working your ass off."

Jackson snorted. "Coming from you, that's funny." He turned to Charlotte. "Camille is a documentary filmmaker."

His sister interrupted. "I work at the local public TV station. He's exaggerating."

"She's a genius. She's being modest, but when we were kids, she would have me dress up as whatever and film me. She was the smallest dictator you ever saw."

Camille threw a piece of bread at him.

"What do you do, Lilianne?" Charlotte looked at the younger of Jackson's two older sisters.

"I'm a resident at TMC." Charlotte must have looked confused. "Tulane Medical Center. It's the big hospital in town. Well, one of them."

Millie pulled bowls from the cupboard and started serving great steaming bowls of gumbo, along with long loaves of crusty French bread.

"It's hard to believe all three of you even got through school, the shenanigans you got up to, and yet here you are, respectable professionals." She grinned. "Well, largely respectable."

Camille got a green salad from the fridge, and for a moment, there was silence, only the sound of spoons at work.

Charlotte put down her spoon and looked at Jackson. "You realize I'm being stalked right now by some wacko, right?"

He nodded.

"And that my dad just got sent to jail for fraud."

Another nod.

"And that if I come and sing with your band, all anyone will talk about is that, and what a bitch I am, and how you're trading on my notoriety, and that I'm just being even more shallow than ever."

A nod and a shrug. "Look, they can think what they want. When they hear you sing, they'll realize that it doesn't matter what your background is. What matters is that you're really talented and have something rare—talent and drive and beauty. And"—here he pretended to blow on his fingernails—"you'll be singing my arrangements, which are brilliant."

"And"—this from Kat—"you'll also look like a million bucks, because I'm going to style you. It's going to be awesome. When's the next gig?"

"Wednesday. Time enough to rehearse with the rest of the band and get ready." Everyone around the table looked at Charlotte. "What do you say, Charlie? Are you up for it?"

She thought about it. About how she was trying to lie low and start over. About how scared she was about this guy who was stalking her, despite everyone else taking it so lightly. And then she thought about her mom singing to her and how nice all of these people had been to her. She owed them. And she owed herself.

"Sure. Why the hell not? I love singing, and people here don't really know who I am, so much."

She hoped.

JACKSON WAS A man of his word. By the time dinner was over, he'd been on the phone to his band, and a rehearsal was set up for the next day.

Millie clucked at him. "The girl's been through a lot, Jackson. Go easy, OK?"

He shook his head, looking at Charlotte. "Nope. She's much tougher than everyone thinks. Just because she's had a pampered life doesn't mean she isn't capable of standing on her own two feet and kicking some butt."

Kat laughed. "Well, she'd have to be standing on her own two feet to kick some butt, or she'd fall on her ass."

"Again," added Charlotte, wondering how long it'd been since she'd laughed at herself.

At first, the thought of performing with Jackson had made her nervous, but now she recognized the feeling as exhilaration. She knew her voice was good, and she'd loved the music he'd taught her, and why not go for it? Besides, she was encouraged by Jackson's faith in her. He was right—she was tougher than everyone thought.

Chapter

TWENTY-SIX

Working with Jackson turned out to be just as hard as his sister had warned her. The easy, affable guy from dinner turned into a focused ball buster once he got in front of the band.

The rehearsal was taking place in an old theater in the Quarter, which was available as a practice space. The curtains were dusty, and the chairs looked as if they hadn't been sat in for decades, but there was something magical about it. Old posters lined the backstage area: King Oliver, Cab Calloway, Fats Domino. Charlotte wondered how many amazing singers had looked out at the auditorium just as she was doing. Startled from her dreaming by Jackson barking her name, she tried to pay attention.

It was hard work, getting two dozen musicians to do what you needed them to do, especially if you were also trying to introduce a new singer. Generally speaking, the band members were young native New Orleanians, like Jackson, with the occasional old-timer. The lead sax player had come out of retirement, he said, to play with Jackson's band, and she was chatting with him when Jackson lost his temper at her.

"Charlotte, are you actually listening to me? Because I'm talking to you."

She spun around, horrified. "I'm sorry, Jackson, I was chatting with Chick." She grinned over her shoulder at the old man. "He's very charming."

Jackson wasn't buying it. "I don't care if he's Prince Charming, pay some fucking attention, or you won't know the arrangements, and when we play tomorrow night, I'll look like an idiot."

Charlotte hung her head. "Sorry, Jackson."

"Fine."

He picked up his baton and told the band to start at the top. Charlotte got ready, and when her cue came, she belted out the introductory verse to "Summertime." It sounded great, and from behind her, she heard Chick calling out, "Sing it, baby." It was a great feeling, to be standing in front of such a wall of music, the bass physically shaking the floor, knowing that you're doing a good job.

After a couple of hours, Jackson declared himself satisfied, and he took Charlotte's hand and shook it. "You did great. I'm sorry if I yelled. The music is really important to me, the band is really important to me, and being successful in my own city is really important to me. I think you're awesome, honestly."

The other musicians were filing out, and Jackson suddenly had a thought.

"Hey, do you want to learn some more songs? I was thinking we might be able to pick up work as a duet. Not every venue can support a big band, and it might be nice to change it up a bit, you know?"

Charlotte nodded. "Your own music or standards like the other day?"

"My own stuff, if that's cool. I haven't heard it in another voice, either, so it might help me refine it." He pulled a pile of manuscript paper from his bag.

"Sure."

They headed for Millie's house, and as they caught the cable car together, Charlotte was amazed at how beautiful the city looked in the sparkling spring sunshine. Tourists mingled easily with locals, young with old, black with white. It was unique.

Back in Millie's living room, Jackson sat down at the piano, and after hesitating a moment, Charlotte sat next to him. In order to see the music he'd propped up on the piano, she had to wriggle closer, and she felt the warmth of his thigh pressing against hers. Despite herself, Charlotte felt herself responding to him. He played the first song through once, a gorgeously modulated mid-tempo love song. *"On the outside you're ice and fire, a live wire that flicks a switch and turns me on, a beautiful fall of gold and green, I've seen you in my dreams forever."*

She picked up the melody the second time through and started chiming in on harmonies, adding depth to his voice, which was warm and sexy. It was a great song, and as she listened to the melody, she closed her eyes and swayed against him on the piano bench. Still playing, Jackson turned his head and kissed her, swiftly and as if it was no big thing. But for her, it felt like sun through the clouds, and she turned and caught his face between her hands and kissed him back, deeply and hungrily. He took his hands from the keys and put them on her waist. He pulled her onto his lap, running his hands along her slender thighs and pulling her against him, feeling her move. The keyboard was pressing into her back, hurting her, but she didn't care. He hadn't shaved that morning, and his rough stubble was warming her neck as he kissed her, biting her gently, making the breath catch in her throat.

He stood up, her legs wrapped around his waist, and slowly made his way from the living room to his bedroom, the bed still unmade from the night before. Gently, he laid her down and moved quickly himself, pulling off his shirt and reaching to help her with hers. Her shoulders gleamed pale against his smooth brown hands as he stroked her, feeling her shudder in the cool air of the room. He tangled his hands in her hair, pulling it forward to watch it drape across her breasts. She was so lovely, so slender and strong, her eyes cloudy with the same desire he felt. She knelt up, still only reaching his broad shoulders, and bent her head to kiss his chest.

"Do you . . . " His voice was hoarse, and he paused, swallowing, feeling nervous with a woman for the first time in many years.

She nodded, unwilling to speak herself, worried that she would start to cry. She felt so vulnerable, even though she trusted him. It was if all those times she'd made love before hadn't actually been her but some other person. This was her, Charlotte, plain and simple, and he wanted her just for who she was, not what she had. Part of her was fearful that she wouldn't be enough alone, without her money and glamour, but then she looked into his eyes and saw how much he wanted her, how simple it really was. She relaxed and let him take her in his arms, closing her eyes and losing herself in the pleasure that followed.

SOMETIME LATER, SHE woke and watched him sleeping, a slight smile curving on his lips. *I put that smile there,* she thought, and reached out to trace it with her finger. His mouth twitched, and his eyes opened, finding hers immediately.

"Well, hello there." He pulled her closer, wrapping his strong arms around her and pulling the full length of her against him.

"Hello." She felt a little shy, despite the passion she'd just shown him.

"You're an attractive girl, did you know that? I expect you know that. People tell you all the time." He was laughing at her, but he meant it.

"It's been said. I've heard it. Although not lately. You can say it again if you like."

He grinned, punctuating his speech with kisses. "You. Are. Gorgeous. Sexy. Strong. Sexy."

"You already said sexy."

"Well, it's an important feature, and I have to say right now, I'm very aware of it."

"I can feel that."

He began kissing her again. "Where was I? Oh, yeah, sexy. Funny. Smart. Talented."

She started to giggle, not just at his words but also at what his hands were doing under the covers. "Don't stop, you're doing so well."

"Don't stop talking, or don't stop doing this?"

She gasped, her face flushing suddenly. "Just . . . don't . . . stop, OK?"

He didn't.

Chapter TWENTY-SEVEN

When they walked into Kat's store together, she raised her eyebrows.

"Well, hello, young lovers." Kat was wearing a 1950s summer dress with a full skirt and wedge-heeled espadrilles. Very *Roman Holiday*. She listened indulgently as Charlotte told her about the rehearsal, and decided to wait until later to get the details of what had clearly happened afterward.

"I need an evening dress to wear for the orchestra gig tomorrow night. Something sexy in the extreme."

Jackson grinned. "Not so sexy that no one looks at the other musicians but something that the singer fronting the band deserves. Classy. Think of it as her grand introduction to New Orleans society."

"Except in a scandalous, nightclubby, jazz-band kind of way." Charlotte was giggling; both of them were still giddy.

Kat tipped her head to one side. "So, sexy but not too sexy, classy, society-appropriate but a little scandalous, and jazzy." She held up a finger. "I have just the thing."

And she did.

When Charlotte stepped out of the dressing room, both Kat and Jackson caught their breath, for slightly different reasons.

The dress was simple in line, suspended by two shoulder straps and hanging straight to the floor. Heavily beaded and folded, it looked like gold leaf, and the heaviness of it made it cling to Charlotte's curves as if it had been painted on. The metallic color made her skin glow and played off the tawny streaks in her hair. When she turned around, she revealed that the dress was almost totally backless, dipping down to the small of her back.

Charlotte was beside herself. "It's awesome. I have never felt so glamorous and gorgeous in my life."

Kat was smiling like the cat who got the canary. "Vintage Worth couture, 1950s. I've been saving it. Apparently for you, as it looks as if it was fitted on." She turned to Jackson. "What do you think, Mr. Bandleader? Good enough for jazz?"

He just nodded, his eyes gleaming. It was going to be one hell of a gig.

ONCE THE DRESS was off again and carefully wrapped in tissue, Charlotte glanced at her watch.

"Shit, I'm going to be late for work." She hugged Kat. "You are so amazing."

"I know," Kat said, airily. "I'm even going to walk you to work. I want to see my dad."

They were half a block away when Charlotte heard her name.

"Ms. Williams?" An attractive young woman was coming toward her, a microphone in her hand. Charlotte frowned and stepped back, and the woman held up her hand. "Don't worry, it's not on." The three friends stopped, wary. "I'm Selena Messier, from Channel Nine . . . " There was a question implicit in her tone, and she waited before continuing. "We have a show you might have seen called *Crescent City Connection*?"

Charlotte took pity on her. "I just got here, Miss Messier, as you doubtless know, and I haven't had time to catch up on local TV. I'm not interested in doing any interviews, and I have nothing to say."

"I just have a few questions. It won't take a moment."

Charlotte sighed. "What kind of questions?"

Selena smiled. "You know, general questions about how you're finding life here in New Orleans, how you're settling in, how your job is going, that kind of thing."

"How do you know I have a job?"

There was a slight pause. "I read it online."

"On the Charlotte Williams Sucks Web site? That's the only site that's mentioned it that I know of."

Selena's smile didn't waver. "I'm a reporter. Your father might have disappeared into the legal system, but it's still a big story, and you moved into my neighborhood. Of course, I'm going to follow up. I'm surprised I'm the only one."

"You're not. Dan Robinson from the *New York Sentinel* is here, too."

That made her smile slip a little. "Really? Have you given him an interview?"

Charlotte shook her head.

"Well, will you at least think about it?" She handed Charlotte a business card. "You can call me anytime at all, OK?"

Charlotte nodded. "I'll think about it. The press haven't been my friends lately."

Selena turned up her smile another one hundred watts. Suddenly, Charlotte was reminded of a baby alligator.

"Well, maybe we can change that."

Everybody smiled politely, and then Charlotte and her friends headed into the restaurant.

DAVID KARRABY WAS glowing with good humor, as usual.

"Kat Karraby, fashion icon, what brings you here to the old family biz?"

She hugged him. "I just wanted to see you, Daddy. How's it going?"

He lifted her off her feet, much to the amusement of Charlotte and Jackson.

"It's going well, darlin', except your momma is getting anxious to see you." He looked at Charlotte. "And she wants to meet your new friend, baby."

"Well, maybe this weekend."

David Karraby looked over her shoulder. "OK, sweetness, I have guests to welcome. I'll see you later, OK?"

Kat laughed as he pushed past her. "Well, 'bye, then." She turned to Charlotte. "Let's get you back to work. And then an early night—that dress is heavy; you'll need to rest up."

CHARLOTTE'S PHONE STARTED ringing in the middle of the night, long after she'd collapsed and fallen asleep. The restaurant had been packed, and she hadn't had time for so much as a drink of water. When she didn't answer, it stopped, and then the texts started. Chime after chime after chime, long into the night.

Bitch

Bitch

Bitch

Bitch

Bitch
Today
You
Die.

Mr. Karraby had given her the morning shift the next day, so she could be free to do the gig in the evening, and she didn't have time to check her messages until she was getting ready to perform.

Her phone chimed, with a reminder from Jackson of the club address, and then she noticed the long string of texts from a number she didn't recognize.

"Are you just going to stare at the phone all night, or can we finish your makeup?" Kat was standing there, holding a dark red lipstick in one hand and an orchid in the other. "You know, I still can't decide if the orchid is right or if we should go with the headband."

"Orchid," Charlotte said absently. "But hang on, I think I need to call the police." She showed Kat the text messages.

Her friend frowned. "That's a little uncalled for, isn't it? How did they even get your number?"

Charlotte shrugged, trying not to let herself get freaked out. She wasn't sure who to call, so she called Scarsford.

It was good to hear his voice, even if things still felt a little weird between them. Scarsford listened to her read the texts and sighed.

"I'll call New Orleans PD. Where is the club again?" She told him. "OK, I'll make sure they send someone over to keep an eye on things. Hang in there, Charlotte."

She wanted to ask him if he was coming back to New Orleans, but he'd hung up already.

Chapter

TWENTY-EIGHT

The club was darker and smaller than the first one she and Kat had gone to, but it, too, felt as if it came from another era. Couples ringed the dance floor in velvet booths, sipping cocktails and chatting quietly. Candles gleamed everywhere, and a giant crystal chandelier hung low over the polished dance floor. The band sat on a raised podium right in the middle, with Jackson directing from the center. It was very stylish, and as Charlotte took her place alongside the piano, she suddenly felt the platform move. It turned slowly, so everyone could see everything.

She looked at the piano player, Dave, who grinned at her. "I hope you don't get seasick," he joked. "You get used to it, but one time when we played here, a trumpeter had to leave in the middle of the set." He shrugged. "But that's brass players for you. Strong lungs. Weak stomachs."

Charlotte smiled nervously. The text messages had scared her more than she was ready to admit, and she scanned the room anxiously, looking for friendly cops or unfriendly faces. She'd hidden her phone in an evening bag Kat had given her, and now she laid it faceup on the piano so she could see if anyone texted her again. When Jackson saw it, he frowned, but he accepted it once she told him what was going on.

"No one's going to attack you during the show," he pointed out. "You're on a slowly turning platform, surrounded by men, in the middle of a nightclub. Just focus on the music, and forget all about the other bullshit." He squeezed her hand. "You're an amazing person, and you're right where you're supposed to be, all right?"

She nodded up at him gratefully, thinking how hot he looked in his evening suit. All of the band members were wearing tuxedos and white shirts, and the overall effect was glamorous and sophisticated.

It wasn't until halfway through the first set that a text came in.

Charlotte had turned off the chime, obviously, but she saw the phone move slightly as it vibrated. She was singing "Heart and Soul" at the time; she waited until applause was filling the room before leaning over to read it.

Nice dress, Charlotte. Gold is the perfect color for you, you thief.

She looked around the room. He was there, in the same room. Another text.

Kat's going to be mad when I rip it apart to get to your heart, bitch.

She felt her head start to swim and looked up to see Jackson watching her. He raised his eyebrows, and suddenly she felt safer. This guy was just a jerkoff, trying to mess with her.

Your dad took everything from me. Now I'm going to hurt him back.

She could hardly text a reply, so she just kept singing and reading the evil texts and trying to stay focused.

Midway through "Satin Doll," she remembered that it was the last song before the break. She was going to find a cop and tell him what was going on. Jackson would come with her. She'd be totally safe.

Couples stopped dancing when the song was over and applauded loudly. Charlotte was scared but also angry. The stalker had ruined the evening for her, and she was sad that she'd been too distracted to notice how well it had been going. She looked around at the happy faces smiling up at her, the people clapping, and then she saw him. One man, standing alone at the back of the dance floor, staring right at her.

Not smiling.

Not clapping.

Just watching.

And as she looked at him, knowing in her heart that it was him, the man who wanted to hurt her, he puckered his lips in a hateful parody of a kiss and melted into the shadows.

"Jackson!" Charlotte pushed her way through the band to reach him, trying not to trip. "He's here, the man who's been threatening me. I saw him."

Jackson frowned. "Are the police here?"

"I don't know. Scarsford said he'd call them, but I don't see anyone in uniform."

Jackson stepped down from the platform and took her hand, helping her to the ground. "Well, let's find someone."

As they moved through the crowd, the man was suddenly there, not an arm's length away. He was moving fast, angling his body past everyone else like a shark. Not very tall but clearly very strong and determined. And furious.

Charlotte gave a little moan of fear and pulled at Jackson's hand. But he misunderstood and pulled the other way. In a split second, she was adrift, dragged by the crowd. Some people were trying to talk to her, to congratulate her on her performance, but she turned and tried to make her way toward the door to the club. Panicking, all she could think of was getting away. Smiling faces loomed up on all sides, but she could hear the heavy breathing of her pursuer, and once she felt his fingers on her shoulder, grasping.

She turned to look, terrified, and he was right behind her, snarling, apparently unworried that anyone would see him.

The crowd thinned, and she broke loose, almost stumbling in her haste. The heavy dress kept wrapping itself around her legs, and she sobbed in frustration and fear. The stalker hissed her name, and suddenly, he was on her, a flying leap knocking her to the ground, a sharp pain in her side making her scream.

Hitting the ground knocked the wind out of her, and for a moment, all she felt was blind panic, animal fear. Trying to scramble to her feet, she could feel the weight of her attacker pinning her down. The club was a riot of whirling lights and yelling faces and above it all the insane muttering of the man who was trying to kill her.

"Bitch, bitch, bitch . . . "

And then he was lifted off her, and Charlotte saw Jackson through streaming eyes, his face contorted with rage, pulling back his arm and punching the madman in the face, doubling him over. Behind Jackson were two cops, and as she rolled to her knees, she saw the doors to the club open and more cops come rushing in.

And behind them, of course, came the cameras.

YOU WOULD THINK the police would have emptied the club, shut the place down, tied it all up with crime-scene tape, and done a thorough investigation, but this was New Orleans. People got attacked all the time, apparently, and so what actually happened was that the guy got arrested and taken downtown, and Charlotte got back on stage and finished the set, to general applause. Cam-

eras whirred, and the club owner decided that the publicity can-
celed out the cost of the broken glasses.

The sharp pain in her side had been the guy trying to stab her
with a short-bladed hunting knife, but God was in the details, as
usual, and the heavy beading on her dress had deflected the blade.

"I'm telling you, couture saves lives." Kat was pale-faced and
hyper. "What if you'd been wearing something less incredible?
You could be dead!"

Charlotte laughed despite herself. She was going to have a heck
of a bruise on her side, and the dress had lost some of its beads, but
both of them were in better shape than they had any right to be.

She'd looked at the man as he was taken away, screaming and
raving that her dad had destroyed his life, taken all his money.
She'd never seen him before, had never met him, and yet he'd
wanted to kill her, had apparently stalked her all the way from
New York. It was incredibly sad.

The police asked her to come down to the station once the set
was over to make a statement, and she was on her way, sharing the
back of a cab with Kat, who was still very chatty. Even though she
was shaken and hurt, she was enormously relieved that it was over.
Maybe now she could get on with her life.

Inside her bag, lying next to her on the seat of the cab, her phone
vibrated, unnoticed.

That was close, bitch.

Nearly got beaten to it.

But it'll be me that kills you in the end.

Getting on with her life wasn't going to be as easy as she thought.

———

WHOEVER WAS BEHIND the Charlotte Williams Sucks Web
site had a field day, posting photos of the guy, photos of Charlotte

walking into the police station, photos of her walking out, shots from inside the club—the whole nine yards.

"Charlotte Williams Nearly Made to Pay!

"Charlotte almost got what was coming to her last night at a nightclub in New Orleans. Local police sources have identified Gavin Albert Paddoray as the man who attempted to stab Charlotte, and we at CWS wish him all the best in any future attempts he's able to make. Charlotte seems to be trying to come up smelling of roses out of all of this, singing with a popular New Orleans band in an attempt to pretend she isn't the spawn of a thieving parasite, and an unholy bitch whore herself."

Charlotte had discovered the new texts from her old stalker while she was at the police station, and the detective in charge of the case had dutifully written it all down.

"It could easily have been Paddoray who sent these. You know how sometimes texts get delayed. Don't panic and assume there's someone else out there, OK? Most of the time, these crazies just threaten anyway."

"He didn't." She inclined her head in the direction of Paddoray, who was now raving about being the angel of death—or Marlene Dietrich, it was hard to make it out exactly. "And these texts clearly refer to him, so how could they be from him?" She was shaken to the core that there had apparently been two people in that club who wanted to kill her.

The detective just shrugged. Last year in New Orleans, there had been more than one hundred fifty murders, nearly half of them committed in broad daylight. The detective had seen things he'd never thought possible. The city was rich in cultural variety, history, and general weirdness. He dreamed of retiring to somewhere quieter, like Baghdad.

Chapter
TWENTY-NINE

A couple of days later, Charlotte sat at a mahogany dining table the size of a small state and decided that a knife-wielding madman might have been easier to face than Mrs. Karraby.

Kat had been right. Her mother, having heard all about Charlotte from both her husband and her daughter, not to mention the local and national news, had demanded an audience. Rather than just inviting her around for coffee, Leila Karraby was throwing a small dinner party. Small turned out to mean twenty people, but Charlotte had been forewarned by Kat and had dressed up. In fact, she had pulled out all the stops, and she could tell from Jackson's expression (she had brought him as her date) that the effort had been worth it.

She wore a pale green Armani gown, tea-length, made of very fine, clingy silk jersey. Simple shoes matched, and she'd twisted her hair into a low, smooth knot. Her makeup was a little more daring. Iridescent green and blue eye shadow the color of peacock feathers brought out the deep green of her eyes, and the barest hint of glitter touched her eyelashes. Her lips were pale but perfectly

drawn and made her eyes seem even larger. From behind, she
looked like an elegant swan, but when she turned her gaze on you,
she revealed a far more exotic creature.

Mrs. Karraby admired the effect from a distance, watching her
daughter's new friend as she chatted to the other guests. To most
people, Leila Karraby was a puzzle. Beautiful, aloof, elegant, she
cultivated an air of reserve that kept most people at a distance. It
had become such a habit that sometimes she even scared the pants
off her own loved ones. But at the same time, she was famous for
helping her poorer neighbors and for chiding her wealthier friends
for not doing more to be of practical service. In the first, terrible
night when the levees broke, Leila Karraby had organized boats
to ferry people from their roofs and had housed ten families in
her own home. In the days that followed, she had been among the
first to venture into the still-flooded Ninth Ward, saving all they
could, before the official rescuers arrived—too little, too late—and
prevented them from doing more. She'd covered sun-bloated bodies, marking each one with a date and time and searching each
face before she did so, hoping to remember them so she could provide closure for a family grieving later on. And she'd worked the
phones, bullying every contact she could think of in every Gulf
Coast state to get off their asses and do something. She never
talked about it, or rarely, but her name was mentioned fondly in
those districts where wealthy New Orleanians rarely ventured.

Jackson knew all of this and had hugged her warmly when he'd
first arrived. Leila was wearing a deep red velvet dress, her dark
red hair loose about her shoulders, and Jackson thought for the
hundredth time how much like Kat she looked. For several minutes, they talked about the rebuilding efforts and what he'd been
doing since high school, and then Leila had dropped her voice and
asked about Charlotte.

"Katherine tells me you and she are an item already."

Jackson blushed a little. He'd known Mrs. Karraby since grade school and still thought of her as someone else's mother. "Well, yes. She's not at all what you would think."

"And what would I think?" Leila was sharp.

"That she was spoiled. Entitled. Shallow." He watched Charlotte talking to Kat on the other side of the room. "She's had a terrible shock, you know, and I think she's holding it together pretty well." He looked keenly at Mrs. Karraby. "Sometimes bad things make us better people. You'd be the first to say it."

She smiled at him briefly. "If there is substance there in the first place, then adversity brings it out. But if there's nothing there, then it just as easily gets revealed." She watched her daughter. "I worry about Kat. I want her to find friends, of course, but I don't want her to be hurt."

Jackson nodded. "I think Kat is stronger than you think, too."

Leila shrugged gracefully. "Maybe. But I am her mother, so she will always get my protection, whether she needs it or not."

At dinner, she sat across from Charlotte and began her interrogation.

"So, Charlotte, I hear you were enrolled at Yale. Have you dropped out?"

Charlotte took a breath and a sip of wine. Needless to say, all conversations nearby had stopped, and she was basically answering for the benefit of everyone at the table. Well, she'd been warned.

"I think I am taking a leave of absence. I contacted the dean, and he graciously allowed me some time off to deal with my father's legal case. Once the future becomes a little clearer, I can make a decision."

"And you were studying law?"

Charlotte nodded.

"Ironic." Leila's voice was smooth.

Charlotte nodded again. Down the table, Kat frowned, trying to catch her mother's eye.

Her father took her hand and squeezed it, whispering in her ear. "Your mother is grilling Charlotte for your protection, baby, and there's nothing you can do to stop her. You might as well have another glass of wine and enjoy the show." He laughed gently. "I have a feeling our Miss Williams might be able to take care of herself."

Leila's garnet necklace glittered in the candlelight, matching the wine in the crystal glasses on her perfectly set table. "And now you're working in my husband's kitchen?"

"Yes. It has been a new experience for me."

"I imagine so."

"But a good one. I hadn't really had to do much until now. It was a relief to discover I was actually capable of doing something constructive."

Leila smiled. One point to Charlotte. "And your mother, of course, was Jackie Williams. A beauty for the ages."

Charlotte inclined her head. "Thank you."

"You take after her."

"That's a very great compliment."

"Are you planning on doing any modeling yourself?"

"No."

"And you recently returned from Paris, is that right?"

"Yes. I spent a year there at the Sorbonne."

"Because you burned down a building at Yale?"

Charlotte's hand wobbled, but she managed not to spill anything. *Fuck.* She had been totally lulled by the pleasant conversation and hadn't seen it coming at all. Deep breath.

She managed a rueful smile. "You heard about that? Yes, I'm afraid a broken heart led me to make a very poor decision. Fortunately, no one was hurt."

"And your father was able to rebuild the building."

"Yes, but whether or not they'll want to keep an embezzler's name on the political science building is an open question."

Surprisingly, Leila Karraby laughed. "Yes, although there's something fitting in it. It's not as if politicians are known for their honor."

Charlotte's face became grave. "Despite what you might have read, my father is an honorable man, in his own way. I would like to believe that the sudden death of my mother made him lose his way. He will pay for his crime, and I hope those who lost money will get it back."

Leila could see she had offended her. But she let it slide for the moment. "Although if they do, that will presumably leave you with very little."

Charlotte made a face. "May I be blunt, Mrs. Karraby?" The other guests went quiet.

"Of course."

"All the money I had didn't make me happy. In the last week or so, I've had more moments of true happiness and satisfaction than I can ever remember in my life before. Even despite being attacked. Maybe it's easy to say because the reality of my situation isn't clear yet, and maybe the novelty of poverty will quickly wear off once it becomes permanent, but for right now, I think I'm pretty damn fortunate." She grinned down the table at Kat. "Just meeting your daughter has been one of the luckiest things that ever happened to me, and that came at no price at all."

Leila was impressed but not ready to show it. "Well, Miss Williams, let's hope it never does."

Charlotte raised her glass. "I'll drink to that, Mrs. Karraby."
Suddenly, her hostess smiled. "You can call me Leila."

ONCE DINNER WAS over, Leila and Charlotte circled each
other cautiously. This being just a "small" affair, there was only
the single dessert table, set up in a conservatory just off the dining
room. It was fortunate that Charlotte didn't have a sweet tooth,
or she might have burst her zipper. Profiteroles formed a perfect
pyramid, vying for title of tallest dessert with a pile of strawberries
that glistened with freshness and threatened to topple into the vat
of whipped cream waiting alongside them. A pecan pie, of course,
and a lemon meringue pie for those who liked their sweet with a
hint of tart. Jackson and Kat had both offered their congratula-
tions on surviving dinner intact.

"Wow, my mother really likes you." Kat looked relaxed for the
first time all night. "I was terrified."

"She likes me? What would she have said if she didn't?" Charlotte was pleased that her friend was happy, but she herself was still
reeling from some of Leila's comments.

"Oh, she would have been much nicer if she didn't like you."
Kat sighed as she looked at the table. "You know, it's just as well
women used to be slightly bigger and that I like vintage clothing so
I can pull off these ten extra my mother keeps on me." She reached
over to dollop some cream alongside her pecan pie.

Charlotte noticed how slender her friend was and smiled to
herself. "You look perfect to me," she said, and a voice from behind
agreed with her.

"A little thin, perhaps, but I understand that's the fashion these
days." Leila Karraby was even more beautiful up close, and she
and Charlotte looked each other over with frank appreciation.

"Did my daughter find this dress for you, Charlotte, or is it one of your own?"

"This one is mine, Mrs. Karraby, but Kat has an amazing collection at her store. You must be very proud of her."

Kat snorted. "She thinks it's just a hobby."

Leila frowned. "Maybe that was true at first, Katherine, but not anymore. You've done very well for yourself, and you've stuck to what you care about. That's all a mother could ever want, to be honest. You're happy, so I'm happy." She smiled at Charlotte. "I expect your mother would be very happy to see how well you're handling what must have been a very difficult experience. I'm sorry if I seemed a little sharp at dinner. It's just my way. I'm actually very impressed with your poise in the face of all this trouble."

Charlotte was surprised to feel tears pricking her eyes. If Leila and Kat noticed, they were kind enough not to mention it. "Well, I hope she would be proud of me. But if she were here, I imagine things would have worked out very differently." She suddenly remembered her mother's friend speaking about Jackie's desire for more children, a dream echoed by her father that day in jail. "I'd probably not be going through it alone, anyway."

Leila squeezed her hand warmly. "If you need any help at all while you're here, a lawyer, or someone to help with the press, just let me know. There aren't many people I don't know in this town."

"Well, thank you, Mrs. Karraby. Your family have been lifesavers. Your husband's generosity alone has been amazing."

"And don't forget I introduced you to Target." Kat was pouting.

"Well, then," said her mother dryly, "that's worth a kidney just on its own."

Charlotte grinned. "If Kat needs a kidney, she knows where to come."

"I'll bear that in mind. Now, I'm going to get another drink. It might be a liver transplant I'm needing at this rate."

Charlotte felt someone watching her and looked up to see Jackson from across the room. He raised his eyebrows at her, and she made her excuses to Mrs. Karraby and went to him.

"How are you doing? Are you OK?"

Charlotte nodded and stood on her toes to give him a kiss.

He lowered his voice. "You know, there's a guy over there who owns an important radio station. I'm trying to work up the courage to go speak to him about our music." He sipped his drink. "But I'm not doing very well."

Charlotte's face lit up. "Let's do a little impromptu performance!" She wanted to help him, loving this new sensation of doing something useful. "I'm sure it would be OK with our hosts."

He grinned. "Something classic or some of our stuff?"

"Hey, your stuff is classic, just not yet."

They went over to the piano, a gorgeous Steinway grand, already propped open.

"Let's start with something traditional. How about 'Summertime'? Ella-style rather than Janis-style, OK? Then we'll shoot forward in time to the ever-popular Ms. Jones. Let's do 'Don't Know Why' and then the new song you taught me the other day."

He leaned closer. "OK, but let's not end up doing it on the piano."

She smiled into his eyes. "On this piano? I wouldn't dare. Maybe later at home."

And with these wicked thoughts in their heads, he played the opening bars of the Gershwin classic.

At first, nobody was paying much attention, presuming it was just the evening's entertainment, but when Charlotte started to sing, the conversations died down. It wasn't just that her voice was good. Lots of people sing well. It was that her voice had an intimacy and power that made it compelling. Every person there felt she was singing just for them, but at the same time, they were glad everyone else was hearing it. Kat, watching from the garden room, smiled.

The classic song over, Charlotte took on the more recent Norah Jones song and made that one her own, too. She had a deep voice with a growl at the ready, but for this song, she sang it straight and sweet, leaving out the pain and subtlety she employed for "Summertime." Then, once everyone was feeling dreamy and warm, she and Jackson launched into "Fire and Ice," the song he'd written, and the atmosphere heated up. Jackson joined in on the harmonies, and the sexy lyrics and funky modulation had everyone swinging their hips.

Loud applause broke out when they finished, and one man came right over to Jackson and pointed a finger at him.

"That last one is a radio hit waiting to happen, young man. Do you have it recorded yet?"

Jackson grinned and shook his head. The man stuck out his hand, and Leila Karraby wandered over to make introductions.

"Ben Albrecht, this is Jackson Pearl. His band, the Pearly Kings, is quite the sensation in the city, you know."

The man smiled broadly. "Of course. I'm surprised we never met before. Your band is very popular, son."

"Thanks, Mr. Albrecht. We have a lot of fun together."

"Call me Ben, please, you're making me feel old. And this lovely young woman is . . . ?"

"I'm Charlotte Williams." She smiled at the older man but dropped her gaze quickly. The last thing she wanted to do was draw more attention to herself. It was funny. When she was performing, she felt safe and protected, but once the performance was over, she felt especially exposed. Fortunately, Jackson didn't seem to know what nerves were, and she was glad he was there to handle the conversation. They were standing close together next to the piano, and behind her back, he took her hand, twisting his fingers into hers. She felt herself relax.

Leila was being a gracious hostess. "Ben owns the biggest radio station in Louisiana, Jackson, although you might already know that."

"Not just in Louisiana, sugar, but in all the Gulf Coast. Get that song recorded and over to me tomorrow, and I'll have it on the radio by the time people are driving home."

"That's fantastic!" Jackson said. "We don't have a record label, though. Does that matter?"

"Not to me. It won't take long, son, with a little radio exposure. You should get it up on iTunes or something, though, for download. I'll make sure it's on our site. You'll get a good start, and I'll get to boast about it when you're taking home your first Grammy." His eyes lingered on Charlotte. "You should take some pictures, too. She's a big selling point. I guess you know that already."

There was a slightly uncomfortable pause, which Leila stepped in to fill. "Charlotte has just arrived here from New York, Ben."

"Oh, really?" His eyes were still on her, and a certain hunger had entered them. Charlotte was familiar with that look. Sometimes friends of her father's had come by the apartment and looked at her the same way. The little girl they'd ignored till then had turned into a sexy young woman, and it was hard for them to shift mental gears. That was the charitable way to look at it, anyway.

Kat appeared at her elbow and smiled at the station owner. "Hi there, Mr. Albrecht. Charlotte, can I borrow you a moment?" She led her away and whispered in her ear. "Is the dirty old man making you feel icky? Come on upstairs. I want to show you my room."

Charlotte was grateful. With no mom at home, she had often played hostess for her dad's parties. Fortunately, he didn't throw them very often, but when he did, she was expected to do the honors. Sometimes recently, that had meant fending off unwelcome advances from men twice her age or pretending that the hand that lingered at her hip was avuncular rather than predatory. Since the roof had caved in on her life, she'd come to realize how difficult some of it had been, how tightly she'd kept herself wound. Since coming south, she seemed to have shed a protective layer of skin, and many things she would have shrugged off before were making her anxious. Luckily, Kat seemed to know this.

Kat's room was at the very top of the house. "That way, I could look down on everyone." She laughed. "Janey's room is much bigger and has its own bathroom, but I like this one better. I persuaded my mother to let me move up here when I was fourteen, which was not a moment too soon. I still like coming back."

"I can see why." Charlotte gazed around. As a former attic, the room had a steeply angled roof and dormer windows set at regular intervals. Each had been turned into a window seat, and the cushions were covered with vintage fabrics in shades of yellow and orange. Even in the dark of the evening, it felt sunny. Wide plank floors were polished to a deep mahogany shine, and old rag rugs were puddles of muddled color. An old iron bed was painted butter yellow and set at an angle in one corner, a traditional candlewick bedspread giving it a timeless appeal. Stuffed toys were clearly Kat's—trolls vied for space with My Little Pony, and in general, the childhood of the early '90s was well represented.

"My God, I had one of these!" Charlotte pounced on a Beanie Baby in the shape of a unicorn. "But mine was purple."

Kat smiled. "I was more of a Barbie freak, clearly." Along one wall ran a single shelf displaying about one hundred Barbies in various outfits. Charlotte looked more closely.

"Where did those clothes come from? I don't remember any of those."

"I have the clothes they came in originally somewhere, but I was an early eBayer and spent much of my lonely teen years styling dolls with vintage clothing and trading handmade clothes with other Barbie losers." She pulled a mock sad face. "I had no real friends to dress up, so these plastic ladies were my only companions." She laughed at herself. "Mind you, I'm not sure real girls would have put up with me mixing patterns and fabrics the way Barbie did." She pointed to one of the dolls, who was sporting vinyl leggings under a tartan miniskirt and a dress shirt with a ruffled front. "That's Ken's shirt, actually."

Charlotte looked around. "I don't see Ken. What happened?"

"He kept pressuring Barbie for a blow job, so she killed him."

"Wow!"

"Well, look at her. She's not one for putting up with crap from guys, right?"

"I guess not. Where did she hide the body?"

"Under the beach house, where else?"

"But seriously, you don't have any Kens—don't you like styling guys?"

There was a pause. "Uh . . . I don't really like guys in general, if you catch my drift." Kat was smiling gently at her, but Charlotte still wasn't getting it.

"How do you mean? You and Jackson are friends. And the guys in the kitchen."

Kat sighed and put her finger to her lips. "Hmmm, how can I put this more clearly? I. Am. Gay. I like men just fine as friends, but I'm only attracted to women. I find women more inspiring, and I love our clothes and the way we look in them, so I tend to style women. But I could style guys, I guess. Never thought about it."

"Oh. You're a lesbian."

Kat giggled. "Now you're getting it. Just one more reason for people not to like me at school, although now, of course, when I run into people, they pretend they were all cool and hip with it back then. But they weren't."

"People are fuckwits."

"True dat."

"Do your parents know?"

Kat nodded, then shook her head. "Yes . . . and no. My dad does explicitly, and my mom does secretly, but we've never discussed it among ourselves. They worry, I think. It's easier for parents if their kids are normal, run-of-the-mill heterosexuals, right? I'm their 'different' kid, but they do their best. My mom knew a lesbian back in college, I think." She laughed again. "And rumor has it that my cousin Brady is a flaming queen of the first order, but he moved to Paris after college." She sighed and looked around at her comfortable and stylish space. "I love it here, but I need to move to a bigger city, I think. Somewhere where being gay is less defining, if you know what I mean."

"I think so."

"I don't find you attractive, by the way."

"Um . . . thanks?"

Kat blushed a little. "I didn't mean it that way. I just meant whenever I tell a girl I'm gay, she worries I'm coming on to her. You're very beautiful, of course."

"Um . . . thanks again?"

"But you're not my type. I like a sporty, no-makeup kind of girl. I'm the stylish one."

"Are you saying I'm out of shape?" Charlotte was laughing at her, and Kat grinned.

"Well, your upper body is OK."

Charlotte threw a troll doll with deadly accuracy, and the two friends giggled.

Standing outside the door, Leila Karraby smiled and headed down the stairs.

Chapter
THIRTY

The next day, Charlotte and Jackson had a fight.

It was over something very small, as these things often are. Jackson had taken Albrecht's advice to heart, and he and Kat were discussing what Charlotte should wear in some photos they were taking to go along with the song.

"What are these photos for, exactly?" Charlotte was curious. "I mean, we're literally e-mailing the man a digital file of the song, right? An MP3?"

Jackson nodded and returned to flipping through the racks at Kat's store. He was in the underwear section.

"I just don't think you need to make her look sexy. She's already sexy." Kat was on the other side of the store, flipping through the evening dresses.

"Yeah, but I want her to look like a pop singer, not a blues singer. If we want to cross over and get big, we'll need to have a more commercial look."

"Does that have to mean slutty?" Kat was losing her cool a little.

"No, but she's gorgeous, and you heard Albrecht, that's a selling point." He held up a white Victorian camisole. "That's not slutty, it's sexy."

"Excuse me?" Charlotte broke in. "Are these pictures just for Albrecht to jerk off over, or are we using them for publicity for the band? Because if it's the latter, then shouldn't you be in them, too? And if it's the former, then why don't I just hand-deliver the song and blow him at the same time?"

Her tone was still cool, but both Kat and Jackson stopped what they were doing and looked at her. And then at each other.

"Don't be like that, Charlotte," Jackson started, and that was when Charlotte lost her temper.

"Hey, I'll be like I want, OK? For the last month, people have discussed me as if I wasn't there or as if they know me when they don't, and I'm getting sick of it. I am a person, you know, not just my criminal father's or my beautiful dead mother's daughter or a rich bitch or a 'selling point.' I would like to represent myself the way I feel inside, and why on earth we should send that pervert any pictures at all, seeing as he owns a *radio* station, is beyond me, and I won't do it."

There was applause from the doorway, making them all jump.

"You tell them, Charlotte." It was the reporter, Dan Robinson.

"Mr. Robinson, what the hell are you doing here? Didn't I tell you I had nothing to say?"

The journalist wasn't ruffled by her rudeness at all. "Miss Williams, you clearly have plenty to say. I would have thought you would welcome an opportunity to express yourself, to see your words in print, to answer your critics. Besides, since that crazy guy attacked you the other day, you're back in the news, and I'd love an exclusive. I think I've proved my loyalty, haven't I? I've been following you since the beginning." He said roguishly, "I've been after you much longer than anyone else."

"Yes, you're very persistent. You and whoever's taking photos of me for that horrible Web site."

Charlotte was still steamed. Kat and Jackson were just watching, Jackson still holding the camisole. Kat made a mental note to check it for fingerprints.

Robinson shrugged. "Well, some people are nuts, and I guess that's true online and off." He looked pointedly at Jackson. "And people follow celebrity, whatever it's for, right? People love to hitch their wagon to a runaway train, don't you think? They don't care if it ends up a train wreck."

"Look, I don't know who you are . . . "

Robinson stuck out his hand to the young man. "Dan Robinson, *New York Sentinel*. And you would be Jackson Pearl, am I right?"

Jackson didn't take his hand but nodded at his name. "Yes, that's me."

"And you're Kat Karraby?"

Kat didn't even nod at the reporter, merely raised her eyebrows.

He laughed. "Well, the gang's all here, Charlotte. Where's Mr. Scarsford?"

"You seem to know everything, you tell me."

"I'd love to talk to you. Can we go somewhere private?"

"No," Kat and Jackson spoke in unison, and suddenly, Charlotte got annoyed again.

"Yes. Of course." She picked up her bag from the counter and turned to her friends. "Don't tell me what to do, OK? Everything's going just a little bit fast, and I'm going to go have coffee with Mr. Robinson and calm down. I'll see you back at the house, Jackson, for the recording."

And with that, she brushed past Dan Robinson and walked out. The reporter grinned at Kat and Jackson and followed her, shutting the door firmly behind him.

There was a moment of silence.

"How long should we wait?" Kat still hadn't moved.

"Let's give them another ten seconds, and then you follow on one side, and I'll go around the block and get ahead of them."

"Can I be Cagney?"

"Is that the blond one?"

Kat nodded.

"OK." He put down the camisole, and the two of them headed after their friend.

DAN ROBINSON WALKED to a small café that Charlotte didn't even know existed. He must have been checking out the neighborhood. They seemed to know him there, and they took a table in the sunny back room.

"So, Charlotte, what's new with you?"

She raised her eyebrows. "I think you know what's new with me. I'm worried about my dad in jail, I'm working in a restaurant kitchen, I've started singing in a band, I nearly got killed by a crazy stalker. You know, the usual young American woman's life. Not the life I thought I was going to have but the life I apparently do have." He was watching her intently, and suddenly, Charlotte needed to vent to someone who knew her before, knew her whole New York persona. She leaned forward. "You know, it isn't so bad. I like working, I like doing something physical."

"Even though it's washing dishes?"

"Sure, why not? I realize more and more that I'm not super-qualified for anything else."

The waitress came over and delivered their tea. Charlotte thanked her, put honey in her cup, and stirred. A group of young people at another table burst out laughing, and Charlotte felt a twinge of envy.

The journalist took out his notebook. "Is it OK if I make notes?"

She shook her head. "No. I'm not giving you an interview. This is off the record."

Dan frowned. "I'm a journalist, Charlotte. My goal is to report the news, remember?"

"OK, but not today. We can talk a bit, and maybe we can do a proper interview later." She raised her palms. "Or we can talk about the great restaurants here in New Orleans and the proper way to serve gumbo and part as friends."

"No, no, we can just talk. But please think about giving me a real interview. People are still very interested in your dad's case— they're preparing a big civil suit now, you know?"

Charlotte looked at her plate. "Yeah, I heard. I doubt it will ever end, actually. We'll probably spend whatever money we have left in legal fees until it's all gone, and then the lawyers will settle."

"Sounds as if you're none too fond of the legal profession, either. It's not just journalists you don't like."

Charlotte smiled wanly. "I don't really know whom to trust anymore. I haven't received a single call from any of my old friends in New York or from anywhere else. My dad is in jail. My mom is dead. My dad's lawyer has his secretary call if he needs information or to let me know that they're taking more money or something." She laughed bitterly. "The bank won't even call me back. All I have in the world are the clothes I wear to work and the few new friends I've made here."

"And your voice. I hear rumors you're quite a talent."

"Maybe."

"Well, maybe if this hadn't all happened, you never would have had the opportunity to sing in a band, right? Aren't you supposed to be getting a degree from Yale?"

She nodded. "You're an optimist, Mr. Robinson. I'm sure there is a silver lining here, and sometimes I can see it. Other times, I'm just tired of looking."

Robinson looked at the beautiful girl across from him and smiled. He had to work out a way to get her to talk about her dad's case. He was running out of time.

"Have you been able to talk to your dad very much?"

"No. He can make one call a week, and so far, it seems to have been to his lawyer. I've stopped taking calls, anyway. People are pissed off at me, I'll tell you that for nothing. I wish I could tell them something positive."

"I guess they want their money back."

"It won't make them happy."

"That's easy for you to say. Theirs was taken away from them."

"So was mine."

"They were duped by a con man."

"So was I. He was my dad, which makes it a little more painful."

Robinson sighed. "You're starting to sound a little sorry for yourself."

Charlotte sipped her tea and shrugged. "Ask me again tomorrow. I'm just trying to take it day by day."

―――――――

WHEN SHE LEFT the café, Jackson and Kat were waiting for her.

"Did you two follow me?"

Kat grinned. "We did. It was fun. But you didn't go very far, so we didn't get to leap into a cab and say, 'Follow that car,' which was what I was hoping for."

"I'll try harder next time." Charlotte was wry.

"Good. Did the guy get you to confess to anything?"

"Yes. I confessed to defacing the *Mona Lisa,* but I don't think he believed me."

Jackson took her hand. "Are you still mad at me? We don't have to send any photos, you're right. Let's just go home and record the song and send it off and let fate take care of the rest, OK?"

Charlotte smiled at him. "I'm sorry I snapped at you both this morning, I'm feeling a little pressured. The Web site thing is upsetting me. The stalker thing is upsetting me. I wish I could be as blasé about it as you two are."

He wrapped his arms around her and hugged her tightly. "We understand, it's OK."

Kat walked off and then turned back. "Come on, you two, stop mooning at each other. Let's go. I want to sit in on the recording part so I can get inspired for fabulous outfits you can wear when you move to L.A. and become famous."

"This is the thing about you, Kat. You like to keep it real."

Kat laughed. "Why on earth would I want to keep it real? Real life is usually very badly accessorized."

Chapter THIRTY-ONE

The recording session went well, although it took much longer than Charlotte thought it would. In the end, they'd decided to go to Kat's parents' house to play, as their piano was so good. They set up a microphone on the piano and another for Charlotte, and Kat manned Jackson's precious computer with its audio recording software.

"You realize I know nothing about sound recording, right?" She'd made a big thing about taking off her white gloves, finger by finger, in order to push the buttons more readily.

"All you need to do is hit record when we start and stop when we, you know, stop." Jackson was laughing at her. "How you managed to graduate from high school I will never know."

"The principal had a crush on me. Or hated me and couldn't wait to see the back of me. Either way."

"She liked you. She always referred to you as Kitty Karraby, like you were a character in a Jane Austen novel."

"Whatever. Are you ready to go?"

Charlotte had been quietly watching them, enjoying the easy friendship they had. When she and her friends got together in

New York, they had usually ended up trashing whichever friend wasn't there. She realized now that they doubtless trashed her when she was absent. These two teased each other, sure, but not with any real malice.

Jackson rubbed his hands together and played a few scales. "Yeah, we're ready. Let's run through it once and see how it sounds."

Seven hours later, having sung it fifteen different ways with several different piano arrangements, Jackson pronounced himself satisfied.

"I think that's it. Don't you think, Charlotte?"

Charlotte was collapsed on a sofa. "Sure, whatever. The first take sounded fine to me hours ago. I trust your judgement."

"Kat? What do you think?"

Kat, who still looked as fresh as a daisy, was playing with a Barbie she'd fetched from her room. "I think you should make a video. Nothing fancy. Just you two singing the song, maybe in the rehearsal place. Unless you want me to reenact it with Barbies, which I could totally do."

Charlotte was shaking her head when Jackson spoke up. "Hey, why not? We can get Camille to film it. She's really good at things like that."

"She is?" Charlotte was doubtful. "I don't know, guys, I'm feeling pretty exposed already."

Kat clapped her hands together. "But that's it! The goal is to promote the song, right? So let's use all the weird press and interest in you to our advantage. We'll make a video, put it on You-Tube, and then e-mail that horrible Web site so they can mention it, too."

"Why would we do that? They'll just say crap about it."

"How can they, when it's going to rock?"

Charlotte still wasn't sure. "Because the truth is irrelevant, Kat. They just say whatever they want to say, and they'll be mean."

Jackson had been watching her face. "How about we compromise? Let's make a simple video, upload it to YouTube, and just see what happens. I can promote it on my band's MySpace page, and we can make a MySpace band page for ourselves. We won't mention your real name at all, just stick with Jack and Charlie, OK?" He came over and took her hands. "Look, Charlotte, if you want to make a living as a singer, you need to trust your talent enough to put it out there. The song is great, your voice is awesome, and I'm sure Kat can pretty us up for the video."

Kat laughed. "She's easy. You, I'm not so sure."

He pulled out his phone and was dialing already. "I'll see if Camille can do it tomorrow morning."

Charlotte walked over to look out the window into the lush gardens that surrounded Kat's family home. It felt so secure there. She was surrounded by new friends who knew her as she really was and who didn't care about her dad. But the rest of the world still hated her. She thought of the guy who tried to kill her. The voice on the phone who *still* wanted to kill her. The woman who'd attacked her outside the courthouse. Did she really want to give them something else to take shots at?

Behind her, Jackson clicked his phone shut. "Great, we're all set. Camille can do it tomorrow, so you'd better pull out some threads for us to wear, Kat Karraby. I'm going to go see about getting that old theater to film in, you know, where we rehearse." He ran over, kissed Charlotte on the back of the neck, and was gone.

OK, then, Charlotte thought. *I guess we're doing it. Better just get ready for the ride.*

THAT EVENING, AFTER her shift, she talked to Kat a little bit about her fears. Kat, as usual, was laid-back.

"Look, it's easy for me to say not to worry, because no one launched themselves at my face in a nightclub or spat on me in public, but I'm still going to say it. Don't worry. First, it was your dad who did something wrong, not you, and it won't be long before people forget all about it. Second, if you spend your life worrying about what other people could take away from you, then you'll be left with very little to take."

Charlotte smiled. "You're very wise, Obi Wan Karraby."

"That is very true. It's my Jedi training."

"But you kind of talk like an inspirational poster."

"Well, sure, but that's because I'm Southern. We all talk like that, like warm molasses on the porch in August."

"You're doing it again."

"Sorry."

FOR THE VIDEO, Kat had dressed them in several different outfits but ended up just putting them in simple men's shirts and dress-suit pants. Camille had been straightforward and had moved the location back to Kat's house.

"Look, this isn't MTV, and we don't have very much time or any budget at all. So let's keep it simple and clean and tell a story. You guys are kicking back at home on a Sunday morning, say. Jackson, you're playing the piano. Charlotte, you're reading the newspaper in this armchair, wearing your boyfriend's shirt and not much else. Curl your lovely long legs under you like this . . . OK, good. And then Jackson, you just start singing. Charlotte, join in, and then if you feel like getting up and wandering over to join him, go ahead. I'll shoot it as it comes."

At first, it was hard for Charlotte to relax, and she was very aware of the camera. But then she looked over at Jackson, who was watching her with affection, looking as gorgeous and sexy and alive as anyone had ever looked, and she forgot herself in the music. She really did love the song, and without really thinking about it, she got up and went to lean on the piano and sing with Jackson. Camille smiled to herself behind the camera as the shirt dropped down just to cover Charlotte's behind but highlighted the slender curves of her figure and the length of her legs. As Charlotte leaned on the piano, Camille moved around carefully to shoot across her brother's profile, catching both his good looks and Charlotte's tousled hair and smooth décolletage as she leaned on the top of the piano. It was simple, yes, but it was very sexy and very well shot. Camille was pleased, and so were they. After half a dozen more takes, Camille decided she was done and went off to edit it at home.

"I'll send it over later on when it's done. It might be late. I've got some other stuff to do."

Charlotte looked at her watch. "Shit, I'm going to be late for work. See you later!"

She hugged Jackson and shot off. He'd sent the audio file to the radio station the night before, and they were all hoping Albrecht would come through on his promise to play it. Half running through the streets of the French Quarter, Charlotte felt hopeful for the first time in ages.

THE RADIO WAS playing in the kitchen, and after some good-natured teasing, the guys let her change it to the popular station.

They were more fond of the local Creole channel, which broadcast fast, French-speaking rock and funk, but apart from mockingly singing along to any Britney Spears song that came on, they put up with it. And actually, Ronnie's routine to "Oops, I Did it Again" was never to be forgotten. He used a colander instead of a space helmet, but it was very convincing.

Suddenly, at around four, the announcer said Jackson's name. Charlotte looked up, thinking she must be imagining it, but she saw that all the guys had stopped, too, and were looking at her wide-eyed.

"Here's something hot off the digital presses. Local hero Jackson Pearl, whom many of you have heard playing in the Big Easy, has teamed up with a singer who might just take them all the way. They call themselves Jack and Charlie, and here's their first single, 'Fire and Ice.' It's clearly homegrown—no big studio involved here—but this is a KCRC exclusive! You can download the song on our Web site and, for now at least, nowhere else!"

And then, in a moment Charlotte would never forget as long as she lived, she heard her own voice pouring out of the radio. The arrangement was simple but sexy and up-tempo, and she was forced to admit it sounded amazing. The guys in the kitchen were dancing around, cheering and hugging her, and she started to laugh out loud for the craziness of it.

Later on, they played the song again. She could hear the announcer grinning as he introduced it.

"We seem to have hit a nerve with this one, listeners. You guys are lighting up the switchboard for it. One more time, it's Jack and Charlie."

When at last her shift was over, she stumbled out of the back door of the kitchen, only to find Jackson waiting for her.

"Did you hear it?" His eyes were glittering in the darkness, his smile gleaming.

"Yes!" She giggled as he lifted her high in the air. "It's weird, right?"

"If by weird you mean wonderful, then yes. My mother's invited every relative we have to come listen to the radio. I had to get out before they threw me a ticker-tape parade between the bathroom and the kitchen." He laughed, still carrying her, turning slow circles in the alley. "You are a star, Ms. Williams. How does it feel?"

She squirmed against his waist. "It feels kind of sexy, actually."

The alleyway was dark, and he carried her a little bit farther down toward the end. Then, pushing her up against the wall, he began kissing her.

"You are the sexiest woman I have ever met," he said, his voice hoarse, as he licked her neck. She still had her legs wrapped around his waist, and although the wall was rough against her back, she wasn't paying much attention. She could feel how excited he was, and her own body was getting hotter by the second.

"Maybe we should go somewhere else," she whispered, catching her breath as Jackson slipped his hands inside her shirt, pulling her close and undoing her shirt buttons with his teeth. Cool night air made her nipples harden as he pulled her shirt open, and then his warm mouth covered them, making her moan gently.

"No, we can do it right here . . . "

It was lucky no one looked down the alley, although all they would have seen was two lovers wrapped tightly around each other.

Once it was over, Jackson whispered in her ear. "Your voice

was so beautiful on the radio today that all I could think about was this."

She smiled against his throat, her head resting on his shoulder, the sweat cooling on her back where it pressed against the wall. "You are the beautiful one," she replied.

Slowly, they covered themselves up again and started the slow walk home.

Chapter THIRTY-TWO

When they got back to Kat's place, Camille had sent the video.

"You are going to flip out when you see this." Kat's eyes were gleaming as she hit play.

After a second or two, Charlotte raised her hand to her mouth, amazed. She looked incredibly, achingly, like her mother. Somehow, being on film changed the way she looked, highlighting only the very best aspects of her face and figure. Even Jackson whistled.

"Wow, you look amazing."

"The camera loves you, baby!" Kat was crowing, dancing around the room. "YouTube is going to eat you up!"

It was strange. Charlotte almost didn't recognize that girl on the screen as herself. The discovery made her less nervous. She wasn't exposing herself; she was sending out a more glamorous version to play her on TV.

She grinned. "Camille is a genius! Let's do it. Put it up!"

She went to pull out a bottle of champagne, and Jackson worked for a few moments, posting it to YouTube.

"Well, for better or worse, there it goes." He stood up and

stretched, accepting a brimming glass of champagne. He raised it. "To old friends, new friends, and tomorrow's adventures."

A quick clink, and they all drank deeply. Whatever tomorrow brought, tonight they were young and talented and happy, and two of them were starting to think they just might be falling in love.

THE NEXT MORNING dawned hot and muggy. The walk from Kat's to the restaurant had become second nature for Charlotte, and she greeted some regular faces as she walked along. People often said that New York was a city of villages, like London, but it was totally anonymous compared with New Orleans. People in New Orleans seemed to want to know more about one another, were curious about the people they saw around them, and were ready to volunteer information themselves. Charlotte knew that the woman who sold her coffee every morning had a daughter who lived in Charlotte, North Carolina, and that the woman remembered her name because of it. She knew the woman's name was Amber and that her daughter's name was Jade, and that was easy enough to remember on its own. Slowly, day by day, she was starting to relax and feel as if she could maybe get through this period of time and get stronger because of it. Maybe.

The shift was hard, and by the time Charlotte was done, she was ready for a long nap, or a quick drink, whichever came first. But, the peace she craved was not to be had. She came into Kat's house to find Jackson sitting at the table looking crushed, while Kat herself yelled at someone on the phone.

"Uh . . . what happened?"

Jackson flipped a newspaper around to face her. It was the *New York Sentinel,* Dan Robinson's paper, and a small headline on the front page leaped out at her:

"Charlotte Williams Feels Bad for the Little People." There was a story inside, and sure enough, it bore Dan Robinson's byline.

"Sitting with Charlotte Williams in a charming café in New Orleans, one can't help feeling a little sorry for her. After all, she's incredibly beautiful and was raised as a New York society princess, only to have her whole life destroyed when her father was arrested for securities fraud. 'It will never end,' she says, 'until we run out of money and the lawyers settle.' Of course, they've already run out of money—and bilked investors claim it was never their money in the first place. Nearly 3,000 individual and corporate investors have filed a class-action suit against Jacob Williams' firm, and Charlotte wishes she could help. 'I'd love to have something positive to tell them, but I don't. I'm washing dishes and taking it a day at a time.' One piece of good news, though: Charlotte and her new boyfriend have recorded a song that's getting a lot of local radio play. Less good is the fact that the radio station is owned by one of those suing investors, Ben Albrecht, who lists a loss of nearly a million dollars in the suit. Guess Charlotte's luck has run out—again."

Charlotte put her hand to her mouth. "Is it true? Is Albrecht an investor?"

"Was he an investor, you mean. Yes, it's true. Someone at the station told him about this, and he pulled the song immediately. Apparently, he's livid and thinks we did it on purpose."

Charlotte frowned. "Why? How?"

"Who the fuck knows? Why would he invest with a criminal? Why would that criminal steal everyone's money? Why would his daughter walk into my house and throw my whole life into disarray?" He smacked the paper. "Look, I don't even get a name check, I'm just 'Charlotte's new boyfriend.'"

"Hey, wait a second, don't get pissy with me. I'm not responsible for any of this."

Jackson got to his feet. "You didn't do it on purpose, I'm not saying that, but it's your dad who's fucked it up."

She got mad. "Yeah, but it was my voice that got us on the radio in the first place, remember? And the video is still out there, right?"

"Yeah, and I guess my slack ass just came along for the ride? Fine. You carry on alone, then. You're certainly more interested in yourself than anyone else." He stormed out, slamming the door behind him.

Charlotte turned to Kat, who was still on the phone. Kat held up a finger—*wait*.

"Yes, Mom. No, I get it. OK, let's talk in a bit." She hung up. "First, that whole conversation you just had was, if you ask me, not that you did, totally unreasonable on Jackson's part. Not that I'm taking sides, but he was wrong, and you were right."

"I agree. I guess he's just really disappointed."

Kat shrugged. "Well, disappointed or not, it's not OK to be an asshole. Second, my mom is going to talk to Albrecht, to try to change his mind. Again, he might have lost money with your dad, but that doesn't mean he should take it out on you."

"Well, that's very nice of her, but it's OK. My dad is who he is, and he did what he did. People can't get to him to shake money out of his pockets or slap him or yell at him, so they look around for someone else to take the blame, and here I am."

Tears welled up and trickled down her cheeks. "I was so happy this morning, and now everything has gone to shit."

"Aww, baby!" Kat came over and gave her a big hug. "Never mind. You look totally worn out. Why don't you go and lie down and take a nap? And I'm sure things will look better when you wake up."

Charlotte nodded, feeling about six years old. Kat walked

her in and drew the curtains, dimming the lights and tucking her in.

"Hang in there, Charlotte, it's going to improve, OK?"

Charlotte nodded and closed her eyes, hoping desperately that things would be better when she woke up.

Unfortunately, it took a little longer than that.

Chapter THIRTY-THREE

The next day, things felt subdued, as if they were happening at half speed and volume. Jackson hadn't reappeared or called or texted, and the radio station in the kitchen was playing Creole music again. Charlotte guessed the guys must have heard about the article, because they were studiously not mentioning the song. They weren't even making fun of her. It was kind of insulting.

Days passed. Jackson stayed away, and Charlotte stopped checking her phone for texts. Kat was careful not to say anything, and they settled into a routine of working, ordering food, and watching movies. Recovery mode. In some ways, it was exactly what Charlotte needed, and she realized again how alone she had been before her world collapsed. Yes, she'd spent her evenings at glamorous nightclubs with beautiful people doing fabulous things, but it turned out that she loved just hanging out in her PJs and watching *Star Trek*. Her friendship with Kat deepened every day, and she loved how the other young woman didn't feel the need to fill every silence with chatter. Somehow they just clicked, and in the gentle warmth of her new friend's affection, Charlotte began to relax and heal. She tried to ignore the sadness she felt about Jackson, reminding herself that in the grand scheme of shitty things that had happened to her lately, a boyfriend was the least of her worries. She put thoughts about her career in music out of her mind and focused on just making it through the days.

When Jackson burst through the door of Kat's house a week or so later, though, she felt her heart leap.

"No, really, come on in," Kat said lazily, licking the butter from her fingers. They were eating popcorn and watching an old musical. "I'd hate for you to stand on ceremony or even observe the niceties of basic manners."

"Sorry, Kat, you're totally right." Jackson was out of breath. He looked at Charlotte. "Charlotte, I owe you a massive apology."

Charlotte gazed at him impassively. It was a good start, but she wasn't going to let him off easily.

He kept talking. "I got angry with you for something that wasn't your fault, and I'm really sorry."

She continued to gaze.

"Then I didn't come and apologize right away because I realized what a dick I had been, and I was embarrassed. And then a day or two went by, and it seemed too late to come and apologize." He made a gesture of frustration. "I just messed it all up. I'm really sorry."

Charlotte raised an eyebrow. He could squirm a little more.

He took a deep breath. "I realize this might seem like too much of a coincidence, but a friend of mine from L.A. just e-mailed me that he heard our song on the radio there. I don't know how it's possible, but that's what he said."

Charlotte frowned and flicked a glance at Kat. "So you came to apologize because things are going better with the song, so you decided to play nice."

He shook his head. "I know it looks that way, but it really isn't. I was on my way to see you when my friend called. I didn't want to not apologize just because it looked weird. I really miss you, Charlotte. I don't care about the fucking song."

Kat got up and went to her computer. Over her shoulder, she said, "Charlotte, why don't you just admit you miss him, too, and you two can hug while my back is turned. I'm going online to see if he's right."

Charlotte laughed. Kat was right. Hugging Jackson felt so good, such a relief. It was OK to need people; she was learning that. You just had to be careful.

"Well, holy shit." Kat laughed. "Your song appears to be getting some serious play. That's awesome." They peered over her shoulder. She'd pulled up a major online music site, and under "New and Noteworthy" was a little plain icon with "Fire and Ice, Jack and Charlie" under it.

"How the hell did that happen?" Charlotte was confused.

"Well, I uploaded it, and I guess it got around." Jackson was smiling. "God bless the Internet. Look, there's even a link to the video."

They followed the link.

"Read that number to me," Kat said in a hushed voice. "I'm not so good at math."

Jackson cleared his throat. "Five million, nine hundred thousand, two hundred and twenty-seven views."

There was a pause, and then Kat slapped Charlotte on the back. "Congrats, you've gone viral!"

"Um . . . great." She felt nervous suddenly.

Kat's phone rang.

"Hello? Yes, this is she." She looked at her friends as she listened to her caller, and they both saw her go pale. "Well, that's very exciting news. I'll have to talk to my clients and get right back to you." She scribbled a number. "Yes, thanks, I have it. Speak to you soon." She hung up. "Well, that was an unexpected caller."

"Who was it?"

"Only the most successful radio DJ in the country. Only the most listened-to voice in America. Only the host of several must-see TV shows and reputedly the highest-paid entertainer on network television."

She paused, not that she really needed to say his name.

"Only . . . Peter Lakeshore himself."

KAT HAD FINISHED running around the apartment and screaming and had regained her elegant calm.

"Apparently, they've been getting requests for your song and went looking for us. They want you to come to L.A., do an interview with Pete, and meet with a record label."

"Why did they call you?"

"Well, he said they'd e-mailed Jackson through his site but didn't get a reply."

Jackson grinned. He was sitting on the sofa with Charlotte on his lap and seemed bemused by the whole thing. "I've been distracted, missing my friend here. I haven't checked the site in a day or so."

"Whatever. Then they called Albrecht's radio station, and even though he hates Charlotte's dad, he's apparently more scared of my mom, because he told them I was your manager and gave them my number. Pete was very excited, he said, and then he disappeared, and some girl came on and wanted to make arrangements. I said I would call her back." She grinned at them. "So what do you say? Fame and fortune are calling. Are we taking the call or blocking the number?"

AN HOUR OR so later, a coordinator from the radio station called to finalize arrangements.

"Hi, I'm Tiffanii-with-two-i's, and I'm the coordinator from KRRK, OK?"

Kat said yes. There didn't seem much else to say.

"We e-mailed you your flight confirmations. Did you get those?"

Kat had this one covered, too, and had already printed them out.

"A car will be waiting for you at the airport, and you should just go ahead and get into it, OK?"

Here Kat paused for a moment, because it begged the question of why they might *not* have gotten in to the car, but she decided that maybe Tiffanii-with-two-i's was also Tiffanii-with-two-brain-cells and let it go.

"Drop your stuff at the hotel, and then the car will bring you to the station. Bring nothing to the station except your most essential items: cell phone, makeup, change of clothes, sunglasses, purse, shoes."

Shoes? Kat moved the phone away from her ear and looked at it. "Do people sometimes show up with no shoes?"

Tiffanii seemed confused by the question. "Noooo, but sometimes they're not the right shoes."

Kat took a breath. "OK, fine. I'll make sure the band is shod."

"Shod?"

"Wearing shoes."

"OK, good. There will be a photographer there, too, for preliminary shots. Do you need us to provide a stylist?"

"No. I'm their stylist."

Kat had been worried that this wouldn't make sense to Tiffanii, but she was wrong. She could hear the other girl making a note.

"Oh, you're a manager-stylist? OK. I'm a coordinator-assistant-actress."

"Cool."

"Right?"

"Sure."

"After we've taken some photos, we'll do the on-air interview with Peter, and the car will take them back to the hotel to rest and recuperate."

"In preparation for what?"

"For dinner with Peter. He has two working dinners tomorrow night before his real dinner, and you'll be the first, so no dessert, OK?"

"Why not?"

"Because there won't be time. You'll need to schedule a separate dessert for your band."

"I'll be sure to do that." Whatever.

"The next day is all at the record label, so not my responsibility, OK?"

"OK. So should I call them to coordinate?"

Tiffanii laughed. "Nooo! Jessika will call you. She's one of the record label coordinator-booker-studio managers."

"Does she have two i's?"

"No, she has a k."

Then she hung up.

―――――

TWO DAYS LATER, the three of them were standing in the airport, surrounded by family and friends. Kat was perched on her vintage Vuitton trunk, dressed for travel in a yellow and pink

Pucci muumuu with espadrilles, giant yellow sunglasses perched on her head. Her mother was fussing over her, and Kat was letting her.

"Now, Katherine, don't forget it's much drier there than it is here, so remember to hydrate well and moisturize heavily."

"And don't forget the sunscreen."

"And don't forget the sunscreen, all the time, baby. You're a Southern girl; we don't wrinkle well."

Kat met Charlotte's eye and looked away, trying not to smile.

Charlotte was standing next to Millie, who was poking Jackson in the chest with a stern forefinger.

"Now, you remember where you came from, and don't forget your manners, ya hear?"

"Mom . . . "

"Don't take any drugs, and don't sign any documents without your own lawyer."

"Mom . . . "

"And be old-fashioned for me and take care of these two young ladies."

"Mom!" He took her by the shoulders. "It's just Los Angeles, it's not deepest Mongolia. I'll call you as soon as we get there, all right? Calm down."

Kat stood up. "OK, let's get this show on the road. Mothers, retreat!"

Charlotte felt a pang of sadness that her own mother wasn't there, but when both Millie and Leila enveloped her in gigantic hugs, she knew she was far from alone.

"Be good, Charlotte," Millie whispered. "Take care of yourself."

Charlotte nodded, smiling, and all three of them headed off to security.

CHARLOTTE HAD BEEN to Los Angeles many, many times, but it was the first time for both Jackson and Kat.

Unfortunately, LAX is not in the most attractive part of town, but anywhere looks good through the windows of a limousine.

Jackson was excited. "This is cool. I've only been in L.A. twenty minutes, and already I'm in a limo."

"And now you're stuck in traffic, so it's a complete L.A. experience."

Charlotte wasn't as wowed by L.A. as the other two, but it was still fun to be there under these circumstances. She was a little nervous, though. She knew lots of people in town, and the paparazzi were there in force, of course, and although no one from the radio station had mentioned it so far, she wondered if they'd put it together that she was who she was. Her dad wasn't in the news all that much right now, while the wheels of the legal system ground slowly on, but it had been only a few weeks since the story had broken. She wondered also how long it would take Dan Robinson to find her.

She'd spoken to Arthur Bedford briefly the day before.

"Did you say all those things, Charlotte?" The lawyer had been to the point.

"Well, I'm not sure. It was supposed to be off the record."

"Hmm. Let me call the editor and lodge a complaint. Maybe that will prevent more sloppy journalism on Mr. Robinson's part, but you should be more careful, Charlotte. Try to stick to 'no comment,' all right?"

She'd hung up feeling like a chastened child, and today, in the sunny brightness of Los Angeles, she tried to forget the whole thing.

SHE WAS ALSO a little nervous because of a conversation she'd had with Jackson on the flight. Although he was clearly very excited, as that initial buzz wore off, she could see him pondering something.

Eventually, she just asked him. "What's up, Jackson? You seem preoccupied."

He turned to her, his face grave, but then he smiled. "You know me pretty well for someone who doesn't know me very well."

She grinned back. "Well, you're not doing a very good job of hiding your feelings."

"I'm not even sure what I'm feeling, to be honest. Here's the problem." He turned in his seat to face her, taking her hands in his. "I think it's fantastic that 'Fire and Ice' is doing well and that people like it. But my first love is jazz, followed closely by the city of New Orleans. I don't want to move to L.A. and become a pop singer, do you know what I mean?"

"Well, that hasn't happened yet. They're just excited about this one song." Charlotte felt her heart sinking, although she was doing her best to keep it hidden.

He nodded. "I know. That's why I think it's slightly silly for me even to be worried about it. But nonetheless, I just needed to tell you how confused I am about this. I know you could have an amazing career as a singer. You're truly brilliant. And for now, at least, I am behind you one hundred percent. But this might not be my thing, longer term." He smiled a small smile at her. "You, now, you might well be my thing, longer term." He bent forward and kissed her sweetly.

Charlotte felt a glimmer of her old self-control coming back. *Hello, shiny shell.* "Well, let's just take it one thing at a time and see what happens. It could all just blow over."

Jackson nodded and squeezed her hand. "You're right, babe. Hollywood is a fickle place, I hear."

Charlotte turned and looked out the window so he couldn't see how anxious she was. *Hollywood . . . here we come.*

THE HOTEL WAS up on Sunset Boulevard, just down the street from the famous Chateau Marmont. As they'd driven up La Cienega, they'd seen the Hollywood sign, and Jackson and Kat had giggled.

"I'm trying very hard to be cool," Kat had said, "but the Hollywood sign is just cooler. There's no contest."

Now, as handsome young men took their luggage and led them into a smoked-glass and gray-slate lobby, it felt as if they were in a movie. Charlotte didn't pay much attention, but as Kat looked around, she thought she'd never seen so many good-looking and well-dressed people in her life. New Orleans was not a slouchy city, and the long history of intermarriage among diverse groups meant you saw some amazingly beautiful people, but as with any other city, there was rough alongside the smooth. Here everyone appeared to have been airbrushed, with the glossy setting on high. Long hair gleamed, skin glowed, muscles were toned, outfits were carefully casual. Everyone looked like a celebrity, or as if they might be a celebrity or about to become a celebrity. It was strange. Even she felt more glamorous, which was an enjoyable feeling. And the weather was outstanding.

The young man behind the desk looked as if he'd just stepped out of an Abercrombie catalog.

"Hello, I am Justin. Welcome to the Hotel Rothko. Are you checking in?"

Kat gave him their names, and he smiled and handed over three thin wands of titanium.

"These are your room keys. Just wave them across the door panels."

"Of course." Kat smiled coolly as if people handed her sticks of ultralight metal every day, and they headed toward the elevator.

―――――――

THEY HAD ROOMS next to each other, which was nice, even if each of them was smaller than Kat's closet back home—perfectly furnished, of course, but minute. The world's squashiest bed faced a flat-screen plasma mounted to the wall, and jeweled lights sparkled on the walls behind the upholstered headboard. You could jump off the bed into the tiny bathtub in the bathroom—something Kat ably demonstrated—but it gave you the feeling of being inside a yacht rather than an extremely small hotel room.

"I guess they had to choose between quality and quantity and went for the former." Kat smoothed her hand across the sheets, noting the fine thread count. For her and Charlotte, used to the very best of everything, this all seemed normal, but Jackson was truly amazed.

"Did you feel the towels? They're awesome!" He chuckled, taking photos with his cell phone to send to Millie. "This whole day has been amazing, and it's not even over yet."

Kat looked at her watch. "Nope, and in fact, we'd better get back down to the car and head over to the station, or we'll be late. I wouldn't want Tiffanii-with-two-i's to get pissy-with-two-s's."

―――――――

THE RADIO STATION was in Burbank, and traffic was terrible, as usual. By the time they got there, it was mid-afternoon, and Tiffanii looked a little bit ruffled.

"We're running late, so it's straight into the studio, OK?"

Charlotte opened her mouth to ask a question, but Tiffanii was already on the move.

"Come, come," she called over her shoulder. "We've rescheduled the photographer for tomorrow, so don't worry about what you look like. Let's just get into the studio."

As no one had been worrying about their appearance at that exact moment, they were all a bit confused, but then Jackson shrugged and followed her. Tiffanii had turned out to be extremely small and slender, though just as gorgeous as every other girl they'd seen, and as he trailed after her, Jackson turned and whispered, "You know, maybe the reason the hotel rooms are so small is that everyone here is half the size of a regular person."

Charlotte giggled. "I know! I feel enormous."

Kat chided them both. "Don't be mean. Tiffanii might have been blessed with an extra vowel, but that doesn't mean she didn't have to work hard to get where she is."

She caught up with the scurrying young woman, who was confidently leading them through a maze of carpeted hallways lined with gold records and publicity shots. "So, Tiffanii, how did you get interested in radio?"

Tiffanii laughed. "Oh, my dad owns the station. I'm just helping out while I wait to get discovered by Hollywood." She pulled open a big double door. "Here we are."

Chapter THIRTY-FOUR

Peter Lakeshore turned out to be two totally different people. When they first met him, he was serious and focused, saying very little as he pulled their song up from the station's impressive computer system. He sat with his eyes closed, listening as the song played.

"You know," he mused, "it reminds me a little of that Sheryl Crow song, 'All I Wanna Do,' but it's sexier than that, and your voice is totally different, much more Sade, but younger."

Suddenly, he sat up and opened his eyes wide, focusing on Charlotte and Jackson. "Are you guys ready to be huge? This single is going to sell a million." Then, just as suddenly, he dropped his voice again. "With a little help, of course. You need to rerecord in an actual studio." He jumped to his feet and shook Charlotte's hand. "You're the singer, right? Not you?" He looked at Kat.

"No, I'm the studio technician," she deadpanned. "I'm a manager-stylist-studio technician."

"Nice," he said, not blinking. "Charlotte, right?" Charlotte nodded. "I want to do a short interview with you guys, so I can put it on air. OK?"

They nodded enthusiastically.

"We can just do it here in the studio now, and then I'll break it on the morning show. You're meeting with the label tomorrow, right?" Not waiting for an answer, he pulled on some headphones and started pressing buttons. He was reportedly in his mid-thirties, but he looked as young as they did and was handsomer in real life than he appeared on TV. He moved quickly, intensely, but also had the ability to slow down suddenly, as if he could switch into relaxed mode whenever he wanted to.

"Where's the mic?" Jackson looked around.

"Above you, we'll hear you just fine."

Lakeshore sat behind his desk, nearly hidden by a huge array of screens and control panels. He had an old-fashioned microphone, which he leaned into. As he spoke, his voice was suddenly the voice millions of people listened to every day, the familiar tones syndicated across the country.

"Well, here's a story. We started playing a track a day or so ago, 'Fire and Ice,' you know it by heart now. Turned out it was made by a duo no one had heard of, Jack and Charlie, two kids from New Orleans. Well, anyway, we have them here right now." He winked at Charlotte and spoke to her first. "So, Charlie, you're the girl half, right?"

Charlotte laughed. "So they tell me." She looked around for somewhere to sit and perched on a stool.

"And are you two old friends or what?"

"No, actually, we only met recently, although I've known his mom forever."

"Your mom brought you two together?"

Now Jackson laughed. "Well, not exactly. She just knew Charlotte before I did. Charlotte grew up in New York, by the way, not New Orleans."

Tiffanii suddenly appeared and handed Peter Lakeshore a note. He read it quickly and raised his eyebrows, all while Jackson was talking.

"So, just to make this already hot story more interesting, it turns out that Charlie is Charlotte Williams, the daughter of Jacob Williams, who just, if I remember rightly, went to jail for embezzling millions of dollars."

Charlotte felt the blood drain from her face. *Holy crap.*

"That is totally true, Peter." Jackson's voice was smooth and unflustered. "Proving yet again that every cloud has a silver lining. She came to stay with my mom to get away from the press, and we met and started making music together."

Peter watched her face and suddenly smiled. "Lucky for you, huh, Charlotte?"

"You can call me Charlie, it's OK. And yes, it was lucky."

"And now that you're here in L.A., you're going to lay down some more tracks, right? And make a video for 'Fire and Ice'?"

"That's the plan, Peter."

"Great. OK, here's this summer's big hit, 'Fire and Ice,' by Jack and Charlie."

And just as quickly as it all seemed about to blow up, it was done, and no bloodshed.

Peter Lakeshore shook their hands and paused for a moment, holding Charlotte's. "People are going to find out anyway. You know that, right?"

She nodded, trying not to start crying in front of one of the most powerful men in media.

"If you want some advice, just take a leaf out of your friend's playbook here." He looked at Jackson and grinned. "Acknowledge it, and move on. You didn't go to jail, and if you knew how many celebrities have shadows in their past, you'd be amazed. Unless you read the trash rags, in which case you wouldn't be surprised at all. Take this chance and go with it. The press will mention it a lot at first, but then they'll move on. Focus on the work, and you'll be fine."

A beaming smile all around, and then he was gone, calling over his shoulder, "I can't do dinner tonight after all, but have fun out there, kids!"

Tiffanii appeared and led them out, and as the door nearly hit them on their asses on the way out, they realized they were free.

"I don't know about you two," said Kat, looking around the early evening of downtown Burbank, "but I'm starving. It's hard holding down three jobs, you know."

Chapter
THIRTY-FIVE

If Peter Lakeshore had seemed a little crazy, the people at the record label made him look like the sanest guy around.

The day started badly.

To begin with, the label coordinator, Jessika, met them in the lobby of the hotel wearing skin-tight leather from head to toe. She was tall, strong, and gorgeous, with wild black hair that snaked down her back. She looked like a superhero or someone from a video game. Kat's eyes had bugged out a little, but she'd stayed calm.

"No limo today, I'm afraid," Jessika said as she led them to a long, low, gleaming Mercedes. "I'm driving you myself. It's not far, anyway." She pointed her clicker and beeped the doors open. Jackson started to head for the passenger door, but Kat shouldered him out of the way, sliding in beside Jessika smoothly. She herself was wearing a black Givenchy sheath à la *Breakfast at Tiffany's* and stood out in the tanned L.A. crowd like a racehorse in a field of sheep.

Without warning, a flash went off, and Charlotte turned at the sound of her name.

"Charlotte! Over here!"

Suddenly, there was a wall of lights and microphones and people's faces. Peter Lakeshore's show reached a lot of people, it would seem.

"You bitch!" A middle-aged man, who otherwise looked totally reasonable, yelled from behind the photographers. "You steal our money, and now you're going to get famous off it! Whore!"

Jessika was out of the car and next to Charlotte in a matter of seconds. "No comment, fuck off, thanks very much!" She yelled as she turned Charlotte around and pushed her down into the car. Checking that Jackson was in, she slammed the door and jumped in herself, squealing out of the hotel driveway at an illegal pace.

"What was that all about?" she asked, looking at Charlotte in the rearview.

"You don't know?"

Jessika shrugged. "I was out last night, I can barely remember when I got in. I haven't had time to read any backstory on you guys at all."

Charlotte sighed and looked out the window. She was getting tired of explaining it.

Kat stepped in. "Charlotte's dad is Jacob Williams, who just went to jail."

"Oh, yeah? Did he kill someone?" Jessika seemed only mildly interested.

"No. He stole a load of money."

"Oh? From that guy?"

"No idea. From lots of guys, so maybe that one, too."

"Oh, well, never mind. It'll all blow over." Charlotte was surprised, but Jessika elaborated. "Look, I've worked with rock stars and musicians and actors and whatever, and they all get in trouble in one way or another. Drugs, girls, money, sex, gambling, fighting, you name it, they do it, and the press loves to make copy out of it. It's much easier than actually reporting something, you know, like investigating something or whatever. And seeing as these people tend to photograph well, it's more attractive news than if Joe Blow punches his girlfriend, because who cares about that?" She leaned back, resting one leather-clad arm on the car window's edge. "If I might quote Emily Dickinson, the great American poetess, 'Fame is a bee. It has a song—It has a sting—Ah, too, it has a wing.'"

There was silence in the car as they all digested this.

"Oh, fuck sticks," said their philosopher-driver-coordinator. "They're here, too."

The Mercedes swept into the driveway of the record label, which looked like any other office building apart from the giant billboards of extremely famous bands, nearly scattering the crowd of reporters and paparazzi standing there.

"Mind you," she added, activating the gate to an underground parking garage, "that lot of shifty characters more or less camps there anyway, just in case Britney or Lindsay shows up."

F. ASPEN, THE hot producer du jour, was born Francis Aspenweiser and changed his name in high school. He'd known for years at that point that he was destined for greatness, and so did everyone around him. Francis, as his family still called him, had formed his first band in elementary school (the Recess) and persuaded his dad to trick him out with a MacBook Pro and GarageBand (with all of the jam packs) instead of a bar mitzvah. He played piano, guitar, sax, drums, bass, cello, and trumpet and couldn't sing worth spit. Which was fine—there were always singers around, and what he really wanted to do was produce, anyway. He worshipped at the shrine of Dre, with side deities Guy Sigsworth and Bloodshy and

Avant. And yet, for all his hipness and fabulosity, he was at heart another twenty-something music geek who loved nothing more than hearing a song that made him want to dance or cry or get laid. He'd heard "Fire and Ice" two days before, thanks to the Internet and an assistant whose only job it was to trawl for new music, and he'd had it on replay ever since.

"Charlie and Jack! Nice to meet you, dudes. Come on in, come on in." He stood up, which still made him only five feet four inches tall, and hugged Jessika. "Hello, gorgeous, how are you?" He was dark-haired and normal-looking, and could just as easily have been a barista or a student, rather than a multiplatinum, multinational record producer with the world at his Chuck Taylor–wearing feet.

"I'm good, F., pretty good, thanks." Jessika peeled off her jacket, sexily revealing a simple white V-neck T-shirt with plenty of cleavage. Kat made a small noise but bit her tongue. "These kids are all yours now, OK? I'm supposed to take them back to the hotel when you're done working, so give me a tinkle, yeah?"

"Sure, Jessika, sure. Can you ask Sandy to send in some snacks and drinks? I'm parched. Is it lunchtime?"

Jessika laughed. "When did you get here? It's not even brunch, bro."

"I got here last night, babe, and you know how it is when I'm in the zone."

The young woman shook her head. "Breakfast's the most important meal of the day, dude. Get yourself some granola and shit." She sighed and looked at Kat. "Honestly, these creative types." She left the room, her perfume lingering long after she was gone.

Charlotte looked at Kat. *Oh, dear.* That was one smitten kitten.

"SO, LET'S HEAR what else you've got."

F. perched on the mixing desk as Jackson headed into the studio just beyond a smoked-glass window. Inside was a baby grand, and he sat down and just started playing. Charlotte stood next to F and watched, feeling enormously proud. Song after song poured out of Jackson, from bluesy love songs to fast, syncopated dance tracks. Somehow, just with his voice and the piano, he was able to convey arrangements and instrumentation, and Charlotte and Kat could tell from his body language that F. Aspen was dying to get started.

He turned to Charlotte. "OK, in you go. Do you know these songs?" She shook her head. "Go learn them, then. I'll be back in half an hour. Have two of them ready to go, OK?" With that, he left the room, and they could hear him shouting for Sandy, whoever he or she was.

ABOUT HALFWAY THROUGH the afternoon, a strange thing happened. Charlotte and Jackson sort of missed it, because they were bickering over which of them should take a harmony part, but Kat had an excellent ringside seat. F. Aspen had been leaning back in his mixing chair, feet up on the console, waiting for Charlotte and Jackson to agree on the harmony. Charlotte started singing the harmony and then switched to the main melody to demonstrate her point, and for whatever reason, she looked and sounded so exquisite in that moment that even Kat caught her breath. F. Aspen suddenly leaped to his feet and essentially ran out of the room.

Jackson and Charlotte kept arguing, but Kat, who'd been watching carefully the whole time, leaned forward and pressed the button that allowed them to hear her.

"Uh . . . guys. I have no idea what just happened, but something did."

They couldn't have cared less.

Jackson was speaking calmly, but his expression made it clear that he was holding his anger just under the surface. "The way I wrote it, I sing the melody here, you sing the harmony, and then in the next verse, we trade places."

Charlotte shrugged. "I realize you wrote it, Jackson, you don't have to keep mentioning it. All I'm saying is that I think it sounds better this way."

"Well, you would, wouldn't you, because all you can hear is you."

"That's just not true. The harmony is vital. It wouldn't sound the same if it was just my voice."

"Well, I think you're wrong, and as it's my song—"

Their voices were getting louder and louder, but when F. Aspen came back in with another man, Kat let go of the button, and suddenly the argument was muted.

"See what I mean?"

F. Aspen seemed to be continuing a conversation he'd already started with this other man, and Kat looked at him curiously. The other man was older, like her dad older, and dressed in what Kat recognized as a bespoke suit. Under it, he wore a Cocteau Twins T-shirt, but the suit had cost more than five grand, she knew that. He was very handsome in a rich, smooth way, and although his face was unlined and relaxed, his eyes were sharp and cold. He turned to look at Kat.

"You're Kat Karraby, the manager?"

She nodded, trying to look as calm as he did.

"Is there a contract between these two?"

She shook her head.

"Or between them and you?"

"No. We're friends. Nothing on paper."

A short smile. "Well, then, nothing at all." He pressed the button and spoke to Jackson and Charlotte. "I'm John Sparks. I run this record label."

The two musicians fell silent. Charlotte turned to face the glass, and Kat saw John Sparks's face grow even more still.

He let go of the button and spoke to F. "You're right, she's smoking hot. And she can really sing?"

"Listen for yourself." Aspen leaned over. "Sing that second song you did, the one that speeds up."

"'Intoxication'?"

"Yes."

Jackson sat down at the piano, and Aspen brought up the playback, with the additional percussion and instruments they'd added earlier. He dropped out Charlotte's recorded track so Sparks could hear her sing live, although once she'd started, he hit record again. "No point in missing another take while we're at it," he muttered to himself.

It was clear to Kat, who knew them well, that the argument they'd just had was working in their favor musically. The song was about sex, basically, about the slow build-up, about the gentlest beginnings turning into the most incredible passion. The song began simply and slowly and gradually doubled in pace until the last verse. Charlotte was clearly giving it her all and letting her anger power her singing.

It was an awesome performance. Her voice was so mellow, so round in tone, but then she would give it an edge, a rasp, a subtle break that made the hairs stand up on the back of your neck. Kat could see that John Sparks was affected, but he was also all business.

He interrupted the song. "OK, so my understanding is that there is no contract between the two of you, is that right?"

Charlotte and Jackson stopped playing and looked at each other.

"How do you mean?" Jackson asked.

"I mean that if the record label wanted to sign just her, it could, right?"

There was a pause. Then Charlotte answered. "Well, yes, theoretically. But no, practically. We're a band, not a solo act."

"But you're the one with the major career in front of her."

"Not without him. Without the songs to sing, I'm just a singer."

John Sparks laughed. Not a pleasant sound. "You've got it backward, sweetheart. Songwriters are thick on the ground, and so are singers. But singers with voices like yours, looks like yours, and a media story like yours are not thick on the ground. But hey, if you don't want to sign with us, don't. I'll find the next big thing somewhere else."

He waited a moment and then shrugged. "Think it over. We'll talk tomorrow." He turned and headed toward the door. Then he stopped. "Aspen, don't record anything else, OK?"

When Jessika turned up to take them back to the hotel, nobody was saying anything to anyone. But the silence was deafening.

Chapter
THIRTY-SIX

As the three of them trudged across the lobby, they were hailed by Justin, the desk clerk.

"Miss Williams? Your room has been changed." He handed her a new wand.

She frowned. "Was there something wrong with my room?"

He shook his head. "No, it was at the request of your record label. We already moved your luggage."

"Oh. Am I still on the same floor as my friends?"

"No. You're on the top floor now."

Jackson gave a snort. "Of course you are. And now the persuasion begins, right? Can't you see that's what they're trying to do? It's a seduction."

Charlotte was exhausted and really didn't want to fight. One of the paparazzi outside the hotel had mentioned the Charlotte Williams Sucks Web site, and all she wanted to do was get to her room, take a shower, change into her jammies, and see what bullshit they were saying about her now.

"Come on, let's not fight. I'm with you, remember? No one is going to seduce me into anything."

But when they pushed open the door of her new suite, even Jackson admitted that the label was looking pretty sexy. A giant room looked out over the city, one wall completely made of glass. A plasma screen folded out of a wall, and a gorgeous modern chandelier ran the length of the enormous dining table. All three of them headed for the white leather sofa in front of the window, although Kat veered off at the last minute when she spotted a leopard-print Eames chair instead.

"I could get used to this," she said as someone knocked on the door.

"It's me," said Jessika, followed by three guys pushing trolleys. "I thought you guys might be hungry." Large silver domes were quickly unloaded onto the dining table and pulled off to reveal steak frites, a delicious-looking salad, three kinds of doughnuts, and a fruit platter Tiffanii could have used as a snowboard. "We can go out for dessert after if you like."

There was silence, followed by a fairly inelegant scramble for the table.

"I didn't realize how hungry I was," Charlotte admitted, once she'd gotten a plate of delicious fries down. She turned to Jackson. "Look, I'm sorry I was snappish before."

"It's OK. It's all a bit overwhelming." Jackson was looking better, too, as he munched his way through a loaded plate.

"I don't want them to sign me on my own." Charlotte reached for his hand. "You know that, right?"

He shrugged. "I'm not going to stand in your way. I already told you, this isn't really my scene. Face it, you and I got into a fight in the studio already, and I just don't want to fight over music. I think I might be better off getting back to where I'm happiest, and that's New Orleans." He paused and smiled at Charlotte. "But I don't want to leave you alone with all these wolves, so let's take it day by day for a bit, OK?"

As Charlotte nodded, the phone rang. Kat went to get it, but after a few seconds, she held it out to Charlotte.

"It's someone called Mr. Edelstein. He says he's calling from New York."

Charlotte looked at her watch. Edelstein was her dad's banker, the man who'd refused to give her any money. It was after nine there. Oh, God, maybe something had happened to her dad. She took the phone.

"Mr. Edelstein?"

"Miss Williams?"

"Yes, it's me. Is something wrong?" *Smart, Charlotte,* she chided herself. *Of course something's wrong. He's a banker, and your dad stole millions of dollars.* As far as he was concerned, something would always be wrong.

But she was mistaken.

"I'm calling with good news, Miss Williams. I'm sorry for the lateness of the hour, but when I heard you were on the West Coast, I thought it might be acceptable to call."

Charlotte sank to the edge of the sofa, confused. "No, it's fine, Mr. Edelstein, but what is it?"

"Your money, Miss Williams. Your personal account. I've managed to free it up for you. Our branch in L.A. should already have delivered a checkbook and bank cards to your hotel. In addition to the ten million dollars or so that is in your account, you have access to a fairly sizable credit line."

Charlotte gasped. Kat and Jackson looked worried, but she held up a reassuring hand. "Are you joking?"

Mr. Edelstein seemed affronted. "No, of course not. I never

joke about money in excess of one million dollars." There was a pause, and then he chuckled. "That was a joke, of course."

"Of course." Charlotte didn't know what to say, so she did what she'd been raised to do, which was to say thank you. Then she hung up the phone and turned to face her friends. "Well, that changes things a bit."

"What happened?" Kat looked worried.

"I'm rich again."

Chapter

THIRTY-SEVEN

It was only much later that Charlotte thought to check the Charlotte Williams Sucks Web site. After the surprising call from Edelstein, she and her friends had ordered champagne and then basically hung out and watched a movie. Very glamorous.

Charlotte had mixed feelings about the money. On the one hand, of course, she was glad to be solvent again, and it meant she could pay some bills and go back to Yale if she wanted to. But on the other hand, she had been getting used to the freedom of not having money.

Jackson was scornful of this position. "There's no freedom in poverty. This is one of those lies the rich make up to make themselves feel better about the massive discrepancy between them and the poor. It's not very freeing not to know where your next meal is coming from."

Charlotte frowned. "I'm not glorifying poverty. I'm saying that wealth carries implications and responsibilities."

"Why? It didn't before."

A slight chill had entered the room. Suddenly, Jackson got to his feet.

"You know what? I'm really tired. Let's talk in the morning and work out what to do once we've all had a good night's sleep, OK?"

Charlotte had started to try to talk him out of it, to invite him to spend the night with her, but she realized she needed time to think as well. Kat was going out with Jessika, "to see some things," and went to get ready. Charlotte was left alone, and she was glad of it.

She turned on her laptop and connected to the Internet. *Let's see what the world is saying about me now,* she thought to herself.

The Web site was at least consistent.

"Charlotte Sings for Her Supper," read the headline, which was inoffensive enough, but the article wasn't very kind.

"Charlotte Williams arrived in Los Angeles ready to steal the careers of harder-working young women. After never publicly showing an interest in music before, she met up with a talented musician in New Orleans and quickly took advantage of him. Now she's meeting with record labels that reportedly are only interested in signing her. How long will it be before she jettisons those she no longer needs? Not long, we imagine."

There was a picture of her taken outside the hotel that morning, looking like every tabloid photograph she'd ever seen. Why did those pictures always look so similar? There was just enough truth in the story to be believable, but they'd twisted her motivation to make her look terrible and selfish. She thought about all the tabloid stories she'd read over the years and wondered how many of those had been true. Not so many, it would seem.

There were links at the bottom of the article, and she discovered that CWS was not the only site paying attention to her now that she was back "on the scene." Other gossip sites wondered which club she'd favor with her first visit, and some had photos of her coming back to the hotel. Great. It wouldn't be long before her local friends got in touch, and she wasn't sure how she felt about that.

The phone rang. Maybe it was Kat.

"Hey there, whore. How ya doin'?"

The voice. Charlotte felt herself flood with adrenaline and wished she wasn't alone. She looked around for another phone, but there wasn't one.

"How did you get this number?"

He laughed. "Well, let's think about that. Your picture is all over the Internet, the name of your hotel is public knowledge, so I just called the front desk and asked for you. Not so hard, huh? Maybe for you, but not for those of us who think for a living."

Charlotte was angry. "Look, I have no idea who you are or why you think it's cool to bug me, but I've done nothing to you, and I want you to stop."

"You've done nothing to me? Actually, your father took all of my parents' money and reduced them to utter poverty, just as they were beginning their retirement. You just watched your dad go to jail, but at least he'll be fed. I watched my parents cry with dread that they'd lose the home they've lived in for the last fifty years. I want to watch you cry and beg for mercy, Charlotte, that's what I want. I want to watch you write me a big fat check to save my parents' home."

"You want money? That's what all this is about?" Charlotte was incredulous. "I thought you were crazy, but you're just a fucking thief."

"It's not thievery, baby, it's retribution."

"I'm not giving you anything, loser."

"Really? Don't you care about your friends?"

Charlotte paused. "What do you mean?"

"I have someone here who wants to talk to you."

There was a silence. Then another voice came on the line. "Don't pay this dickhead a fucking cent, Charlotte."

"Kat?"

"I mean it, Charlotte. He's full of shit. He doesn't have the balls to do anything to me."

Another silence. And then a scream that Charlotte would remember for the rest of her life.

"Your friend was very, very wrong, Charlotte. She's bleeding now, so I suggest you hurry."

In the background, Charlotte could hear Kat crying brokenly. Suddenly, she was filled with an anger so pure and hot that everything started to move very slowly.

"Where are you?"

"Close."

"What exactly do you want me to do?"

"I want you to come and meet me, baby. I want you to write me a check for five million dollars."

"I'm not sure I have a checkbook. How do you even know I have money?"

Another chuckle. "I know everything about you, honey. Everything worth knowing."

"Really?"

"Yes. And I know there's a checkbook waiting for you at the hotel desk, and I know there's a taxi stand out front, and I know that if you hurry, maybe your pretty little friend will still be alive when you get here."

Charlotte looked around for her shoes. For a second, she wondered about calling Jackson to come with her, but no, this was her problem. She didn't need to drag another friend into this mess.

Chapter
THIRTY-EIGHT

The Grove is one of the biggest tourist attractions in L.A. It brings in more visitors than Disneyland and has a fountain that dances in time to Frank Sinatra. However, as far as Charlotte was concerned, it was a major pain in the butt. Forty million people appeared to be swarming over every inch of it, and as she scanned the crowd looking for a glimpse of Kat, she started to feel overwhelmed. Maybe she should just call the police.

"Charlotte?"

Turning, Charlotte was surprised and taken aback to see Dan Robinson standing there.

"Jesus, Mr. Robinson, you scared the shit out of me. I can't talk to you right now. I have a bit of an emergency."

Dan looked concerned. "Can I help? What's going on?"

Charlotte ignored him. She didn't have time for the reporter right now.

"No, really, can I help? Have you lost someone? It took me a while to find you, you know, since you left New Orleans."

Charlotte was distracted. "Yeah, well, I was a little bit pissed with you, to be honest. I told you we were talking off the record, but you went ahead and published an article anyway. But really, we can talk about this another time."

"Yeah, my editors got a call from your lawyer. They weren't very happy about it."

Charlotte wasn't really listening. The voice on the phone had told her to come alone. He had assured her that he would be watching her, that if he saw she had company, he would hurt Kat again. Charlotte walked a few steps away from the journalist, in the hopes of shaking him, but he was as sticky as ever.

"Mr. Robinson, you'll have to excuse me, I'm really busy right now."

"Well, will you promise me an interview? I'm fascinated by your story, Charlotte. I want to write about it."

Charlotte flashed him a brief smile. "Well, look, Dan, let's talk tomorrow or the next day, OK? I'm trying to find Kat, and she's lost."

"Is she?"

"Yes. I have to go now, Dan." She turned, frustrated, and started to make her way through the crowd. Robinson was annoying, and she was scared that if she told him the truth about what was going on, the voice on the phone would see her talking too much and hurt Kat. She had to face this alone.

The Grove was located next to the old Farmers Market, and the crowds moved between the two places easily. A free trolley ran between them, and as one passed Charlotte, she jumped on, thinking maybe she would see Kat from the top deck.

It was empty up there, and Charlotte moved from side to side, searching the crowd and trying to ignore the rising panic she felt. Was this always going to be a possibility? That mad people would endanger her friends, herself? If something happened to Kat, she would never forgive herself and never rest until she found the man responsible.

The trolley had stopped at the Farmers Market end of the track and was taking on passengers for the return trip. Peering over the edge, she saw Dan Robinson getting on and frowned. Really, he was the most persistent and irritating man alive. She heard someone mounting the metal stairs to the top deck and wasn't surprised when it turned out to be him.

"It's nice of you to think of helping, Mr. Robinson, but I'm really better off alone."

He stood there, saying nothing. She noticed he was wearing the same outfit he'd been wearing in New Orleans. He looked at her strangely.

"Are you OK, Mr. Robinson?"

"Call me Dan."

"Are you OK?"

He nodded and suddenly smiled. "Did you bring your checkbook, Charlotte?"

She gazed at him in horror. "What did you say?"

"You heard me." He chuckled, a sound she recognized for the first time. "Who else could it possibly be but me, Charlotte? You're so focused on yourself, you never really see anyone else, do you? No wonder Kat was so easy to pick off. You never considered that she might be in danger. All she knew was that she'd seen me with you before, and when I stabbed her, she was really surprised." He laughed again, apparently delighted.

Charlotte sank onto one of the trolley seats. "But . . . why?"

"Why? I told you. Your father destroyed my parents. You're going to make it better for them. Plus interest, of course. From the day the story broke, that day in the park, I knew I was going to get to you, going to take our money back. You're weak, Charlotte, and

I am strong. You're young, your money will sit in the bank, and by the time you're the age my parents are, you'll be rich again if you don't do anything stupid."

Charlotte was angry. "What, like invest my life savings with a criminal?"

His face flushed. "Your father was a very convincing con man, Charlotte. You've inherited that skill, and people like Kat and Jackson believe you really care about them, when all you care about is who's going to look out for Charlotte."

The trolley started up again with a jolt, and Robinson grabbed the rail for support.

"Anyway, although this has been a pleasant chat, your little friend is bleeding to death in a car on the top level of the car park, and I'm in need of that check."

He pointed at her. "If you do anything to stop payment on it or try to track me in any way, I will pick off another one of your friends. Or I'll wait a few years until you have children, and I'll grab one of them. But I'm an honorable man, and if you give me the money, I'll run away somewhere nice and sunny and never bother you again."

"How can I possibly trust you? You can't even keep a conversation private."

Robinson pulled a knife from his pocket. Its blade was still wet with Kat's blood.

"I actually don't give a shit if you trust me or not. All I care about is that check. Write it now, or I'll kill you and then go back and finish off your friend. I'm just too pissed off at this point to accept anything other than lots of money or your dead body. Your choice, Charlie."

As she stood there, she realized she could hear people laughing and talking, that all around her, stores were doing business, movies were playing, popcorn was popping. It reminded her of when her father was arrested in New York, this sense of life going on while hers stood still. In a moment like this, money became utterly irrelevent. She reached into her bag and pulled out her checkbook. The trolley stopped; something was wrong. She looked at Robinson—he knew it, too, and was frowning. She looked over the edge of the trolley rail. Everyone was getting off the trolley, and fast. They were right next to the fountain, which was going through one of its regular light and sound shows, its jets shooting impossibly high in the air, level with where she was sitting. People were looking up at her and pointing.

She looked over at Robinson again and saw why.

Scarsford. Gun drawn, he was standing at the top of the stairs.

"Hi there, Charlotte," he said softly. "Are you OK?"

She nodded. "Kat . . ."

"We have her. She's on her way to the hospital now." He lifted his arm and pointed his gun at Robinson. "Dan Robinson, you are under arrest for extortion and assault with a deadly weapon. Why don't you put down your knife and come with me? There's no need for this to get out of hand."

Robinson looked irritated. "What the hell? Why are you even here? She's not under your protection."

Scarsford didn't move. "The SEC and the FBI are both keeping an eye on Miss Williams in case any of her father's victims decide to take vengeance into their own hands. We've been watching you ever since we discovered you were responsible for the Web site."

"You are? Why?" Charlotte was confused.

"For fun, you stupid bitch. Torturing you was the only thing keeping me going." Dan Robinson threw down the knife suddenly. "You know, this is really just too fucking annoying. Everything works out for you, you spoiled cow, and now I'm going to have to go on the run without even the satisfaction of killing you." He turned amiably to Scarsford. "You're spoiling all my fun, Agent Scarsford. And she didn't even fuck you."

And with that, he turned and jumped off the trolley, directly into the still singing fountain.

Chapter
THIRTY-NINE

When Kat woke up, the first face she saw was Charlotte's.

She spoke through cracked lips. "What am I wearing?"

Charlotte's mouth twitched. "A hospital gown."

Kat carefully tipped her head so she could see. "Gray? Really?"

"It's not actually that bad on you, to be honest. It sets off your hair nicely."

Kat closed her eyes. "Oh, good. And presumably, I'm attractively pale?"

"Like Garbo in *Camille*."

Kat smiled. "And I'm going to live?"

Charlotte nodded. "Yes. You're going to be in here for a few more days, though. But that's just as well, because it's a freaking madhouse out there."

"Why?"

"After Robinson jumped into the fountain and impaled himself on a floodlight, the crowd at the Grove all pulled out their cell phones and tweeted photos all around the world. In about thirty seconds, the press showed up, and Scarsford and I barely made it out alive."

Kat smiled wearily. "Oh, it was Scarsford. I thought I was hallucinating. He saved my life, you know."

"Mine, too."

"He's a bit of a stud. If I liked guys, I might go for him."

"He's handsome."

"And heroic."

"And back in New York already."

"Just as well. Did you call my parents?"

Charlotte nodded. "Your mom got here this morning. She just popped out for breakfast. We didn't think you were going to wake up for a while."

"So you were just sitting there, waiting?"

Charlotte grinned. "Yup. If you think I'm letting you out of my sight for quite a while, you're very much mistaken."

Kat smiled back at her. "OK, then, I think I'll go back to sleep."

"Do that. I'll be right here."

"Thanks, sweetie."

Kat's eyelids fluttered, and she slipped back into sleep. The doctors had been very worried about her for a while. She'd lost a lot of blood.

Charlotte sighed and watched her friend sleep. There was nowhere else she would rather have been in the world.

DAN ROBINSON THROWING himself into the fountain had been horrific. Charlotte and Scarsford had both rushed down to see if they could help, but it was too late. Security at the Grove was tight, and even though medical personnel got there very quickly, Robinson had died at the scene. He was only twenty-nine.

Sometime later, Charlotte, Jackson, and Scarsford had been

waiting outside the operating room as the doctors inside had tried to stem the internal bleeding that was threatening Kat's life. Jackson had come as soon as Charlotte called, and he hadn't let go of her hand since he'd arrived at the hospital. Charlotte had begun to cry.

"It's my fault Robinson is dead. Whatever he did, he did because of my dad. Now his parents have lost all of their money and their son."

Scarsford had shaken his head. "You're just feeling guilty. He was an adult; he made his own choices. He published lies and hateful stories about you online. He made allegations you couldn't respond to. And he kidnapped Kat and hurt her badly." He'd smiled at her. "She's going to be fine, though."

"No thanks to me, right?"

Jackson had pulled her into a hug. "No thanks to your dad, Charlotte. He started this whole thing by stealing money. Don't forget, you didn't do anything wrong."

Scarsford had nodded in agreement. "Regardless of what I might have thought."

Charlotte had kept crying, sobbing into Jackson's chest, holding him tightly. She'd felt safe for the first time in weeks.

THE MEDIA WAS having a field day.

"Embezzler's Daughter in Mega-Mall Murder!" was one good headline.

When Charlotte and Jackson left the hospital, the photographers pushed one another into traffic to try to get a shot, leading to "Paparazzi Injured by Charlotte Williams, Sues!" Back at the hotel, she smiled at the guy who opened the door for her, giving rise to the classic "Charlotte Williams Laughs at Tragedy" article, which alleged that she was a heartless cow who only cared about her career and who considered the death of Dan Robinson to be "annoying."

If she had learned one thing through this whole experience, it was that whatever you did, the press wrote what they wanted. There was no point in fighting it. The headline that never appeared was "Charlotte Williams Visits Dead Journalist's Parents and Gives Back the Money Her Father Stole," but then, that would be too long, anyway. And no one saw her do it, because by then, they were feeding on someone else's tragedy.

JACKSON AND CHARLOTTE closed the hotel-room door behind them and locked it. Wordlessly, they moved to the sofa and sat, still stunned by everything that had happened.

She looked at him. "Are you going back to New Orleans?"

Jackson shook his head. "Not right now. I'm sticking with you until all this mess settles down and you're ready for me to leave. And who knows, maybe I'll change my mind about L.A."

She smiled at him. "I don't know if I'll ever be ready for you to leave. Why don't we forget about the record company and just hang out and make some music? I have enough money now for us to rent time in any studio in town. This has all happened so fast, let's just slow it down and take our time."

It was hard to resist her, the beautiful face he'd come to care about so much, the lovely body, and, more important, the warm hearted woman he knew he was falling in love with. She was smart and brave and unique.

"You're a persuasive woman, Charlotte Williams." He tucked her hair behind her ear and kissed her. "OK, we'll take it slow and see what happens. I don't know if I'm an L.A. kind of guy, and

New Orleans is my home. But hey, as long as I get to write and play music every single day, I'll probably be fine."

There was a knock at the door. Jessika.

"Hey, handsome duo. John Sparks sent me to give you both a message, although, of course, I forget exactly how he said it." She looked totally different today, wearing a long white dress with a beaded hem, her hair braided like Pocahontas, no makeup at all. She caught Charlotte eyeing her with surprise. "I change my clothes a lot. I like to mix it up, you know. Anyway, John says basically that he'd changed his mind, that he wants both of you as a band if you're interested. After you left yesterday, he listened to all the tracks and realized how fantastic you sound together." She laughed. "Besides, there's so much buzz about you right now, he can't resist building on it. You have a day or two to think about it." She turned to go. "I'm going to go visit your friend Kat at the hospital." She paused and blushed. "Do you think . . . do you know . . . do you think she would mind if I visited? I mean, we don't know each other very well. We were going to go out last night, but that asshole kidnapped her before we met up." Her eyes clouded briefly. "I thought she'd stood me up, actually. I waited for her for ages."

Charlotte tried to suppress a smile. "I think she'd love to see you. You should definitely go. We'll talk it over here and let you know later today."

"OK, sounds like a plan." Jessika left, looking more cheerful.

"Hmm, seems like maybe Kat has a new friend." Jackson was looking thoughtful.

"Yup. That's a nice surprise."

Charlotte stood up and went to look out at the view. "We don't have to take the record company's offer. We could record the songs ourselves and distribute the music online. It's been done."

"Using your money?"

"Sure."

Jackson sighed and came over to stand behind her, kissing the back of her neck.

"As I said, I just don't know. I wish I could promise you I'd stay, but I can't."

Charlotte sighed, and suddenly she realized it was fine. She turned and hugged him.

"It's OK, I get it. I've decided that life is about doing the things that make you happy, not the things that please other people. If you can please other people, that's a plus, but as long as you're not hurting anyone, you're golden." She squeezed his bottom. "But will you stay until there aren't crowds of photographers everywhere?"

Jackson laughed, picked her up and carried her to the bed. "Well, that might take longer than you think, because I have a feeling you're about to become famous for all the right reasons, rather than the wrong ones." He laid her down on the bed. "And now I think you should go to sleep, tempting though it is to keep you awake a while longer." He grinned as she reached up for him.

"I'm not that tired. Why don't we talk it over a bit more?"

He grinned and lay down next to her.

Chapter

FORTY

In the end, everyone got what he or she wanted, which was unusual.

Once Kat was out of the hospital, the three friends found an apartment in Venice, near the ocean, and settled down to write an album. Well, Jackson and Charlotte did. Kat turned around and launched her assault on the fashion world of L.A.

Once the songs were written, Jackson took Charlotte out for dinner to celebrate.

Abbot Kinney Boulevard was thronged with people on that warm evening, and as they made their way to Joe's Restaurant, Charlotte marveled at how quickly she'd come to love this funkier area of Los Angeles. An eclectic mix of edgy fashion and art spaces, along with your standard tattooed weirdos and chainsaw jugglers, Venice Beach was somewhere she never would have gone before her world changed so dramatically. Now it felt like home.

But it didn't feel that way to Jackson. She knew what he was going to say before he said it.

"You're going home, aren't you?" She took his hands across the table.

He smiled at her. "How did you know?"

"You stopped mentioning New Orleans a week or so ago. I realized that it probably meant it hurt too much to talk about it, because you missed it so badly." She grinned. "It's OK. I'm happy here, Kat's fine, and if you think I won't be coming to visit you every other weekend, you're wrong."

He looked enormously relieved. "Are you sure?"

She nodded. "Honestly, it's fine. Before my dad . . . before things went wrong, I always wanted my needs met first, do you know what I mean? Now I realize that I'll be OK whatever happens. I'm stronger than I thought, you know?"

Jackson nodded, thinking again how cool Charlotte had turned out to be. "You're a pretty tough cookie, that's for sure."

"Well, you had something to do with it."

He laughed. "I don't think so. I think you were born tough, you just didn't realize it."

She shrugged and called the waiter over. "Well, whether that's true or not, I'm a hungry tough cookie right now, so let's eat."

THE ALBUM WAS being released the last week of summer, and the weather in Los Angeles was still baking hot. Kat met Charlotte at Smashbox the week before the release, dragging a rack of swimsuits and vintage cover-ups across the parking lot.

"Hey, babe." Charlotte kissed her friend. "How was the *Vogue* shoot?"

In the previous few months, Kat had taken the city by storm and had been getting work styling the young and hip, as well as advising the older and wealthier on their vintage-clothing collections.

"Are you kidding? I met Grace Coddington in person. I honestly thought I was going to die. She is the most brilliant, the most amazing . . . "

Charlotte listened to Kat going on and on, watching the play of expressions across her friend's face, feeling the usual wave of affection she felt every time they were together. Whatever crimes her father had committed, his actions had led to her making probably the best friend she would ever have, and she was grateful.

They went into the facility, which housed recording studios, rehearsal spaces, practice rooms, and video-editing suites. They were there to shoot the back cover of the album. They'd shot the front the week before, an homage to the famous *Vogue* cover of her mother, Charlotte naked, her arms folded across her chest, wearing the gorgeous agate and diamond collar her mother had left her. She'd dedicated the album to her mom, and it all felt right to Charlotte. On the back, Kat wanted to shoot her in a 1970s string bikini, possibly with a cover-up, sitting on the sand, looking relaxed and natural, no makeup at all, her hair loose.

"Did you have fun with Jackson last weekend?" Kat had been busy that week and hadn't seen Charlotte for a few days.

Charlotte nodded. "Yeah, it was great. The Pearly Kings got picked up by a New Orleans label and are working on a CD. He's thrilled."

"Good." They pushed open a studio door, where an assistant was spreading sand next to a scrim.

"Why aren't we doing this at the actual beach?" Charlotte was smiling as she followed Kat.

"Are you joking? It's, like, ninety-three degrees out there. I'll freckle!" She pointed to a large wooden packing case, set to one side of the room. "What the hell is that? Is that a prop?"

Charlotte grinned. "No, it's a birthday present for you."

"It's not my birthday."

"No, but it will be at some point. Open it."

Kat narrowed her eyes at her friend but grabbed the crowbar that was sitting on top of the packing case. Prying carefully, she muttered under her breath about splinters.

Inside the case were layers of tissue paper, and as Kat started to lift them off, her voice went up an octave or two.

"Ossie Clark . . . a Celia Birtwell print . . . oh, my God." She lifted the deceptively simple chiffon dress from the case and looked at Charlotte with wide eyes.

"Keep going." Charlotte started looking through the swim-wear, trying not to show how pleased she was by Kat's thrilled response.

"Holy shit. Alaïa . . . " Rustling of tissue paper. "Zandra Rhodes . . . the sleeves! Missoni . . . Ungaro . . . Lagerfeld . . . Calvin Klein . . . Lacroix!" Suddenly, Kat turned to Charlotte. "This is your mother's collection, isn't it? I just realized. There's nothing here from . . . "

"From after she died. Nope. It all stops in the mid-'90s. But it should be a good start, right?"

"For what?"

"For your new store. I signed a lease on a space on Main Street yesterday. I thought you might need some stock to open with." She smiled. "There are three more cases waiting for you at the store, but we're going to need to stop and get another crowbar. I borrowed that one from Smashbox."

Kat stood very still and looked at her friend. "Are you kidding me?"

"Not at all."

"You rented me a store?"

"Yes."

"In Santa Monica?"

"Yes."

"Do you know how exciting that is for me?"

Charlotte laughed. "Yes, which makes it very exciting for me, too. Listen, Kat." Her voice grew serious. "You've been the best friend I've ever had. Never once have you made assumptions about me because of my background. Never once have you judged my father harshly. And never once have you hesitated to call me on my bullshit or help me react like a sane and normal person rather than the spoiled bitch I was raised to be."

Kat frowned. "I hope you're not getting all gooey here. It could easily become awkward."

Charlotte grinned. "Nope. Not gooey. But I'm not the person I was, and the person I've become is a better person because of you. You're awesome."

"That's true."

"And you're very stylish."

"I'm glad you mentioned that."

"And I love you."

"That's nice. I love you, too, you idiot. Now, can we get on with the squealing and jumping around part? Because I'm really having a hard time staying calm about the store, and I feel the need to leap."

Charlotte laughed, took Kat's hands, and jumped up and down with her. Maybe Kat would never know how much Charlotte appreciated her, but Charlotte knew, and she knew how valuable true friendship was.

It was priceless.

ACKNOWLEDGMENTS

Thank you to my family, Michael Baum, Nicole Perna, Jan Miller, Nena Madonia, everyone from Atria Books, Jonathan Ehrlich, Robert Strent, Randee St. Nicholas, Andy, Rachel, Abbi Waxman, and Simone.